TRUE NORTH

STEPHANIE FOX

True North

Copyright 2022 © Stephanie Fox
www.writtenlikeafox.com

All rights reserved worldwide.

No part of this publication may be replicated, rewritten, redistributed, or given away in any form without consent of the author.

This book is a work of fiction. Names, characters, places, and incidents are either products of the author's imagination or are used fictitiously. Any resemblance to actual events or persons, living or dead, is entirely coincidential.

Dedicated to everyone who supported me while writing this book, and everyone who has given me a life lesson in what it truly means to be yourself.

Chapter One
August

With a deep sigh to clear the stagnant mood in my body, I focus my eyes on the red brick building that is my destination. My parents coughed up twelve-grand for me to live here for the year; a college dormitory with six floors of replicated windows, a courtyard area of fresh mulch, and a few scraggly plants that seemed to have suffered over the summer. Squinting into the afternoon sun, I can see the campus where my fifty-grand a year tuition was spent. The grass is literally greener on that side of the street. Chemical showers and sharp mower blades have made each geometric patch of green look like a slice of golf course. The centerpiece rising star is a brick building in shades of mortar and ivy, and its grand bell tower fist-bumps the cloudless blue sky well above the small modern facilities flocked around it.

Tugging my suitcase into the building, I weave around clusters of other incoming freshmen and drag it to the fourth floor and a blue plastic plaque that reads Suite 412. I'm panting from the stairs, but it's the door's decor that makes me pause. Apples decorate the door; so trite. Not that I can think of something better off the top of my head. Staring me dead in the eye are two red construction-paper apples the size of my palms Scotch-taped to the faux-oak door. Each one has a brown paper twig, a green plastic leaf, and black lines of letters in thick scrawls.

On the left apple, 'Jason Jethro' is written. My roomie must not have noticed the apple yet, with his full first name and unspeakable middle name exposed to the world in soulless black on brimstone red. I've heard him correct every coach, teacher, and classmate in high school that he is Jase, not Jason. Someone told me when Jase was in 3rd grade, he spit in the face of a 5th grader that tried to tease him about the Jethro thing at recess. The names Jason and Jethro together equivocated a dark ritual to summon demons.

On the right is my apple. It's the same black penmanship, but my apple's red skin is dusty and likely made from cheap construction paper forgotten for years and reused as a last resort. It looks like me; dull, boring, recycled. If I touch it, it would probably feel like me; coarse, shedding, and faded. I frown, seeing my own first and middle name exposed. Christian James. No one calls me Christian either. I heard Jase correct every coach, teacher, and classmate in high school that I am Ian, not Christian. No one ever mentions my middle name because people don't care if your middle name is James.

Opening the door, I enter a shoebox of a hallway. In front of me is an open door to a bathroom, on the left is another faux-oak door, labeled 412 A, and on the right, a poster of a three-quarters naked woman is taped to the door of 412 B. The titty door is the entrance to my freshman year of college, my 'abandon all hope ye who enter here' of a personalized modern Inferno.

Jase's loud voice greets me as I enter our cramped

dorm room. It's cramped because Jase moved in a week ago, and his stuff is taking over two-thirds of the room. Everything he owns is black, and the place looks like a death shrine. "Ian, you look like you got a tiny bit of sun. I don't remember having that in Minnesota."

I reply, smile as if nothing is wrong in the world, and throw my suitcase up on the empty bed. "Spent most of the summer at home being a nerd reading books."

The way my luggage bounces, I know the mattress is going to suck. Of course, he left me the twin bed and desk closest to the window. The battered bed and equally battered desk beside it are the only things the black hasn't touched yet. I flip open my suitcase and frown. I shouldn't be a Judgey McJudgerson. My wardrobe looks pretty bland in greys and navy. At least black is an edgy color.

"That's why your hair stayed dark. Missed you, bro," Jase says, and I hear him blowing a wet kiss from his closet cranny that looks more like a crevasse.

Our reunion after a summer spent apart by choice is over, and that's it, we're back to being bros, I guess. Even though I haven't seen him since graduation in June and only spoke once on social media to decide who was bringing what for the dorm, he acts like everything is normal. If there is even a way to quantify normalcy with him. I'd been expecting more of a 'hey, how have you been, what'd you do all summer, what classes do you have?' reunion if he was going to act like nothing happened. I don't know why. I guess after four years in high school together and an explosive graduation party that destroys everything, you just fall back in stride with a fresh start because it's college.

Jase flops into his camp chair, farts, and starts his Xbox he's conveniently set up on my dresser. "You see our suite-mates out there?"

"I don't think so," I answer and grab a handful of my

storm-colored shirts. "There is a ton of people out there though."

"I hope it's a couple of pussy bitches. I want a lackey this year. I'm disappointed our RA isn't hot." Jase sighs wistfully, tapping his controller to navigate the main menu of the game he chose.

I try not to get in the way of the cords for his controller and headset while I jiggle a dresser drawer open. "I'm sure there will be plenty of girls moving in this weekend that meet your standards. Sick of looking at sweaty football guys last week?"

"Yes, I am."

I can hear his annoyance directed at me. I drop the t-shirts in the drawer and give him an apologetic look as I scuttle back to my suitcase. With a shake of his head, his unkempt black hair flops from one side of his face to the other. The color is a near-perfect match for his black American Eagle t-shirt. And everything else he owns. Sometimes I wondered if that black dye on his clothes leached out of his heart. Other times I wonder if it somehow leached into mine.

I want college to be different from high school. I don't want to be his unassuming partner in civil unrest or silently observe him bullying any physically or mentally short-changed peers. How can anything be different, though, when I already know he hasn't changed? Even if I changed at all, I haven't changed enough. He hasn't changed at all.

"I'm going to get the rest of my stuff," I sigh and jump over his bed to avoid messing with his gaming lifelines. I'm not asking him for help. I'd be happy to never ask him for a thing for the rest of my life, but this situation is going to make it impossible.

After I finish unpacking, I follow Jase for dinner because I don't want to look like an idiot looking for the cafeteria, when he stops me outside our suite door. My stomach grumbles in protest at the added seconds between it and food.

"Hey, look at that," Jase says with genuine interest.

The dry erase board outside our door catches my eye. Some passerby had drawn a fat penis wearing a Superman cape. Nodding approval, I agree, "Looks just like you."

"One, my nuts are twice that big and my dick's three times as long. Two, I'd be Batman." Jase rolls his eyes as if he's relaying some universal knowledge. "I meant Shelly's dumb apples," he says and points to the red construction-paper circles taped to our suite door.

"Who's Shelly?"

"Our RA."

"What's wrong with the apples?" I ask. He's going to bitch about his name.

"One says Chris Samuel, and one says North Dakota. Why would someone come all the way from North Dakota to go to school in the middle of nowhere, Illinois? What's in North Dakota anyway other than Fargo?"

Now it's my turn to roll my eyes. Although, I am impressed Jase knows the location of Fargo. "We came from Minnesota. A state that touches North Dakota." Jase's squinting is starting to look like a glare, so I continue, "His name is North Dakota. Like first name North, middle name Dakota. Just like the other apples."

"No one has that name. It has to be where he's from,"

Jase says with a snort.

"It's a strange name," I relent. His logic is still dumb. "But maybe his parents hated him. Maybe his parents had fifty kids to name after fifty states."

"No way, they'd have a reality show if they had fifty kids."

"Maybe they adopted them all." To hit home the point that I'm more right, I point to the remaining apple and ask, "Do you think this other guy came from the State of Chris Samuel?"

"Shelly probably couldn't remember the kid's name. That's why she put that."

I want to tell him how stupid that sounds, but if I do, he'll just come up with an even dumber reason for why he's right. It's easier just to shut up. In the back of my mind, I hear the whisper of a church mouse commenting my backbone hasn't gotten any stronger.

Jase reaches over and rips an apple off the door, the one named Jason Jethro. He mutters under his breath while he crushes the paper in his fist, but I can't tell if he's cursing me for disagreeing with him or Shelly for using his abominable names.

The door swings open, fluttering the three remaining apples. Instead of a six-foot-eight intimidating suitemate I'd built up in my mind to thwart Jase's lackey idea, a kid just taller than my shoulder steps into the hall. He's wearing a camouflage ball cap, a slim-fit grey Wisconsin Badgers t-shirt, and a red buffalo plaid shirt. I'd imagined an extreme athlete, like an Olympic powerlifter or something, and gotten a sports fan allergic to air conditioning. Jase is going to eat him alive.

Jase grins and drops his crumpled apple on the ground. "Well hey there, suitemate. Which one are you?" It's a wide grin because he has a huge mouth, but also because it's fake. Automatically my mouth makes a tight-lipped smile. If I smile genuinely, it makes up for his falsity.

The kid wraps his blue lanyard around his hand, the one they handed out downstairs with the key cards. I say kid, but he has to be at least eighteen like me. He is eyeing Jase with bright-colored eyes full of suspicion. I think he got picked on in high school, not because he's short, but because of how watchful he is. In the three seconds that passed, I feel like he has thoroughly analyzed his surroundings and processed all the minute details, including sizing Jase up as a bully and labeling me another jock asshole.

Completely unfazed, Jase continues, "Are you Chris or, uh, Northie?"

"Dakota," he growls, his voice a rumbling mid-tone. I'd expected a higher pitch either because of his size or Jase's intimidation, but he's got a good grumble. The suspicious look in his eyes shifts to a contemptuous glare. If looks could kill, then this kid is the grim reaper in jeans and flannel.

I might have underestimated him.

Jase replies, "So your name is North Dakota. Ian here thought you were from North Dakota." Jase laughs and elbows me hard, right in the ribs. "Haven't seen you around yet. I must have missed you moving in or something while I was at practice. You a freshman? You seen your roommate yet?"

"My name is Dakota. Yes, I'm a freshman, and no, Chris isn't coming." Dakota's rich voice lays on condescension while he moves to step past Jase. Oblivious as usual, Jase backpedals toward the elevators to stay in front of him. I follow.

"So you've got that room all to yourself?" Jase asks.

"Yes, I do."

"Huh. You know," Jase says with amazement as if

the idea had just flown out of an angel's ass and blessed him. I can't see Dakota's face, and the back of his neck isn't expressive, but I feel Dakota's not fooled. "You could move your bed into our room, and we could make your room an entertainment room. Like, have a bedroom and a party pad. That'd be pretty awesome, wouldn't it?"

Before I can even process Jase's proposition, like the logistics and the odds I was getting the bunk bed set up, Dakota is snapping off a response. "Yeah, trade my privacy off so you can rule over the entire suite." He scratches the air with two fingers on each hand as he drawls the word 'awesome'. "Can't believe I'm going to pass on that one."

"Come on, Northie, I'll sweeten the deal. Ian can do your homework for you. He's smart. You'll get A's."

Dakota tilts his head back and rolls his palms up, and asks an omnipotent entity above the ceiling tiles, "How about you just fuck off?"

I'm floored. My new suitemate isn't giving Jase an inch. I was ready to do his homework. I definitely underestimated him.

"Think about it, Northie," Jase chuckles and presses the elevator button while shrugging off the rebuke. "Don't be a dumbfuck. Now or the rest of the year."

Great, day one and we're already on threats. Freshman year, I'm going to live with two people who hate my guts to some degree.

Dakota leans back against the door to the stairway, the push bar giving in to his weight with a shrill chirp. I catch his eye as he backs through the doorway, and seeing the hardness in his eyes, I mouth the word 'sorry'. I can't help but feel embarrassed that this is my first introduction. Not that I'd bothered to make an introduction, I just stood there next to Jase who sounded like an idiot. I'm guilty by association. I wish I'd made some effort to make my own impression instead of just being impressed.

Dakota hesitates like he's not sure what planet I came from, then shakes his head and disappears into the stairwell. I'm so sure he thinks I'm an idiot.

Chapter Two
September

I have a foreboding feeling when Jase and Alex start talking about a house party, like a nauseated storm is back building in my abdomen, promising at least an F2 tornado. Since I'm sitting at my desk, I see the courtyard, hear their loud talking, and feel their eyes on my back. I only have my first week of classes under my belt, so I barely know Alex, but he's on the football team with Jase so he's become a standard fixture in our room or at the cafeteria. I won't complain because Jase has someone to talk to about football so I don't have to listen to it. He kind of fades into the faces of Jase's other teammates that ebb and flow through my daily life, circling Jase like some mundane school of indiscriminate fish.

It's the college part of the party that has sweat blooming on the back of my neck. I don't know people here. I don't know the unspoken rules. It's probably not any different than high school, but maybe it is.

Partying came as a package deal with being on the lacrosse team in high school, so it isn't a new concept to me. Show up, get shit-faced trying to impress everyone around you for some reason. Believe that those around you are your "people" because you can all stand around and hold Solo cups together. It's fake, they were all fake. Somehow during the summer of my eighteenth year I finally figured that all out, but a shitload of good it does me now.

For some reason, I thought my freshman year was going to be different. I thought Jase was going to be better, that a summer's time and new surroundings would fix our broken friendship. I thought I was going to be different, that I was going to be better. For college I dropped sports, my hometown, and a lot of my so-called friends, all in an attempt to drop my high school life somehow. New surroundings and everyone around me but Jase are new people, but a week and a half in, I feel like freshman year of college is just a continuation of high school. I have use of half a mini-fridge in my room. That's all that's changed. I'm still technically under a roof my mom and step-dad pay for. So-so cafeteria food. I drive the same restored 1992 Jeep Cherokee, wear the same clothes, go to classes, do homework, and do a lot of studying. Now I can add parties to the list. It's routine.

No, it's worse than routine. It's evidence of how scripted and boring my life is. Everything is decided on what to do, where to go, who to hang out with, what to act like. I hate it. I want to be different. What happened to college expanding your horizons and all that bullshit? I don't know where I went wrong or when I became just another stereotypical douchey bro. I've graduated from a high school douche to a college douche now, I guess.

I have the potential for more. At least, I think I do.

"Where is this party at?" I ask. There's a downdraft in my esophagus as I close my Civil War textbook and spin my chair around to face them. They look like twins in their dark wash jeans, team t-shirts, and black hair.

Alex grins, "The Magician's Lair."

A stupid name for a dumpy house a few blocks from campus. I've been told it's a shithole, and for some reason, it was said to me with genuine pride in that fact. From what I've heard through Jase's new friends, it's the closest place to drink underage near campus. Middle-class houses with absent parents aren't a thing anymore; apparently, it's going to be rundown college rentals.

"Sounds awesome," I drawl.

Alex shakes his head. "Rather sit here and read about a bunch of dead dudes? Lame, Ian."

Yes, I am lame. Thanks for pointing it out, Alex-I-Don't-Even-Really-Know-You. I would rather hang out with a book about dead dudes than go to a stupid house party with you. I think you and your party sound stupid.

I have no balls, so I say none of that out loud. And I know I'm going to follow Jase like always, so what's the point in making a wave? There's just some magnet buried inside me that draws me into Jase's orbit, just as it has since middle school.

Jase claps loudly and jumps out of his camp chair. "We need to get Ian some booze and some bitches, stat. Ian hasn't gotten laid all semester. He's been crabby."

"We're like a week into the semester," I argue. He acts like I was such a promiscuous sex god in high school. Maybe I should take it as one of his roundabout praises, but it's hollow when it's not true.

"And? Change out of that stupid Lincoln t-shirt, too, even if it looks good with your pretty brown eyes. It's creepy," Jase says. "You're going to have a hard enough time getting girls because you're a History major, don't flaunt it."

I look down at my t-shirt. It's grey, of course, with

Abraham Lincoln's photo in black. Beneath it is a quote, 'I'm not really a fan of the theater'. I think it's funny. When I bought it this summer, I thought it would make me a little edgier than bland-high-school-Ian. Apparently, it didn't work.

Alex says, "That settles it. We're going to the Lair. I'm going to text Drew and tell him we're going." Pulling out his phone, he starts screen-tapping.

Jase pulls off his t-shirt to trade it for another black one in his closet. "Just put it in the group text."

More people I don't know that well. I used to like being part of the crowd, but I am more so looking forward to being lost in it.

Jase shakes out his new shirt and says, "Hey, we should bring our neighbor with us."

"The vampire kid?" Alex asks.

"Yep. I need to butter him up a bit."

"Vampire kid?" I ask. "Joey next door? He's into were-wolves, not vampires."

Jase sighs in frustration. "No, dumbass, our suitemate Northie. I've barely talked to him since he moved in. Water in the shower is like the only sign he's around. He must only go out at night."

"Only goes out at night, like someone who maybe has night classes?" I muse out loud and emphatically tap my index fingertip to my chin. Alex smiles, but Jase is glaring.

"Shut up, Ian. Let's get him shitfaced and see what's up. I'm not going to live with someone I don't know."

"Just leave him alone." I sigh as I walk over to my dresser and pull open the top drawer. I've seen plenty of Jase's attempts to be 'friendly' with our suitemate; asking to skip ahead in the laundry room or the cafeteria, asking for cell phone chargers and wall plugs, et cetera et cetera et cetera. The best was Jase holding the suite door closed so

Dakota couldn't get in, with me emphatically telling him to let go while Jase cackled until Dakota just power kicked the door open a bit then left.

"I'm going to go invite him. It's the polite thing to do." Jase says it like he's leading a human rights movement. The idea of Jase doing anything out of politeness is beyond comprehension. He's my best friend, but that doesn't mean I'm blind to his flaws. Why he won't just be honest and say he wants to try to manipulate Dakota to get something for free or mess with him for entertainment purposes is beyond me. What's to hide exactly? Especially from me. I know better.

I blurt out, "He won't come with us. I'm sure he thinks you're an asshole."

"He probably thinks you're an idiot," Jase fires back while tugging down his excessively tight t-shirt. "I'd rather be an asshole than an idiot." Jase leaves our room and steps across the tiny shared hallway to police-knock Dakota's door. I pull a plain navy t-shirt out of my drawer and hope Dakota's gone.

Someone belts out from inside Dakota's room, *"Hello from the other side."*

Pausing with my hands grabbing my grey Lincoln shirt, my mouth skews into a smile. I hear the click of a doorknob and Jase's stuttering, "H-hey." Shaking my head at the Adele reference, I smile harder because it went over Jase's head.

"Hello from the outside," Dakota answers in a normal voice.

Jase says, "Uh, hey, suitemate. We're heading out to a party. Want to come?"

"I don't drink," Dakota responds as I pull my Lincoln shirt off. I feel the static of the cotton fabric rubbing over my dark brown hair. Tossing the shirt into a broken-down grey laundry basket, I bite my lip.

"Even better," Jase says, overloading the enthusiasm. "You can be our designated walker and make sure our drunk asses make it home. Come on, you'd be doing us a favor, and I'll get you a Pepsi or something. Ian's having a dry spell, and we're trying to get him laid, you could help with that too. It might take all of us to knock her out and drag her back here."

My body pauses my exterior movements, guts, heart, everything but my brain. It's like I'm hearing Jase for the first time. I used to laugh off comments like that—locker room jock talk or whatever—but at this moment, I don't see anything funny about kidnapping and raping someone. He sounds like such a disgusting human being.

Reflecting on high school reminds me that I'm just as shitty of a human being, though. I stood by like a gutless wuss and never said anything when Jase talked like this then. I'm still standing by, not saying anything.

Announcing the status of my sex life to someone who doesn't know me is kind of him too. I learned long ago not to tell Jase anything about my sex life, but sharing a room with him makes it hard to hide the lack thereof. Not that I care about my lack of it, but I care about the incessant belittling over it. He acts like if I'm not notching my bedpost, I'm some kind of failure as a man.

Pulling on the blue shirt, I'm surprised to hear Dakota say, "I'm not going to become an accomplice to rape, but I suppose I can handle the rest of that. Give me a minute."

Dakota usually brushes Jase off with a cold shoulder, so this is a new behavioral development. I'm curious.

I get my shirt on right, then grab my keys, wallet, and phone, and join Alex and Jase in the hallway outside the suite. The apples are long gone, and there's a fresh dick on the whiteboard. One Jase is compelled to draw hair on.

Dakota steps out a moment later. His t-shirt is grey like the one I'd abandoned, with blue text across his chest that says '(adj.) ephemeral'. He looks comfortable in the fitted tee over white sleeves, his broken-down jeans, a red baseball cap with a W on it, a beat-up pair of black Converse, and a smug-looking smile.

Dakota exudes this relaxed confidence that somehow eeks through his clothes. Jealousy tinges my skin an invisible green. I always wanted to buy cool points with a pair of chucks, but I just look like a poser or something when I try them on. My humorous Lincoln t-shirt wasn't fit to be seen in public. My head is misshapen or something, so I look stupid when I wear hats. There are just some people that pull themselves together, and I need to accept I'm not one of them.

"Let's go," Jase says with a clap of his hands and leads the way to the stairway, Alex right at his side like a trained dog.

Falling in step beside me, Dakota asks, *"Hello. How are you?"*

I hum a moment. "You really asking, or is that another Adele lyric?"

"You caught that. You've impressed me."

The green jealousy's gone, and I feel a golden hue of pride from his praise. "It's on my Top One Hundred songs list." I tuck my chin to see where my feet are landing on the concrete stairs. "You going to apologize for talking about yourself? Tell me you hope I'm well and ask if I ever made it out of that town? Or tell me it's not a secret that both of us are running out of time?"

My shoes squeak on the landing, and I look over at Dakota as we turn the one-eighty corner for the next flight of stairs. His expression looks thoughtful as he shrugs a shoulder. "We may be running out of time," he muses.

"We're dying every second after we're born," Alex calls back to us, his words bouncing around the stairwell.

"Gotta live in the now."

"Thanks for the verbal memento mori," I shout to Alex.

Dakota says, "I'm wearing a memento mori."

Looking at him, my first guess is the black chucks, black being death and all that. I second-guess myself, though, because he doesn't strike me as that simple of a character. It might be the t-shirt, but I don't know. I'd rather look stupid and ask questions than make a wrong assumption.

I ask, "What's ephemeral?"

Jase answers as his feet hit the ground floor. "A man acting like a chick."

"That's effeminate," Dakota says, his voice reminding me of a disappointed sick-of-this-shit teacher.

"That's what I said."

Dakota pulls his shirt away from his chest and lowers his voice to me, "it means lasting for a brief time."

"What are you two whispering about?" Jase grouches.

"Ars moriendi," Dakota announces as if he were a magician at the prestige of his trick.

Alex snorts. "Arse. They're talking about ass."

So quietly I barely hear it, Dakota mutters, "They're fucking idiots."

My golden glow burns a little brighter that I'm not included as one of 'they'. Acknowledgment that I'm not an idiot feels too good, so I won't ask what an ars moriendi is. Google can tell me later.

The Magician's Lair is just as disgusting as I was

told. Walking up the broken concrete stairs and crossing the bowed-plank wood porch, you can taste bitter cigarette smoke. Stepping inside, there's a fog of harsh music, smoke, and cat piss. The smoke is a healthy blend of cigarette and pot exhalement garnished with fruity vape pen clouds. My mouth tastes like I licked a dusty houseplant and chased it with a shot of essential oils. The acidic tang of cat piss in the air makes my skin feel greasy. I wish it were human piss because I feel bad knowing cats live in this hellhole.

When Jace finds our own corner of space, I refuse to sit on the couches. While Jace, Alex, and Drew look comfortable on the dinged yellow corduroy loveseats, I've got a metal folding chair putting my ass to sleep. I have my feet hooked on the rungs because the matted tawny carpet might ooze something into my shoes. Dakota is perching on a step ladder next to me, the promised cup of cherry Pepsi in his hand. I don't recognize the music screaming above the cloud in the air, but Dakota is tapping his foot on the floor like he knows it.

After a painful-to-listen-to discussion about some football game, Jase's meteor-black eyes turn to Dakota. "So, I had someone tell me you're a music major. That music appreciation teacher Professor Chen is smoking hot. I don't know how you get any work done in her class," Jase says. This is new. And makes me suspicious. In the last twenty minutes, he hasn't said a word to Dakota. He pulls out a pack of red-labeled Marlboros and continues, "I seriously thought about learning the French horn or something so that I could take some private lessons."

Drew nudges Jase and chuckles out, "Or maybe the trom-bone."

Impervious to the stupidity, Dakota replies, "She's out of your league," and tips back his plastic cup of soda.

"I fucked a teacher last year; I'll do it again if I have

to." Jase plucks a cigarette out of the package before holding it out to me, then laughs. "Sorry, Ian, forgot you're a pussy. Here Northie."

Dakota eyes Jase for a long moment, that grim reaper glare creeping in. I don't know how he can turn on the intensity like that. Jase just keeps holding out the pack of cigarettes like an eager child at a petting zoo trying to lure in a stubborn animal.

"Here, Dakota," Jase says.

Holding that intense gaze, Dakota reaches out to pinch the end of a cigarette and slowly drags it out of the pack. There's a weird old-western standoff vibe I'm still getting, even as Dakota lights the cigarette off the nearby trying-to-cover-the-cat-piss-smell Walmart candle.

I hate that Jase is ripping on me, and I hate that I don't know why Jase is attempting to suck up to Dakota. Trying to knock Jase's cool points down, I correct him, "She was a student teacher, not a real teacher." I want to add the rest of the story, mixing drugs, alcohol, and blackmail into his tale of penis triumph, but I'm afraid to push it that far. Immediately I feel scared I even thought of it and shift my attention to Dakota. "Those things will kill you."

Dakota takes a long pull off the cigarette and exhales, politely blowing the smoke away from me. "No, they won't." His voice has such smooth confidence he almost makes me believe it.

"Northie's got more nut hair than you, Ian." Jase chuckles and blows his smoke. He's challenging me with his dark eyes, daring me to say something. Which is pointless; he knows I'm not good at comebacks or being witty. I press my Solo cup to my lips and try to make my eyes dead. It's just sticks and stones, and he's drinking.

Jase's mouth twists in a satisfied smirk, and his eyes stop boring into mine and look to Dakota. "Ignore Ian.

He brought his vagina tonight. See why I can't get him a fuckbuddy, much less a date? None of the girls I've met will even take him as a pity case because he can be such a bitch."

This is the part where I'm supposed to laugh it off like it's funny he's teasing me. Like his words are some kind of friendly banter. I would have done it four months ago in high school without thinking, but now the sharp thing in my chest isn't a chuckle.

Dakota is going to laugh and smile, maybe nod along or join in with a witty remark. That's the game Jase is playing. The same one children play; you build a pack by picking on one of the weaker ones. You become friends when you have a common adversary. For some reason, I'm the adversary tonight. I shouldn't feel like it's a mystery why.

Flicking my eyes to Dakota, I'm surprised. No laugh or smile is touching his lips, just the white paper of his cigarette. Beneath that shadow from his ballcap, his dark eyebrows are pinched a little, rejecting Jase's laser eyes and acid words. He doesn't look the least bit amused, but I can't read his feelings. The tip of his cigarette flares like a dying sun.

Jase throws another splash of gas on the kindling of this fire he's building. "You saw what happened in the laundry room. I couldn't even get Ian to talk to that blonde moving her laundry."

Pulling the cigarette out of his mouth, Dakota says, "I don't think that's the problem. Ian probably doesn't have the same taste in women you do." Dakota snuffs his barely dwindled cigarette on the candle jar lid and shifts his eyes to meet mine.

Even through the cat-piss-pot-smoke-haze, his eyes are fervent. They're tasting my brain to decide on swallowing me whole or spitting me out. He can probably see the colors of my soul and tell me my future now.

"Ian seems like he'd go after a sweet girl with a brain." His eyes leave mine and turn on Jase. "While you seem to take advantage of girls with poor self-esteem and emotionally pressure them to sleep with you. Or they just put up with your dick because you have six-pack abs or something superficial like that. It's definitely not your personality," Dakota scoffs.

Alex bites his fist, looking at Jase, who frowns and puffs off his cigarette. I can see the wheels turning in Jase's head and smell the rust burning off them. Dakota just built a pyre next to Jase's little campfire, and Dakota's holding a bigger gas can.

"Don't deny it," Dakota smirks a little. "The only name I hear coming from that room is yours. You know. 'Harder Jase.' 'Already, Jase?' 'No, don't put it there, Jase.' 'Oh, size doesn't matter, Jase.'"

My jaw unhinges as my eyebrows reach for my hairline. My eyelids bloom, letting the smoky piss air nibble at my corneas. Maybe there's even smoke from the invisible inferno.

Alex and Drew start laughing through their guts, punching Jase in the shoulder, repeating Dakota's words like pop culture one-liners. Jase's eyes are menacing, but his lips pull back into a bitter smile. You have to laugh it off if you're the ass end of the joke, but I don't think he's ever been the ass end before.

I wish I could learn Dakota's magic. When people talk shit, it's just easier to laugh along at someone else's expense, or your own expense, but Dakota isn't having any of it. He takes no shit and can dish it right back. Dish it better. He's even taking the shit directed at me and throwing it back harder. I'm in awe. If he were a girl, I'd probably be in love.

Jase points his finger at Dakota and yells over Alex and Drew's laughter, "You know I've fucked more chicks at this school in three weeks than you have your entire life, Northie."

"I know you have." Dakota shrugs and takes another sip of his drink. "I just told you I heard them."

I'm waiting for Jase to explode, scream, jump off the couch and punch Dakota. I don't know what exactly, but something violent and dramatic. Instead, Jase laughs forcefully. "I hope you're having fun beating off in your room listening to me." He sets his drink down and asks Alex to grab a deck of cards. Like a cheap lighter, Jase has flickered out. No spark, no smoke, no fire, no incendiary bomb. "Let's play Pyramid. I'll grab some refills. You want more Pussy Pepsi, Northie?"

Dakota corrects Jase, "Why yes, Dakota would like more cherry soda."

We're not very far into our first game, and I know something's not right. I sense it; something about Jase's smirk, the way he and Alex keep exchanging glances. Then the way Drew is eyeballing Dakota. I'm not privy to whatever is going on, and I probably don't want to be.

It takes another game while speculating before realizing what they've done. I can see it in the way Dakota is swaying a bit, and he's squinting at his cards, rubbing at his forehead. I give Jase my disapproving stare, but he ignores me. The damage is done, but I subtly move Dakota's cup under my chair so he won't sip any more of the poisoned Pepsi.

Guilt is starting to make it hard to read my cards. Maybe I should say something. Jase would be pissed, though, and I do have to sleep in the same room as him. It's not likely he'd smother me in my sleep, but it's a possibility. He would definitely make my life miserable if he chose to. I bite my lip, pinching the flesh between my teeth hard enough to feel my pulse.

Dakota drops his cards on the table, standing up fast. He loses his balance, side-stepping and catching the arm of the corduroy couch to keep from hitting the floor.

I bounce to my feet, knocking over my half-full cup. Drew and Alex start screeching like feces-flinging howler monkeys.

"What a lightweight, Northie," Jase hoots. "I hardly gave you anything."

"Shit," Dakota squeaks. His skin turns into Greecian alabaster as he stands upright and takes a step away from the couch.

There's something in his voice that prickles my neck. Everything I've seen in Dakota has been self-assured and in control. I can taste the flavor of fear. It's more bitter than the smoke, burns more than the cat piss, and thumps worse than the bad music.

"Good luck walking across the room," Jase says.

I snap, "Jase, what the hell?"

"What? I'm just having a little fun," Jase says and shrugs like that absolves him.

Jase would happily watch Dakota fall and break his face or something, but I can't. As Dakota takes another side-step, I grab his shoulder.

"I can't drink," Dakota croaks. As he grabs his head, he knocks his hat off, which I catch before it hits the ground. His eyebrows scrunch, and his pallid skin makes me nauseous for him. "I'm going to get sick."

"Ian! He's going to barf on you," Alex giggles. "You

are going to get some action."

I glare at Jase and demand, "What did you give him?"

Holding one hand over his mouth to gargle his words, Jase mocks me, "Paging Nurse Ian, need a diagnosis for Northie."

"How old are you?" I snap and grab Dakota's bicep. Muscles are taut beneath his t-shirt, as unyielding as wrapped leather when I dig my fingers in.

More monkey howling.

Ignoring the three morons, I whisper, "Not my circus, not my monkeys. Let's go."

I'm pissed. Pissed at how immature Jase and 'my' new friends are. We're all supposed to be adults. Pissed because I don't know why I'm the one constantly cleaning and patching up behind Hurricane Jase. Pissed I somehow didn't see this coming. Pissed Jase got the better of Dakota.

There's a line outside the bathroom, and by then, Dakota's half-keeled over. I abandon the bathroom idea and head outside. No one says anything while I push our way through the house's funk fog.

We get outside to the front porch, where it's now pouring rain, of course, and Dakota starts heaving over the railing. To keep him from falling into the bush he's puking on, in case the shitty railing inevitably collapses, I grab him by the waist. It feels awkward, just standing here hanging onto his flanks and t-shirt while he spews into the bushes, all nonchalant. It's easier to help girls puke; you can hold their hair or rub their backs or something other than just stand there. If I knew him better, I might have some kind of joke to break the awkward air, but I'm afraid of making the situation any worse. The rain has my back, though, falling harder to fill that void.

I'm soaked and cold when Dakota stops heaving. Water is dripping down my neck, following the path of my spine to flow between my shoulders. It flattens my hair out to cover my forehead. It's running down my face. Flicking my tongue across my bottom lip, I taste the rain. It's cool and flavored like overpriced bottled water.

Dakota stands up straight, and I let the fabric of his shirt slide through my fingers. It's the only dry patch on his shirt. Everything else is soaked and tacked to his skin.

The first words out of my mouth are, "I didn't know. I'm sorry."

"You say that a lot," he croaks while turning away from the bush.

"I think there's a couch inside somewhere. Maybe try lying down for a bit?"

"No, dorm. I can't smell this place anymore." He pants and wipes his hand across his face. "I'm going to be sick. Sicker."

"I'll walk you back," I offer.

"No," he says weakly, shaking his head. Water has plastered his dark hair down too. The rain makes him blink rapidly when he looks up to meet my eyes. "I can get back."

"And fall in the street and get hit by a car or drown in a puddle or something. Come on." I reach over and set his hat on his head. Lot of good it does now. "Even if you puke on me, it beats hanging out with those idiots."

There's a shake in his hand as he situates his hat.

"Let's go." I hope my voice leaves no room for discussion, and in a moment, Dakota nods and shuffles to the stairs.

It's a long walk back to our hall, and the horrible weather doesn't make it enjoyable. There's no natural beauty of lightning or pleasing rolls of thunder, there's just a constant stream of water. Striking up conversation seems futile when Dakota stops twice more to throw up on the sidewalk. When we make it into our brick building's bright lobby, I'm debating on putting him to bed or in the bathroom, and he whimpers like a dying dog. It's the only way I can describe the sound as he grabs my arm, pulling me down as his knees buckle.

"Hey, we're almost there," I try to assure him as he sinks his knees then palms to the commercial-white tiled floor. I say, "like sixty-two seconds away from our bathroom," as I crouch beside him. When he lifts his chin, there's a weakness in his eyes as they focus on mine.

The close gaze surprises me. His eyes are two-toned; right eye blue and left eye green. Not a speckled mix either, or a shade of difference, but cobalt and emerald. It's peculiar but somehow naturally complimentary, like a dazzling ocean and secret forest. Remarkably, they're different colors yet express him in perfect sync.

His eyes go blank; the world around the ocean and forest turns to midnight. Shoulder going lax under my palm, he bellies down like a dog and presses his forehead into the tiled floor.

I touch his wet shoulder and squeeze hard. "Dakota?" My voice squeaks as panic scratches across my lungs. I squeeze his shoulder harder. "Hey?"

I hear a female voice behind me asking if everything's okay. Looking up, I see Shelly approaching, and I've never been this happy to see her pinned red hair. Dakota moans again, but it morphs into this sick growl as his entire body tenses and trembles.

"Hey! Ian, roll him over," Shelly barks. The shriek of her sneakers on the lobby echoes. "He's having a seizure. Get him on his side."

Trying to be gentle, I push Dakota onto his side and hold him there. Shelly falls on her knees and slides the last few feet towards us, pressing her hands between his head and the hard floor.

"Don't hold him," she says, and I snap my hands to my chest.

I've never seen someone have a seizure. On TV and in movies before, sure, but never right in front of me. I don't know what to expect. Foaming at the mouth, flopping all over the floor, and Shelly is going to whip out something to shove in his mouth so he doesn't swallow his tongue or something? I don't know where RAs keep that sort of stuff, but they prepare for things like this, right?

By the time my mind runs through everything I think will happen and I ask Shelly what to do, it's over. He shook and jerked and twitched, but that was it. Not as dramatic as what I've seen on film but ten times scarier. My heart is pummeling my ribs, fear has torn up my stomach, and now both organs are on the brink of failure.

Dakota's shuddering has stopped, but his half-open eyes are dead. The low groan escaping his lips is the only thing convincing me he's alive.

"I think he's done," Shelly whispers.

"I-is he okay? You don't want me to call an ambulance or something?" I ask as internal sensations overwhelm my body. There's the pity in my metaphysical heart but hot anger in its blood. Guilt, too, for not stopping this, and an embarrassment that this is the aftermath of my friend's actions.

Shelly gives me a gentle smile. "I think he'll be fine. I have a cousin who has epilepsy. I've seen a few of her seizures." As she talks, her fingers are stroking Dakota's wet hair in a slow movement that reminds me of a mother calming a child. I wish there were something I could do, some kind of comfort or reassurance I could give, but my mind draws a blank. I'd look stupid if I started petting him.

"He's epileptic?" I ask.

"I don't know. He didn't tell me he was. Where were you guys going or coming back from?" Her eyes squint. "You both stink."

I sigh, and without hesitation, I throw Jase under the bus. "The Lair. Jase's idea. Dakota wasn't drinking," I quickly add when I see the look on Shelly's face. "But Jase spiked his drink with something."

Shelly's scowl carves deep into her features. "Jase needs to watch his act. Freaking idiot. He's going to be a thorn in my side this year." She huffs. "How much did you have?"

"Nothing, and after all this, trust me, I'm more than sober." Looking down at Dakota, those pity and anger emotions inside me smush together and manifest as a deep shame. This fiery guy I've been envying is laying here helpless, and I should have known better. I clear the nerves out of my voice and look up at Shelly's scowling face. "He's not moving. Shouldn't we call an ambulance or something?"

Shelly's expression calms, the angry lines in her face softening. Her tone is reassuring as she says, "He should come out of it in a minute or so, then we can get him to his room."

I exhale and run my fingers through my hair, sending water down my neck. I imagine the top of my head looks like a sewer rat—wet and brown. I already stink like one. I hate crouching here and waiting with nothing I can do. I pick up his hat.

It feels like an hour until Dakota comes around, lashes blinking over his bleary two-colored eyes. He rolls onto his back, groaning softly and fidgeting with his feet. I don't know what to do, so I just stare at him.

Shelly takes control of the situation, rubbing his upper arm and smiling at him.

"You okay?" she asks.

"Maybe," Dakota murmurs.

"Good. I think you about gave Ian a heart attack." Shelly laughs, and Dakota screws his eyes shut. I don't mind the joke at my expense this time and feel my lips turning into a stupid smile. God, I'm an idiot. "Let me know when you're ready, and we'll get you up to your room."

"I'm fine."

This is the first time I've heard doubt in his voice. There's a warble in it that hints he's scared. Everything I've seen of him has been spunky attitude and bleeding confidence, and hearing the insecurity in his voice hurts. He's broken, and it's my fault.

Shelly smiles and shakes her head. "Sorry buddy, I gotta sit with you awhile and make sure you're doing okay." Piercing dubstep racket blares from her hip, and she makes a face before silencing her phone. Dakota struggles to sit up, and as I reach out, he pushes my hand away.

"I'm fine. Just want my toothbrush and my bed."

Shelly smiles. "Maybe some dry clothes too." The front doors open, and a few students walk in, looking at us with curiosity. Dakota and I are the accident, Shelly's the police, and everyone passing by is rubbernecking. "Alright, let's get you off the floor before we're a sideshow attraction. Ian, grab him."

Dakota's cotton-covered upper arm is cold and soaked under my grip as Shelly and I pull him to his feet and flank him to the elevator. I feel so awkward, like if I don't help him, I'll look like a douche, but I'm insulting his masculinity by helping him. I try to catch his eye, to give him the 'it's okay, I get it' look, but his eyes are on the ground. I can't tell if he's embarrassed or angry. Maybe he thinks I was in on it, Jase being my friend and all. Guilty by association. My soul is melting at the thought.

"I'm sorry about this," I say as the elevator dings and opens to our floor.

"Did you put something in my drink?" he asks. There's a bit of his usual confidence in his voice, but it's rough from exiting his raw throat. The three of us step out onto the denim-blue carpet of our floor.

"No, but-"

"Then you don't have to apologize."

"We all know this was Jase." Shelly sighs a little. "Dakota, if you want to I-"

"I just want my bed."

Reaching our suite door, Dakota pulls his arm out of my grasp. He goes straight to the bathroom, leaving Shelly and me in the small hallway. The sound of an electric toothbrush and running water echoes out of the tiled room. Shelly reaches over and bumps her fist against my shoulder.

"He'll be fine," she whispers. "I'll keep an eye on him for a bit."

That was it? I was an accomplice to almost killing my suitemate, and now I just leave? I feel like she's excusing me to go back to the party, but I want to hide in my room like a punished child.

"Okay," is all I say and reach into my pocket for my keys.

I guess I'll just read about a bunch of dead dudes. I can't fuck things up doing that.

* * *

I'm sitting at my dorm room desk half-ass typing an

essay, but my thoughts are wandering. I try to push aside the 'hey, your suitemate almost died or something this weekend' thoughts. Outside my window is a fading afternoon, with people walking across courtyards and down wide pathways. Checking the time, I realize the last afternoon class time ended. The thought crosses my mind of going for a run, but the nerd in me doesn't want to go anywhere until I get my essay somewhat written. I need to take advantage of the relative quiet to work. I can hear music from Dakota's room that sounds like an epic movie soundtrack. Joey next door is playing a first-person shooter, but the wall muffles his chattering. Neither bothers me.

I had left the room's door open, so I hear the suite door bounce off the wall announcing Jase's arrival. I swing my chair one-eighty and see he's looking psyched up and angry. With the sleeves torn off his black shirt, I can see his arms are flexed with tension. His yellow baseball cap is shadowing his eyes, but the twist of his lips says enough.

"Hey," I greet him with a bland tone. I want to say, 'what the fuck is your problem,' but I don't want to piss him off any further. Something made him this angry, and he is looking for a scapegoat. I don't want to be that goat.

Jase makes a disgusted face as he drops his backpack on the floor. "What is that shit next door?"

"What shit?"

"That sound from Dakota's room. I can hear it in here, and it's going to drive me crazy." Jase tosses his phone and earbuds on his desk. "I have homework to do. I'm going to shut him up." He then moves to our small hallway.

I want to get out of my chair, but my ass is rooted. I don't want Jase talking to Dakota after what happened. At the same time, who am I to step in between them? Dakota didn't ask me for protection from Jase or anything. They'd been doing a great job of not speaking to each other the last three days.

Jase's fist slams on Dakota's door, and he yells, "turn that shit down!"

"*Turn down for what?*" Dakota screams back in the best Lil Jon impression I've ever heard. I snort as a laugh escapes my throat.

"Your music fucking sucks, and I don't want to hear it."

I laugh harder that the joke went straight over Jase's head.

"*What?*" Dakota purrs in his Lil Jon voice.

"Your fucking music, turn it down!"

"*What?*"

"Turn it down!" Jase rage-screams.

"*Okay!*" Dakota screams back, and the music cuts completely.

Jase stomps back into our room; I silence my laughter and wipe the smile off my face. He goes to his dresser and yanks open a drawer.

"He is such a little shit," Jase snarls. "I swear to God I'm going to kill him before this semester's over."

I know he's sardonic, but it flips a trigger inside I didn't know existed. Anger grabs all my glee by the throat, then flips it and slams it to the floor like an exaggerated WWE power move. It takes control of my mouth. "What the fuck is wrong with you? You could have killed him Friday night, and now you're making jokes about it?"

"That's a bit overdramatic." Jase scoffs and pulls a black t-shirt out of his drawer. One that still has sleeves.

"It's not a coincidence you slipped him alcohol and god-knows-what else, then he puked the whole way home and seized right inside the doors of our hall." I lower my voice to an angered hiss. "He has a seizure disorder, and look what you did."

"Oh, settle down, Ian, Christ," Jase argues and slams the drawer shut. I'm pretty sure anyone within fifteen feet of our dorm walls can hear him.

"Why should I settle down? What the hell were you thinking? He said he didn't drink. Why did you spike him?"

Jase pulls his sleeveless shirt off then throws it against the wall. I have a feeling he is imagining my face on that wall. "They say that if they're holy rollers. I've done it to tons of people before. I didn't know he had a medical whatever, so that's not my fault. And since when did you get such a high horse? You've never had a problem with it before. What makes you Judge Judy's executionary?"

"It's judge, jury, and executioner, and you don't see me doing that shit, do you?"

"You've watched and laughed, and you never said any- thing about it before."

"I'm saying something because you seriously messed with someone else's life, and it's not right. What if he walked home by himself and collapsed in the road and got hit by a car or choked on his vomit or something? It would have been your fault if something happened to him."

"I put some alcohol and Ritalin in some soda at a college party. Even if something did happen, it's not like they could prove it was me. They couldn't come back on me for it."

My hands are clenching as he pulls out clean jeans. He's so fucking apathetic, and it's butane on my internal rage-fire. I want to scream as loud as my lungs can take, but I don't want anyone but us to hear this conversation. "I'm not talking about you getting in trouble. I'm talking about someone else being injured or dead because of your stupid actions. Does that not bother you on some moral level?"

He gives me a dead-eyed glare. "Ian, he didn't fucking

die. I didn't know he was allergic to alcohol or an appeale— app—"

"Epileptic," I snarl. I don't even know if he's an epileptic but I'm going to run with it.

"Whatever. I didn't know, so it's not my fault."

"What the hell is wrong with you? How do you go through life assuming nothing could go wrong with you doing stupid shit like this? Do you ever think of anyone but yourself?"

His index finger flicks out and stabs the air in my direction. "Last I checked, your opinion doesn't count. I don't know what's up your ass, Ian, but you have been a moody mother fucker since school started, and you're probably making this up just to be a dick."

"Don't believe me, then ask Shelly. She was there."

He mocks me in a nasal tone, "Ask Shelly she was there." He slams the drawer shut. "I'm going out. If I were you, I'd go to the library or something in case I still feel like punching your face in when I get back."

"What, like Evan and Matt?"

Jase's nostrils flare, but a minuscule spark flashes in his eye. "Don't fucking bring that up."

"Why not?"

"Because we're friends and friends keep shit like that quiet. What the hell is wrong with you, Ian? Are you going to get that stick out of your ass at some point?" He snatches his keys up and backs out of our room, giving me the finger before crashing out the suite door.

I can feel anxiety in my throat like a cattail shoved down my gullet. I try so hard not to think about Evan and Matt, but there it just erupted out of my brain. Deep down, I know they have a lot to do with my aversion to Jase. Instead of just throwing down about it, I apparently shoved a stick up my ass.

Maybe he's right. That giant stick is making me overly sensitive. Maybe pulling the stick out is accepting what happened happened, and there's nothing I can do to change it, and if I can't forgive, I should forget. I'd committed to showing up at this school and being roommates. I'd had the idea of a new start. Things divide and quarter friendships, but time and effort are supposed to heal. There will always be scars, but things can be made whole again.

Maybe this wound is too deep though. Our friendship was held together with butterfly bandages, and now Dakota has ripped them clean off and forced the raw edges apart. I learned a lesson, I changed my point of view, but Jase hasn't. What happened to Evan and Matt scared me, creating a deep fundamental fear. It shook my world in a way that only privileged kids experience; reality kicking down the door of my protected life and making me see what evil indeed lurks beyond my safe borders.

I realize I never forgave him for Evan and Matt and won't ever forgive him for Evan and Matt, and I'm not sure I can forgive him for Dakota either. Now, how do I live with my former best friend, with a stick up my ass because I hate him?

* * *

After watching Jase poison our suitemate, I don't have the desire to go anywhere with him. The way Jase blows off the whole thing irritates me, and just hearing anyone breathe the word 'party' puts me in a bad mood. I can't confront him anymore, so I try to avoid him, which is hard when I live with him.

Making distance between us has sanded the edges of my anger. Forgiveness is off the table, but things in my brain have made it complicated.

I don't understand what happened between us. I used to look up to Jase because of his popularity and how he could attract a crowd with him in the middle. Maybe the summer apart refocused my view on things. I don't want to follow Jase anymore. I want to change him, and I want to fix his flaws, maybe. I want to make him care, to realize his ass-backward selfish mindset is wrong, but at the same time, how do I push that when I have to share my living space with him? I don't like finding his used condoms in my pillowcase, so I feel like all I can do is just keep the peace, which means swallowing everything I want to say or do and appeasing him by dropping the subject and ignoring him, which wears on me.

Of course, life is going to challenge my convictions. With my backpack on my shoulder, exhausted from a day of class after a fitful night of sleep, I enter my dorm room to find it dark. The lights are off, the curtains shut. Jase is a decapitated head on his pillow because his black clothes and black hair blend into his black bedding. Something is wrong.

Non-committedly I say, "Hey."

"Hey." There's a broken quality to his voice. I can hear it in just that single word.

Letting my backpack slide to the floor, I sit on the edge of my bed so I can face him. "What's up?"

He breathes deeply through his nose, and it sounds as if he's trying to suck in the urge to cry. That raw quality no one ever sees from him comes through his words. "Bailey called me. And called me. Then she started texting me. I had to turn off my phone. I should block her number, but then I'd miss the call that she's finally dead."

I swallow hard to gain a second to gather my thoughts.

"So," I say. "She must be out of jail." Maybe his exiled

mother is the answer to his amped attitude and cruelty.

"Yeah," he snorts. "You know she just wants money. We should take bets; drugs, alcohol, or a lie about needing rent to get a clean slate."

I'm not lucky enough to be a gambler. "She doesn't know where you are, though, that's a plus."

Jase winces and slaps his hands to the sides of his head. "Thank God. Remember when she lurked outside school in her slut shorts and bikini top, then offered us meth? I fucking hate her. If I could pull all her DNA out of my body, I'd pay a million dollars for it."

I'm not sure what I can do for him except point out the obvious. "Give it a day or two, and she'll be on someone else. Maybe block her number for a few days?"

"And miss the possibility of getting that phone call she ODed and died?" Jase snorts. "No way."

I bite my lower lip.

* * *

I don't have any real friends. Without Jase and his circle of friends, I wouldn't even have fake friends. Plenty of people to say 'hey' to in class, and that acknowledge me outside the classroom, but the groups of friends printed in those glossy college brochures haven't manifested. A Friday night, I'm feeling incredibly lonely and Jase invites me to Shelly's floor social in the common room. I fling aside my conviction for companionship and follow Jase to the social.

There's a nostalgia to the atmosphere. It feels almost like old times; hanging out with no purpose really, just companionship, bullshitting with each other, and talking to a cute blonde that Jase introduced to me. I can't remember her name for the life of me, but she has short-cropped hair and stork-long legs.

It's like picking up a bad habit. I know letting the semi-silent treatment drop between Jase and me is wrong, but it feels so comforting and familiar. Maybe I'm a junkie like his mother, too weak to find a different path than what's in front of me.

Shelly has bigger balls than I do, walking right up to Jase when she arrives and striking up a conversation by reminding him of the floor rules of quiet hours and city ordinances on public intoxication.

"Shelly, I know, ease up," Jase says. He's flippant, like he's talking down to an annoying younger sibling.

"Just follow the rules, Jason," she warns.

I love Shelly for the fact that she calls him by his full first name, even to his face. It's a touchy-feely thing Jase and I have in common, hating our full names, so it's like a guilty pleasure listening to her use it on him and not me.

Jase huffs and puts his arm around the redhead he's been flirting with.

The blonde asks me a question, and I turn my attention to her. Before I can answer, Shelly's loud voice calls out, "Hey, Dakota!"

Shelly is waving and using her friendly smile. Looking around the blonde, I see Dakota standing in the hall, wearing khaki shorts and a blue hoodie with what looks like a radish on it. Looking distrustful, he tips his hand in a tiny wave, and he has that grim reaper grimace for a smile.

"Come on over," Shelly calls and waves at him before half-turning to face us. "Behave," she growls. I know she's speaking to Jase, but I feel condemned for standing near him.

Dakota comes over, eyeing us when Shelly starts talking again. "Let me introduce you. This is Shana." She points to the redhead standing next to Jase. "And this is

Veronica, and they live on the other end of the hall." I silently thank her for naming the blonde.

Veronica's head tilts. "I think we have English together. With Newton?" she asks.

"Yeah," Dakota sighs a bit. Jase mutters something under his breath, and Dakota gives him a death stare. I get this happy little flutter seeing Dakota back in fighting form.

Veronica nods. "I'm horrible with names, but I definitely remember North." She smiles softly. It's a sweeter smile than any she's given me so far. I should probably be jealous, but there's nothing in my heart that twinges. Dakota has way more working for him than I have.

"Newton's roll call skills could use some work," Dakota replies with a shrug. "I don't want to be confused for a Kardashian, so Dakota is fine."

"So, are you from North Dakota?" Veronica asks.

"No. I'm from Wisconsin."

I try not to laugh. Dakota has that disappointed teacher expression again.

"You like football?" Jase intrudes.

The tone of Jase's voice ripples my brain. There's something beneath his surface. I'm looking at a calm navy blue lake surrounded by spring bloom that hides the cold deep waters where anything could be.

"Not really," Dakota says.

"That settles that then. Just Packer fans, cow fuckers, and alcoholics in Wisconsin. Now I know what you are." Jase grins in triumph, and I have the urge to wipe it off his face. I mean, he almost killed the kid, now he's making fun of him?

"Ri-i-ight." Dakota's chin bobs up then down, his grim reaper face melting into a sarcastic wash. "I obviously molest cows in my spare time."

"At least you admit it, cow-fucker."

Shelly snaps in with her authoritative voice. "Jase, aren't you an adult? If you're going to be rude, you could just shut your mouth." There are daggers in her eyes, and Veronica shifts her weight nervously. I can't hear the racket of conversation in the room. The energy Jase is making is sucking in the focus of the room. Shelly's voice is drawing it deeper.

Jase ignores her, oblivious to the emotion rising around us. Continuing to stare Dakota down with his crooked faux smile, he takes a step toward Dakota. "Aw, come on, Shells, just trying to bond with my little suitemate. Trying to make friends."

"Sorry, no friend slots open," Dakota says with a half-smirk and a shake of his head. "The only open role in my life right now is Reappearing Jackass. You'd be a perfect fit for that, however."

My jaw sags in a gape. The girls start giggling, and Jase's lips go wry. That rippling in my brain murmurs it's going to get ugly. Jase's mouth writes big checks, and his temper can cash them. I know his fuse is non-existent now. Sliding my foot back, I shift my weight, bracing for the explosion. Veronica steps away. Shana moves back. Dakota stays right where he is.

"Pretty mouthy there, cow-fucker," Jase says.

"You think I have a pretty mouth? Dude," Dakota exclaims, loud enough for every soul, alive or dead, in the room to hear. "Are you hitting on me?"

There's a guttural echo in the room as diaphragms constrict in preparation for loud laughter. Jase's mouth widens into a teeth-baring smile. He's a starved wolf closing in on its prey. His left bicep tightens while he takes an aggressive step forward.

Grabbing his elbow, I dig my fingers in to hold him in place. "For shit's sake, Jase, leave him alone."

Jase turns his wolf eyes to me, with surprise softening his glare. I can hear a devastated 'et tu, Ian?' in my head. Flashing back over the last four years, I realize I have never, ever stopped him. From anything. A verbal discouragement, yes, but I have never put myself between him and whatever or whoever his prey was. I'm walking into traitor territory now. No wonder he's shocked.

"Shut your fucking mouth Ian," he sneers and hits my wrist with an open fist.

Part of me wants to leave, to walk away and wait for all of this to dissipate, and another part of me wants to punch him right in the mouth. I've never swung a fist in my life, but it's tempting. I might land one good punch on his face, but that would be it. He'd pound my face into the floor and keep hitting. I've seen it result in blood and fractures.

Dakota turns away first and walks away. Jase does this bro-chest pound and foot stomp while saying something. I think he's trying to signal his supremacy, but he looks like a demented rooster. The peanut gallery is a choir of disappointed boos. Shelly starts talking.

I hate everyone.

Turning my back on all of them, I leave the common area. The ruckus fades behind me as I walk down the hallway. The air is cooler, and I breathe it in and start exhaling my anger. Each inhale increases the anxiety, however, and the overwhelming need to apologize. I get to the suite door, and Dakota is keying the lock. For all his cool bravado a minute ago, his hand is shaking enough for his keys to kiss rapidly.

I can't stop the forces of my nature and have to fix this. "Jace is always an ass, don't take him seriously," I say. My voice sounds casual, like nothing exciting has happened in the last 90 days, much less 90 seconds.

Dakota curses, dropping his keys. Crouching to pick them up, he looks up and gives me a deep look. I can't read it very well. Maybe three feet separate us, and as he stands, I notice his eyes again.

Without thinking, I conversationally-stupidly blurt out, "Contacts?"

"No," he sighs and breaks our shared look. His hand is steady this time, keying the lock. "Just another shitty gift from my parents. Heterochromia."

"Oh," I say as he pushes the door open. I follow him into the entryway that separates our rooms, he going to his door as I remember what I was supposed to be talking about. "Look, I'm really sorry about Jase."

Dakota opens his door but doesn't cross the threshold. Instead, he leans against the doorframe, looking into his room. "You know, you apologize for him a lot."

"He's been my best friend for years." I sigh as if those words somehow explain everything.

Turning halfway around, Dakota tilts his head. "Is he?"

He holds my gaze another moment as if waiting for me to answer his question. I have no real answer, and that bothers me.

I should say something, but before I can think of that something, the door to his room clicks shut, followed by the turning tumblers of the deadbolt.

I don't know what to say, and I don't know what to think.

Chapter Three
October

Not hanging out with Jase outside of our room means no extended social circle and a lot of time by myself. This time around, I don't care about being lonely, but it's bothering me that my social life is built on a foundation of Jase. Doesn't anyone like me for my personality, not just because Jase and I are friends? Am I so dull that I'm only likable around him? Jase and my's relationship has been rocky since school started. Are high school friendships strong enough to make it past eighteen?

I start dissecting my life, and when I don't like what I see, I look for a distraction. I study a lot, but Dakota's simple question keeps creeping up on me; is Jase my friend at all?

"It still bothers me." I'm complaining to my twin brother over the phone. Staring out the window over my desk, I flick the end of my highlighter against my open textbook to make that satisfying hollow thump-thump-thump noise.

"It bothers you because Jase is a douchebag, and deep

down, you know it. You just ignored it in high school so you could be accepted and moderately popular."

I roll my eyes at Ben's words. "I don't think he's a complete douchebag. He's just being extremely unjustifiably douche-baggy."

"You know eventually that assholishness is going to rub off on you. Especially living and breathing near him as much as you do now. Then when you come home for a holiday I'll have to kick your worthless ass," Ben chuckles into the phone. He has one of those easy laughs that lightens his deep voice.

"Well, I'm not coming home for fall break, so I have to raincheck you on that ass beating."

"Thanksgiving then." He pauses for a drink, and I just know it's a bottle of Pepsi. "How's it going with the neighbor? The one Jase tried to kill?"

"Yeah." I sigh and lean my elbows onto my desk. "I've apologized to him a couple of times but don't think I'm making friends."

"What do you have to apologize for? Jase needs to, and if he hasn't said anything by now, he's not going to. You can't make Jase a good person. No matter how hard you try, you can't change a person on the inside. Only Jase or Jesus can do that."

The repetition of one of our grandmother's famous lines makes a corner of my mouth twitch.

"And we know there's only one of those people Jase believes in."

I know deep down Ben's right. I think. I can't make Jase change. Maybe I can guide it or inspire it, though? How much time had we spent together in high school? That had to give me some kind of influence on him. We'd even gotten over 'the incident'. Maybe not over it, just ignoring it. "I apologize because I feel bad about the whole thing, and it feels like I should have done something different. Jase still talks shit, and the guy deserves an apology."

"Yeah. From Jase. You're not Jase's secretary. You don't need to be his bitch anymore, Ian, you're in college now, make new friends and outgrow the old. And you feel bad because you don't care if people treat you like shit, but you have a bleeding heart for anyone else in trouble. You just don't act on that. So you double your shitty feeling because you see bad things happen to people and feel bad for them, then guilty you didn't do anything about it. You're just passive. I got all the aggressive. And Ian, as long as you're Jase's friend, that guy doesn't give a shit about your apologies and is never going to trust you. Which means you can't fix it. Move on." Another swig of Pepsi. "I've got to go. Break's over, and I have to get back into class."

"Enjoy twisting wenches or wrenches or whatever it is you do there."

"Turning wrenches. Later, Bro."

"Bye, Benjamin."

I hang up the phone and drop it on my desk. The next bang against the veneer is my forehead.

* * *

The dorms are quiet; most people have evacuated to either downtown or home for fall break. Break isn't long enough for me to justify the long drive home to Minnesota, but Jase justified it and left at noon. I don't go out on the town. I stay in my blissfully quiet dorm room under the guise of working on the paper I haven't started yet. I try, but I can't focus on it. I start surfing the internet and lose a few hours before cracking a Red Bull and forcing myself to work on my essay.

Digging through my backpack, I realize I can't find

my textbook. Groaning, I search through my desk, and still nothing. I'm kind of afraid it got sucked into the black hole that is Jase's three-quarters of our room, or I left it in the library, but I remember reading it in the bathroom. Specifically, leaving it on the counter with a highlighter marking my page.

Thanking the college gods, I open the door to my room, then frown. The bathroom door is shut, and I can hear the shower running. Dakota didn't go home or go out. Or not yet anyway. I sit back down at my desk and check my phone—8:03 pm.

Taking a swig of my energy drink, I start pulling up articles I've found to use for sources. I left my door open so I can hear when the bathroom is vacated, and leave one ear open while I start skimming web pages that are relevant to my assignment.

8:12 I still hear the shower running.

8:22.

    8:27.

       8:31.

At 8:35, I get up and walk back into the hall, wondering if my mind is playing tricks on me. It's not—the shower is still running. Feeling weird, I put my ear to the door and listen, expecting a giggling girl or other strange noises.

The beating rain of the shower is all I hear, and it gives me a brisk walk through a graveyard at midnight feeling. Like that moment in the movies when the music fades, and everything's moving in slow motion so dread pours over the audience.

I knock on the door and call out, "Hey?". There's no answer, and I box my knuckles harder. "I don't care if you smuggled your girlfriend in or something, but I left my book on the counter." Still nothing, just water, which is even weirder because the pattering of the artificial rain isn't changing like it does when someone's moving in it. Swallowing hard, I knock one more time with a prickle-haired fist. "Dakota? You okay?"

There's no answer. I'm not that worried about my book now, but what am I supposed to do? Call security? What if he's in there nailing his girlfriend really, really quietly on the floor? Do I just call Shelly? And on what, a case of Suitemate with Selective Hearing I Have A Foreboding Feeling About?

I wait, shifting my weight from foot to foot, but no epiphany comes.

Grabbing the handle and twisting it, I crack the door enough for steamy air to escape into the entryway and slap my face on the way by. "I need to grab my book," I call out, but still no answer. I take a deep breath of the wet air and push the door open enough to step inside just enough to reach the counter.

The first thing I see is blood.

Dark blood on the ivory tile floor is half-covered by a frayed and faded blue towel. Dakota is shirtless and sitting on the floor in an awkward position, half-slumped against the wall. His hand is pushed over the lip of the shower. More blood streaked across his skin. His right hand is clamped over his left wrist. The water circling the drain is stained pink. I feel my jaw dropping to make an exit for my stomach somersaulting up my throat.

He slit his wrist. While I was sitting at my desk, he'd been lying here bleeding out, trying to kill himself. There's blood everywhere, and he's just staring at me with this horrified surprise.

"What the hell are you doing?" I shriek, my voice cracking. Grabbing his discarded t-shirt off the floor, I kneel beside him. "Give me your arm." He doesn't move, just stares at me with this half-gone half-dumbfounded look. "Give me your fucking arm. What the hell is wrong with you?" I slap him upside the head harder than I mean to, making him flinch and my fingers sting.

He relinquishes his left arm, and it looks terrible with a deep gouge in his skin, so I wrap the shirt tight around his forearm. I turn the water off. It feels like a thousand degrees in the cramped bathroom.

"Christ all-fucking-mighty." I exhale and grope my hoodie pocket for my phone. "What the fuck were you doing?" I can't stop myself from screaming at him. Adrenaline shakes my fingers, streaking humidity and blood across the screen and making it impossible to unlock my phone.

"Don't call. You don't have to call," he finally speaks.

"Of course I'm going to fucking call. You're dying in the bathroom. Why isn't this fucking phone working?" my voice cracks.

"I didn't mean to. I'm not dying. Don't call 911. Please. You know how much an ambulance ride costs?"

My fingers stop fighting my phone, and I glare down at him. "You try to kill yourself, and now you're worried about how much an ambulance costs? Are you crazy?" Maybe that was a rhetorical question.

"I didn't try to kill myself, and I didn't do it on purpose! I'm not going to die right now," he gasps and bangs his head against the wall. With a heavy rise and fall of his shoulders, his lungs drag in a deep breath for a quick exhale.

"You need paramedics and-"

"I need stitches. I don't need a big scene. I just need stitches. And a new shirt."

"You're not funny," I growl.

Dakota snarls, "I'm not going anywhere in an ambulance, asshole."

Stalemate. My choices are to call an ambulance and

wait here for how long with him arguing with me and causing a huge scene when he refuses to ride in said ambulance, or to keep him calm and take him myself.

"Fine, no ambulance, but I'm taking you to the hospital myself. I don't do suicidal roommates."

"It's was an accident!" he howls. "If I wanted to be dead, I'd be fucking dead."

"Don't say shit like that. I'm getting you a shirt, and we're going."

Chapter Four
October

Apparently, they have rules at Memorial Hospital that differ from emergency rooms in movies. Unless you're family, they don't let you past the waiting room. They don't tell you anything after you've waited around an hour. I leave my number with the front desk clerk, but I hear paper crinkle when I turn my back to leave.

I go back to my hovel of a dorm room, but I can't sleep. Every time I close my eyes, I see Dakota on the floor and his blood making a run for the shower drain. I can't concentrate on my paper, so I scrub the bathroom so there are no questions. When I finish cleaning the red out of the grout, my fingers are raw.

I don't know if I should tell someone or not. Is it my place to say something? Do I call Shelly? I have no idea how this kind of thing works; was there a suicide accident report I should be filling out? Or a 'I-think-he-slit-his-wrist-but-he-said-he-wasn't-what-do-I-do' protocol? I'm an adult. There should be some kind of practical action to take here, but I can't think of anything, and I don't know who to ask.

Calling the hospital twice gets me nowhere. I could have lied and said I was his brother or something, but I realize I have no idea what Dakota's last name is.

I don't hear him come home. The cops never come to my door, so I assume he's still alive in the morning. I can't get any answers out of the hospital still, so I nix the idea of driving back to the emergency room. I don't have his number to call him either.

I want to call someone, to voice the thoughts going through my head. I flip through my phone several times, looking for a number to call, and find none. Most of the people in my phone are friends from high school I haven't talked to in months or college acquaintances you meet up with for lunch, not call when you're freaking out over the half-dead body you picked up last night.

I frown hard when I get to Jase's number. He's supposed to be my best friend, but the title seems hollow. I wouldn't know where to start. Sympathy and understanding are what I need, and Jase is the last place I'll find it. I think of calling my brother but dismiss the thought. I almost break down and call my mother, but I know she'll blow it out of proportion. Although, is there even a proportion for something like this?

I'm alone in this. I'm starting to feel alone in everything.

* * *

The library is quiet Saturday afternoon, but the lack of noise just makes the racket in my head louder. I can't concentrate when my mind keeps going back to walking into the bathroom and finding Dakota. This guilt hangs on my neck like a lock and chain. I could take it off if I wanted to, but I just can't. Flicking my music app onto something obnoxious, I try drowning out the images and force my brain to forget Dakota and focus on Lee and Lincoln.

As I'm reviewing my notes on The Battle of the Wilderness, movement catches my eye. Looking over the top of my laptop screen, I see Dakota walking across the library. I'm not a psych major, but didn't they hospitalize you or institutionalize you or something after you try to off yourself? I have been having visions in my head of him handcuffed to a hospital bed in a crisp white room, glaring at the wall, but here he is. White long-sleeved shirt, but no straight jacket.

He doesn't notice me or even look in my direction, he just heads for the back racks. Fidgeting in my seat, I try to rein back my brain that is spooling like a jet engine. Now that I've seen him living and on the loose, I have too many questions.

Pretending to work, I watch and wait for him to come back to the main room so I can corner him. Confrontation isn't my style at all, but it's going to happen now.

It feels like an hour passes, and I can't wait anymore. I hit the save button and leave the table, hoping the half-asleep work-study student at the main desk won't let anyone take off with my stuff. Heading into the back area of the library, I pretend to look at the identity placards on the aisle ends while I scout for Dakota.

And there he is, pale as a ghost in ripped jeans. There's a slit through the fabric on his left knee, the bottom hems are worn through, and the chunky frayed pieces trailing are his silent ghost chains.

As I walk down the aisle, he looks up at me, then back to the book he's putting on the shelf. I was expecting embarrassment or something, but I just got an unimpressed glance.

"Hey," I say.

"Hey," he answers, fingers still touching the book's spine as he meets my gaze. The lighting is dim, and the color difference in his eyes is hard to see.

"What…" I start and stop—all these questions in my head, and no tactful way to ask any of them. Thoughts just explode in my head, 'What happened at the hospital? How did you get out? Did they put you in a straight jacket? Why did you try to do it in the first place?' Clearing my throat, I try again, "When did you get back?"

"That unintelligible time of darkness that's either late last night or early this morning."

"They didn't keep you?" My voice squeaks a little, which is embarrassing.

"Why would they? Some fluids and stitches then out the door. No one noticed the brain damage from you cracking me in the head."

I know we're alone, but I still glance over my shoulder to check. Lowering my voice, I meet his gaze again and say, "Stitches don't fix being suicidal."

"Suicidal?" He repeats, mouth twitching into a half-smile. Exhausted as he looks, there is a spark in his eyes, something mischievous and powerful. He's in perfect control. "If I were suicidal, I would have done it before signing up for student loans."

Mixed emotions dance on my gut. How can he be so nonchalant? How is he always so funny? How does he go from being suicidal to being his normal self? Or what I know as normal?

His voice softens. Dakota takes a step closer to me and pulls the sleeve of his right arm up to his elbow. "It's a coping habit." Thin lines mark the underside of his forearm, flicks of scars hashmarked across his skin that I never noticed but seem so painfully obvious now. "I wasn't trying to off myself."

It hits me like a flood that I have no idea what is going on beneath his confident bravado. Everything I know about him is thick ice on a winter lake, and below the ice, there's darkness, pressure, and suffocation. "I..."

"You don't have to say anything," Dakota says and tugs his sleeve back down. "I already heard it last night. Here, visit this website and call this hotline next time you're being stupid. Talk to someone. Stop cutting yourself. Bye."

I cringe at his words. "I wasn't going to say that. I've just been trying to figure this out. All night I was wondering 'why the hell would my suitemate try to kill himself?'"

His eyes roll. "I wasn't-"

"I believe you. I'm just saying that's what I was thinking. Now I'm wondering why you need to do that to yourself. You seem like a normal, happy guy."

"You wouldn't understand, Ian."

"I don't understand. That's why I'm asking," I hiss. My fingers are pushing through my hair in a tell of my anxiety. "I'm never going to get that image out of my head. I've got your blood all over the seat of my car, and I'm going to look at that every day and wonder—"

"Sorry," he interrupts.

"Sorry for what?"

"About the car."

"I don't care about the fucking car." My hands turn into fists of frustration. "I just need to know why. If I know why then maybe I can help. Maybe it's selfish, but I don't want to live with eternal guilt if you accidentally kill yourself or something and everyone's asking me why I didn't do anything. I'm going to be that idiot on the ten o'clock news saying, 'Oh he was quiet and kept to himself, I shared a suite with him, but I didn't see any signs or think he needed help'."

He studies me for a long moment, letting my words hang in the air. Then he starts chuckling.

"It's not funny," I growl.

Staring him down, I notice little things; the softening of his bi-colored eyes, the falling of his shoulders as his laughter drains. His Adam's apple bobbing as he swallows. There's a twitch at the corner of his mouth as if he's suppressing a smile or joke.

I exhale and shake my head, forcing my voice to soften. "Just, if you need something or need to talk, I'm across the hall. If you don't want to come over because of Jase or something, you can text me, and I'll come over. Do you have your phone?"

"No, it's in my room."

"Do you have a piece of paper?" I ask, plucking a pen from behind my ear. I search my pockets, and he searches his to no avail.

"Here," he says quietly, pulling up his sleeve and offering his bandaged left wrist. "Write on that."

"This is seriously fucked up." I shake my head but take his arm and start writing gently.

"Probably." He smiles a little, watching me scrawl the memorized numbers.

As I write, my eyes wander up his arm. There are a few inches of skin between his bandage and the cuff of his shirt, and the inches are measured in more hash mark scars. My stomach sinks at the reality- this person I've been revering for having his shit together obviously doesn't. At least not all of it. Does anyone? If someone like him can lose it, then I don't think I'll ever keep it together.

Pulling out of my grasp, Dakota examines my penmanship before tugging down his sleeve. He grabs his book off the shelf with a "See ya."

* * *

I'm slammed with homework the next few days. It keeps my brain occupied at night, but not enough. I don't see Dakota, and I'm worried that my number rubbed off his arm or something else dire. I'm probably being over-zealous, but I can't help it. People don't typically bleed that much around me or require emergency room visits, and I'd like to keep that number low. It's all I can do to keep from beating down his door and asking if he's okay. Checking my phone is now a constant habit.

"Did you fuck someone hot this weekend or something?" Jase asks.

"What?" I ask, looking over my shoulder. He's lying in his bed, staring at me over his tablet, his eyes piercing me with suspicion.

"You keep checking your phone. Some girl do you and promise to call?" he starts laughing. Before I can answer him, he snorts and goes back to his tablet. "Grow some balls and be the man in a relationship for once. Just call her."

I frown and set my phone back down on my desk. Face up, though, just in case.

* * *

I can't put my finger on it, but something feels off. My brother would tell me it's the barometric pressure of the changing weather, and I can hear his voice perfectly. He's the concrete thinker, and I'm abstract; changing weather feels like evil foreboding and foreshadowing just like it symbolizes in every blockbuster movie. I will argue world history would be completely different if more people followed their gut feeling. Ulysses S. Grant followed his gut and stayed home instead of attending Ford's theater, but Ben doesn't consider that quality evidence.

Whatever it is, I don't feel right. Walking across the courtyard trailing Jase and Company under a blackening sky on our way to floor social, I start imagining Dakota on the floor of his room. His wrist is bleeding, he's losing consciousness as I'm heading for a free spaghetti dinner.

Out of habit, I grab for my phone so I can check my messages. I wish Dakota would have texted me something, anything, so I'd at least have his number. I can't find him on social media, not that I'm a pro at stalking. It'd ease my mind if I could just ask if he was okay and get a response. Maybe that's why he hasn't messaged me, and he knows I'd be annoying.

My phone isn't in my back pocket. I fumble through the rest of my pockets and find nothing. Stopping in my tracks, I sigh.

"What's wrong?" a male voice asks. I look up and see everyone standing there looking at me.

"I forgot my phone. I'm gonna grab it. I'll see you guys there."

There's a chorus of 'sures' and a snort from Alex. "Dude, disconnect for a few hours. You'll live."

"Ian's hiding an ugly girlfriend or something." Jase rolls his eyes. "He's always checking his phone now. I think she's sexting him all day because she's too fat to leave her house."

Without another word, I go back to our dorm hall.

Taking the stairs two at a time, I'm back at my suite door in no time. I have to release my crazy before it rips out of my chest. Before retrieving my phone, I go to Dakota's room and knock on the door. I listen and hear nothing. I knock again, a little firmer.

"Hey, uh, it's Ian."

A long moment stretches out before I hear Dakota's voice. "It's open."

My hand is twisting the knob before I can think, then it pushes the heavy door, and I step into his room. It's dark, and no lights are on. I'm surprised how clean the room is. Every other dorm room I've seen has been somewhere between a shitpit and cluttered. The empty bed and furniture intended for his roommate are pushed against the wall to my left. Staring at me from the wall is a blonde character on a poster-sized Hellblazer comic cover. A bunch of band posters are taped to the long wall. I recognize Fall Out Boy, Johnny Cash, and Dierks Bentley, but the others are foreign to me. His bed is pushed up to the far wall on my right, near the window with opened shades. It takes me a second to realize he's in the bed, curled up under a dark-colored sherpa comforter.

"Don't feel like free food tonight? Shelly got Alalanzo's catered and free movie in the student center. Best Italian food in town."

"No, just *California dreamin' on such a winter's day.*" His voice is soft memory foam, leaving an indent around my brain. *"All the leaves are brown, and the sky is grey."*

"Isn't that a song?

"Yeah. "California Dreamin'"". By The Mamas and The Papas. I think. I have a headache," he says quietly.

"You need anything?"

He pulls the cover a little tighter around himself and grunts.

"Okay," I sigh. I can't help it. That hopeless feeling is creeping into my body again. "I left my phone in my room, just wanted to, uh-"

"Check on me," he says. I feel self-conscious, and he

doesn't comfort me with his usual grim smile. "Don't want to be that guy on the news talking about your dead suitemate with spaghetti sauce on your shirt?"

"My luck, it would be on my face, not my shirt."

He laughs in his throat, and with a quick 'hang on', I go back to my room, but I don't grab my phone. I grab a bottle of Excedrin out of my desk and snatch a Mountain Dew out of Jase's 5/8ths of the fridge, then go back to Dakota's room.

I start talking as I approach his bed. "My mom gets migraines sometimes, and I get headaches sometimes. This always helps me take the edge off." He opens his eyes and looks at me oddly. I hold out the can, "I hope you're not a Mormon because the caffeine really helps."

Cracking a small smile, he sits up in bed, takes the can, and pops the tab. "Not a Mormon."

"Well." I shrug and hand him two tablets. "I don't see any sacrificial blood rituals laying around, so you can't be into anything too weird."

"I cleaned up after the blood sacrifice earlier."

Setting the pill bottle down on his desk, I think about the bloodstain in my Cherokee and I laugh. It's sick humor, but it strikes something in me, like laughing at the horror makes it less powerful. Without asking for an invitation, I drop into his desk chair. An expensive Mac, an iPad, and a few other gadgets I don't recognize are neatly organized on his desk. There are five black instrument cases stacked on the floor, and I wonder what's inside.

Turning away from his toys and back to him, I ask, "So that's what I interrupted in the bathroom then? Blood sacrifice ritual?" My skin feels hot as soon as the words leave my mouth. I'm not good at joking around, and this is why I don't try.

To my surprise and relief, he chuckles a little and sets

the green soda can down on his nightstand. "A sacrificial offering to the God of Shower Drainage does make for a cooler story than just saying I had a moment of weakness. Or maybe you're just bad luck for me. What stupid thing haven't you gotten to see me do yet this semester?"

"I must be Super Anti-Hero guy or something," I say.

"Mmm," he muses. "Super Anti-Protagonist Guy. They'll call you The Sap for short."

"That would be Super Antagonist Guy. The Sag. That's a horrible name."

"Screw it," he says, settling back down in his bed. "We'll just call you Lucky."

"I like that one. It's an interesting name. I could shoot clover leaves out of my belly button or something."

His forehead crinkles, creasing his eyebrows as he says, "You've got an interesting name."

"Says the kid named North Dakota," I snort.

"We're the same age, so I'm not a kid," he quips. "And Ian isn't that common of a name either."

"First, I was held back in school so I'm probably older than you. Second, Ian's short for Christian. My dad went by Chris, and I hate the name Chris, so Ian was all that was left."

Dakota's dark eyebrows uncurl. "You really hate the name Chris, or do you hate your dad?"

His question catches me off-guard. I clear my throat, stalling as I pull an answer together. I don't want to open the can of mental fuckery that is my dad situation. I have no idea how he even noticed the can. "I don't know him, so I can't actually hate him I guess. Christian is better than Christopher, at least."

"I like Christian. At least you can get a nickname. My

first name is North; what the hell can I do with that?"

"No-no?" I offer.

"Sounds like a bad dog."

"Orth? Ort? Nor?"

His right eyebrow twitches, for a moment making a cinnamon-colored arch. "Hence why I go by my middle name. Which is almost as bad."

"Dak? Ko-ko?" I say.

"I hate those. Call me Dak or Ko-ko, and I'll call you Chris."

"I could call you D?"

"I'm more than just dick."

"Kota?"

"That sounds like a pet name."

"Alright, Dakota it is." I laugh and lean back in the chair. "You've probably been asked this a hundred times before, but why did your parents name you North Dakota to begin with?"

"It was my mom. She got a little crazier the older she got or something. I have two brothers, one older one younger." He pauses and takes a drink. "She had something about how she was never going to get off the farm, and she decided to name us after places she wanted to visit. So, we got states for names."

"That sounds kind of cool, actually," I say.

"My older brother is Montana, which isn't so bad. I thought I got the shit end of the deal with North Dakota until my younger brother was born. His name is Pennsylvania."

I can't help the rockslide of laughter that falls out of my mouth. "For real?"

"Swear on my grandmother's grave. He goes by Pen. He's a junior in high school but super smart, like will graduate early probably smart. I think he still gets teased, though."

I wave my hand between breaths. "I'm sorry, I shouldn't laugh."

"You should laugh. It's hilarious. Who names their son Pennsylvania? I mean, she had forty-eight states left to pick from and she chose that one? And it gets better. My brothers got cities for their middle names. She had to make Dakota my middle name, so I escaped unscathed. My brother Montana got Missoula for a middle name and Pen got Erie."

"Are you serious?"

"Swear. You can't make shit like this up."

Thunder rolls outside, and rain starts to pour, tapping at the window. My laughter dies out, leaving the two of us alone with each other.

My eyes are still wet from laughing, and I rub my right with the back of my wrist. "I'm sorry, I shouldn't have laughed," I say.

"Ian, you apologize way too much for stupid shit. Constantly."

I scuff my foot against the carpet, and feel like a child being corrected. "I can't help it. Habit, I guess."

Dakota rolls his eyes. "More like a side-effect."

"Side-effect?"

"I've noticed you kind of just follow your buddy Jase around and apologize for him."

That habit makes me jump to the defense. "I know Jase is kind of rough, but he—"

Dakota interrupts. "He's an asshole. Absolutely no redeeming qualities. I don't get how you two are friends, with you having a moral conscience and him lacking one."

"Well." My lips pull back into a tight frown. "We went through high school together, and I was on the lacrosse team with him for four years."

"So?" he interrupts again. "There's a guy who lives two farms up from me back in Wisconsin that I went to school with since Kindergarten, that doesn't make us friends. Just because you've been around someone for a period of time doesn't mean you automatically have an unbreakable bond. If you're sports bros, the bro-ing stops once the season is over."

"I don't think that's true."

"Uh-huh. Still no explanation on how Jase with no ethics can make friends with you."

"I don't think he has no moral conscience. He's kind of hard to understand. Yes, he's an asshole, and I don't exactly condone ninety percent of his actions, but I don't know. He's just been my best friend since I joined the lacrosse team. Maybe opposites attract." I finish lamely.

"Did you really pick him to be your friend, or is it just that he accepted you as his?" Dakota asks. This perk to his eyebrows tells me he knows the answer to the question. Yet I don't.

"What… what does it matter who picked who as a best friend?

"I didn't say that. Did you pick to be friends with him, or did you just get accepted into his fold? Friendship is just like a romantic relationship. Ideally, things are balanced." He holds his hand out evenly, demonstrating the idea of balance as if I'm not familiar with the concept. "Little sway back and forth, but everything stays on the fulcrum. If you didn't build a relationship, there's no fulcrum." He twists his hand vertical. "Then you've got one person who decided this is what it's going to be, and they're on top, and the person that just goes along with it is on the bottom. And they stay there. And it never changes because there's nothing to pivot on. You're never going to have an upswing."

"Oh." When have I ever been on the upswing?

"You two don't have a fulcrum. Does he give two shits about you? Are you really important to him because of what's inside or what's outside?"

Dakota's question hangs in the air, and his expression softens as another crash of lightning breaks the sky. I guess I do know the answer if I have the balls to admit it; I'm sure there's half a shit given, and it's what's on my outside that counts.

I hate how easily Dakota seems to read me, finding all of my flaws, but at the same time he's not being an asshole about it and making fun of me. Maybe that's the trade-off, I don't make a big deal about him being an epileptic wrist-cutter, and he won't make a big deal about me being a lost-puppy loser.

Sighing a little, he closes his eyes and leans back into his pillow. "Life is too short to have people in your life that don't give a shit about you."

I stare at his window, watching the rain weaving pathways on the glass. "What if you get rid of those people, then there's no one left?"

"It's not that bad, being alone."

"Says the kid who cut his wrist in the bathroom."

"For the last time, I was not slitting my wrist and I was nowhere near dying. Stop calling me that; I'm not a kid compared to you just because I'm shorter than you," he hisses. "And there are monsters out there worse than loneliness. Way worse."

Chapter Five
October

I duck back into my suite with the intention of just swapping books out. Muffled noises warn me I'm not alone, and when I enter Jase and I's room Alex is talking to Jase and asking, "Your suitemate?"

No surprise, Alex is spread out on my bed, hands behind his head to air out his pits, and they've both just come back from the gym. My lip curls at the thought of sleeping under a man-musk-scented comforter. I can't do laundry tonight, so I better get used to the idea.

Jase answers, "Ian's been trying to tame it. When I came back from floor social last week, Ian had infiltrated its natural habitat. Isn't that right, Ian?" Jase asks as he twirls in his desk chair to face me. Alex doesn't move off my bed.

I roll my eyes and start swapping books out of my backpack.

"Where are you off to already?" Alex asks.

"Study session," I say.

Alex whines, "Are you serious? Ian, it's Friday night. I

thought we were all going out?”

“You guys can still go out. Send me a text where you end up, and if I finish early, I’ll join you.” My voice sounds convincing enough. I hope.

“Who the hell studies on a Friday?” Alex asks.

I lie. “Some people in Dakota’s history class I’m tutoring.”

“Oh for fuck’s sake, here we go with Northie again.” Jase sighs, then rolls his boulder-black eyes in a big production. He looks to Alex and complains, “If they become best friends in the world, then Ian might forgive me for that party at the Lair.” Jase turns his sour eyes on me. “What’s the big occasion tonight? You going to get him to eat out of your hand?”

I shoulder my backpack and grab my keys. “Whatever, Jase.”

“I’m not texting you shit, Ian. You don’t want to go out with us, then stay here and study dead dudes.”

“Guess that’s the beauty of it being my birthday.” I grin and back out the door. “I can do whatever I want.”

Jase has been planning on what to do for my birthday as a newly-minted twenty, a lot about the local strip club and the local dive bar that serves you if you look old enough or possess a credible-enough fake ID. I feel like it is his way of trying to smooth things over between us. Yet not once did he ask me what I wanted to do. Now here we are, my birthday or not, they were going out. I feel stupid I never noticed it before; celebrating in my honor was an excuse. It was never about me.

It’s a relief to leave them, get out of my room, out of my suite, out of my dorm hall. The night air is cold, and the sky ebony above the street lights. Walking across campus, I see few people outside, and the ones I do see are in Milford University hoodies and jackets. The library is a glowing beacon, light blooming out of its glass walls, and

I hurry toward it. Book stacks and quiet places to research are strong arms open to offer me an embrace of solace. A building full of dead dudes is more comfortable than my own dorm room.

When I get inside the warm building, I exhale in relief. Sitting at one of the back tables is Dakota, face inches from his laptop screen.

"Hey," I say and set my book bag down on the oak tabletop.

Dakota looks up, smiling around a candy cane. It looks like a fishing hook caught him. He pulls the red and white swirled candy hook out of his mouth. The dye from the swirl of the stick has reddened his lips. "My favorite suitemate that is conveniently a history major, welcome."

"Not that I have much competition for favorite suitemate." I chuckle and pull out a chair. "Christmas candy?"

"They're already stocking it at WalMart." Dakota shrugs and pokes the peppermint stick back into his mouth. He pushes his laptop aside, and I see the white lettering on his black t-shirt. 'How to do Maths: Write down the problem and cry'.

I'm envious of how his personality just oozes out of him. His clothes, his wit, his facial expressions, quirks, they all work together to make his identity. Everything expresses him. If I closed my eyes I could imagine an aura of all the bits and pieces that make him and I'd know it was him without seeing him. He just has this charming persona that is unique and just so him. I feel like a cookie-cutter replica of average that just fades into the crowd. No one could identify me without calling me by name. I don't even know if I have an aura.

I ask, "You're not majoring in History or Math, I take it?"

"Music," he mouths around his stick. "Hence a bad

grade in history right now."

I sit down and ask, "Which teacher do you have?"

"Acklund."

"He's pretty intense. What's your topic?"

"Uh…"

Leaning my elbows into the over-laquered tabletop, my lips twist themselves wry. "So we have some work to do."

Dakota and I push through the library's glass doors, and the air slaps my face with its chilled thickness. The light posts on either side of the walkway are humming from their electric life source.

"*Black as night, black as coal,*" Dakota calls out to the empty courtyard, gesturing to the charcoaled sky above us. "*I want to see the sun, blotted out from the sky.*"

His words wiggle recognition out of my brain. "Wait. That's familiar."

"*I want to see it painted, painted, painted black.*"

I smile with satisfaction. "Rolling Stones."

"You're speaking my language." Dakota catches my eye and grins. "Sorry I kept you out so late."

"Trust me, I didn't have anything better planned. You've got your paper finished now, ahead of schedule. You may make it to Spring semester."

"Maybe. A Friday night and you didn't have anything better planned?" he asks with a raised eyebrow. "Or were you worried I'd kill myself if I didn't get this paper finished?"

He laughs, but I frown.

"What?" he asks.

"Funny, but I feel guilty for wanting to laugh."

"Why?"

"Death is so absolute."

"It is absolute, so why be afraid of it?" He shrugs one shoulder, making his backpack bob. It's a well-worn grey nylon bag with a chincy red rabbit's foot clipped to the main zipper.

"I'm not afraid of death exactly," I say. "I'm afraid of its mode of transportation."

We walk a little way down the sidewalk, our footfalls tapping the cool concrete. The slapping of the soles of his Chucks echo louder than the soles of my Nikes. Just like his soul echoes louder than mine.

Dakota stops, and I do too. His two-colored eyes look dark when his gaze meets mine, and his breath is wispy. Before I can ask him what's up, he says, "Don't worry about trivial mortal things like that. If you did know how you would leave this world, then what? You couldn't stop it, couldn't change it. Knowing wouldn't do you any favors, so maybe the mystery isn't so bad? Maybe that's the charismata."

My inner nerd opens my mouth. "Sarah Winchester, the heiress to all the Winchester fortune, was told she'd die if she didn't keep building, so she spent the rest of her life building a crazy mansion with carpenters working 24/7 so she wouldn't be dragged to hell by ghosts. It didn't work out, still died in the end and lived a lonely life up until that. Amphiaraus was a Greek King in mythos who foresaw his defeat and death in a battle and still went through with it."

"And he spent his last days wigging out over it, didn't

he? Wasn't worth it, was it?"

I put my hands in my jacket pockets and sigh. "He tried to warn everyone, but the battle still happened, he still died, et cetera. He also got eternal damnation from Dante Aligheri for sorcery, so worth it, maybe not. Maybe there's not a point in enjoying those days instead of stopping it either." I look up at the starless sky and exhale, watching my smoky breath fade into the darkness. I start talking, and I don't know why I'm telling this to him. "My grandmother was diagnosed with liver cancer two years ago. She tried all the treatments and everything, tried to change her ending I guess you could say. They gave her two years, and she died nine months after being diagnosed. She made the most of it as well as she could, but you're right, she couldn't stop it."

"I'm sorry. I know that's tough."

I exhale in a soft moan. "It really sucked. My mom was a single mother until we were in junior high when she met my step-father Troy and they married our Freshman year. There was a lot of time she was swinging two jobs, so we spent that time with our grandmother."

"How many?" he asks.

"How many what?" I blink and refocus on his eyes instead of the stars. They are just as deep and infinite.

"You said we. How many siblings do you have?" he asks as he rubs his forehead.

"One then, two now. I have a twin brother, and my mom and Troy adopted a girl after they married, so a younger sister too. Not by much; she's sixteen." My phone blares, and I apologize as I fish it out of my pocket.

"That's a face," Dakota says as I look at my screen.

"Dumbasses." I sigh and show him the screen. There's a picture of Alex with his face smashed into a stripper's chest. Below it is the text 'Happy Birthday, glad you're not here'.

Dakota yelps. "It's your birthday?"

"Yeah. Woo-hoo," I roll my eyes and twirl a finger in the air, then slide my phone into my back pocket.

"What the hell are you doing hanging out with me doing homework on your birthday?" Dakota asks.

I snort loudly. "Jase planned my quote unquote, party. I know what I'm missing out on, and it's not much." My voice is so convincing, and the words sound so much cooler than the truth; if I'm not with Jase, I have no friends, and I'm not sure I want those friends.

"College guy skipping out on his free stripper party? You sick, or do you really think I'd off myself over a paper?"

His humor forces me to smile. "No, I don't," I say. " I just don't see the point. I had a girlfriend in high school, and I know what boobs feel like. I spent four years of high school partying with Jase and I'm no better off. Maybe it's time to try something different."

"Well let me buy you dinner, or breakfast, or coffee or something, since it's your birthday." He starts walking, and I fall in step beside him. "I think the caf has those packaged cupcakes in the vending machines."

"Those are so gross."

"Well, if we hang out there long enough, the morning crew will come in and we get first dibs on the fresh donuts."

"I don't know if I can stay up that late in my old age," I joke.

"Fine, we won't stay that long. Just pick something for me to buy you to ease my conscience." He flips his head to stare at me with narrowed eyes, then makes a slicing motion with his index finger against his forearm. "Or else."

"There is something seriously wrong with you, you

know that, right?"

"Something is humorously wrong with me. You laughed."

I'm not too old, I lied. We get first dibs on the morning donuts at 7 AM and leave the cafeteria to wander back to our dorm. I can't clearly remember the last time I stayed up this late just talking to someone. Probably with my ex-girlfriend Sarah, but I can't grasp a peaceful memory of it. It's like knowing there's big fish in the lake but you can't catch anything. I can't find a high school memory of peace with anyone outside of family; not studying, not at a party, or just hanging out. All that team spirit and camaraderie from being on the lacrosse team seems so empty now. It was what I wanted then, but it's not enough for me now.

Being around Dakota feels comfortable, like a cozy sweatshirt I forgot I owned, and I'm grateful I put it on.

"Question," I ask before swallowing my last bite of Bavarian cream. "How did you end up here at Milford?"

"What about you? You're from Minnesota. What are you doing here in BFE Illinois?"

There he went, turning the questions back on me. I've noticed he likes flipping the subject away from himself. Maybe that's why I enjoy his company; he seems legit curious about me, like I'm number one. Maybe he's hiding something, but I want to believe it's me. I don't want to believe in a falsehood, though, so I ask, "Are you really that interested in my life or do you just have something to hide? You deflect."

He chews his bite of donut before answering me. "I came down here because this is where my mom went to school before my dad knocked her up and she had to drop out. She always wanted me to come here because of their music program. I was able to write one hell of an essay and managed to get a scholarship from the alumni association or something, I don't even remember. Your turn."

I sigh. "I ended up here because of a girl and Jase. Sarah and I were dating during senior year, and she was going to State, but I wanted to go to a smaller school. Milford has a really good education program for a wannabe History teacher, and bonus, it's only a half-hour drive to State. Jase got an offer to play on Milford's last-place Division III football team. I applied, was accepted, and my mom and step-dad are willing to pay for it." The fact that my parents are paying my way makes me feel ashamed. It sounds as if I'm still a child, not paying or making my own way, even though I'm not the only one on campus with an education fund. It makes me feel dirty when most of my classmates are on borrowed cash, and I just happen to have a wealthy step-parent. I brush the guilt aside for the sake of the story. "Sarah and I broke up the week before school ended and I decided to come here anyway. Jase was still coming here and we were set to be roommates, and best friends stick together and all that."

"Huh," he muses as I open the door to our suite.

"Where the hell you two been all night?" Jase asks. He's exiting the bathroom, stark naked, barely covering himself with one hand and peering at us with bloodshot eyes.

"Out," I answer.

"Hunting bitches," Dakota adds with his sarcastic glee. I think Jase doesn't pick up on the sarcastic element, which gives me a kind of righteous satisfaction.

"Must not have gone well, I see you came back with each other. Oh sorry, Ian, I should warn you, that Veronica chick is sleeping, so try to keep quiet."

Jase doesn't move, he just stands there as the moment

stretches. There's a smug fog in Jase's eyes, a tint over his reddened sclera like he's challenging me. He's flaunting it, as if bedding some girl I talked to once proves something. I don't know what I'm supposed to be jealous of, and I hope that shows on my face.

"So move, bitch, get out the way," Dakota mutters.

"What?" Jase asks, his brow furrowing as the song's tune pops into my head.

"Ludacris," I say.

"What's ludicrous?" Jase asks with a small shake of his head as his eyes squint into their judgemental peering state.

"Never mind." I roll my eyes as Dakota starts snickering. "As long as she's not in my bed I don't care. I'm going to sleep."

"Well hurry up and go to sleep then so I can wake her up for round three." Jase laughs and shakes his hand covering his dick. With his non-dick hand, he opens the door and leads the way into our dark room while his bare ass glows from the hall light.

* * *

"Come on, we're going to be late," I growl at Jase, who is moving around our room at a speed sloths would find slow. "Midterms, remember? Those are tests?"

"Yeah, I know. I need my hat."

The thought of leaving him behind so I make sure I'm in class early crosses my mind, but I don't want to be called a bitch for it later. Rationally, there is enough time to walk across campus and be sitting in my Psych class ready for my test. Maybe enough time to also tie my shoes.

"Alright, I found it. Let's go, bitch."

Well, so much for that.

Jase slides his black ball cap on with one hand and yanks his backpack off the floor with the other. "Start quizzing me."

As if cramming in the last ten minutes is going to help him master the foundations of life before his exam. He slept through most of Bio in high school, and I can't imagine he's taken an interest in actually learning anything. I don't think he's interested in anything specific academically, has picked a major, or has thought of anything past college sports. At least he has a grasp of reality and doesn't dream of being picked in the NFL draft or making the Olympic lacrosse team or something else unrealistic.

"Ian, come on. Cells," Jase huffs when we enter the elevator.

Of course, he doesn't have any flashcards or notes, so I have to scrape my brain for information on cells and cellular processes. My lack of memory is irritating him, and his demanding more insistent as we hustle down the sidewalks to get away from the dormitory halls and toward the lecture halls.

Jase is stumbling through an acid-trip explanation of cellular respiration when I hear singing. I interrupt him, "Do you hear that?"

"What?" He listens, then shrugs his shoulders. "It's singing. Probably some fat chicks because it's about to be over."

My eyes tumble clockwise. My ears are trying to catch the words twirling in the air.

Jase starts singing along, *"Tommy's got a six-string in hoc."* Thank god he's quiet because he sings so off-key sea sirens would cover their ears.

Rounding a sharp building corner brings us to a bricked hardscape that splats out to three overlording classroom buildings. Right in the middle of it is a bronzed statue of someone that donated a lot of money to the school at some point, and standing on his pedestal are five guys and two girls in blue Milford shirts. They are belting out lyrics, and rounding them is a loose crowd; some watching, some clapping in time, some singing along, some walking past on their way to exams.

That includes us walking fast and Jase singing. And Jase clapping me in the chest and accusing me, "you're not singing."

Probably because I don't know the words?

"You don't know this song?" Jase yelps.

To hide my slight embarrassment that everyone around me knows the song and I don't, I look past him. The singers on the pedestal are fist-pumping the air, mimicking their audience.

"Dude, it's BON JOVI!"

I recognize one of the singers, but it's not anyone I know named Bon Jovi. White long sleeves under his slim-fit blue shirt and that signature red baseball cap. "And that's Dakota."

"The singer!"

"Yeah, there." I gesture, and somehow Dakota senses my pointing because he looks right at me. I even get a thumbs up in acknowledgment.

"Northie?" Jase asks, slowing his step and squinting his eyes.

Dakota must have read Jase's lips because Dakota's thumbs up turns into the middle finger. *"Whoaaaaaaaa we're halfway there, whoa-oh, living on a pra-yer."*

* * *

Reason number three thousand and fifty-two why Jase is popular is his car. His high school graduation present was a brand new black Yukon Denali, and when you have a vehicle that you can illegally cram fourteen people in for midnight food runs, you get popular on campus. There's nine people stuffed into the SUV tonight, but I get my ceremonial position riding shotgun. I guess this means we're still 'bros'. I feel a mix of satisfaction and shame twisting around my spine, like the snake of sin that tempted Eve was embracing me and whispering in one ear. Not only am I drinking from the poisoned well, I'm enjoying it.

As we cross town I try to think of something else. The history of the term shotgun pops into my head. Back in the days of western expansion, there were always two men seated on the driver's bench of stagecoaches. One drove, and the other had a shotgun at the ready in case of trouble. So who was more important; the one with the driving lines in his hands that decided on the direction, or the one with the shells that decided who to use them on?

"This song is awesome," Jase howls, silencing my thought by jamming his finger against the steering wheel's volume control. He's a horrible singer, but it doesn't stop him from belting out the words.

Comfort embraces me, snuffing the snake inside me. Maybe it's nostalgia that's romancing my mood, but Jase's Yukon buzzing with laughter and overworked speakers puts a smile on my face. No serious talk, just loud music and jokes. It's so reminiscent of my last few years of high school it feels like I'm normal.

I've slid into a comfortable but bad habit. I'm justifying

it that Jase has been less of an asshole the last week.

"Hey, we almost there?" Alex asks when the song ends, leaning into the front of the cab between Jase and me. His black suit smells like Goodwill. At least I laundered my suit.

"Patience, Alfred," Jase rumbles in his best Batman impersonation and flips his turn signal on. I don't know how the hell he can see through his kid-sized costume mask, but he whips into the parking lot of a nightspot called Cover Ups. We circle the lot twice and don't find a space, so Jase drives his SUV up onto the berm separating Cover Ups from the strip mall next door. If I'd done it, the cops would be ticketing me before I stepped out of the vehicle, but Jase will get away with it.

I slide out of the front seat then put my black stovepipe hat on. I wish I had thought of this costume sooner; I'd have grown an actual beard instead of just scruff that itches my jawline.

"Batmobile, lock," Jase barks, then hits the alarm button on his key fob. He's wearing a Batman t-shirt, a yellow belt, a kid's costume mask, and a black trash bag around his neck. I doubt anyone's fooled.

Someone nudges me on the shoulder. "What movie are you from again?" asks the muscled guy painted green as we walk toward the entrance.

"It's Ian. He has to be a famous dead dude." Jase answers. "Abraham Lincoln."

"Dead Abraham Lincoln?"

Scowling, I pull the felt hat down tighter on my head. "Yes, Abraham Lincoln is dead." I can hear Jase chuckling at my expense.

Cover Ups' main door is plastered with posters advertising their Halloween party. Other than being a nightspot for eighteen-plus, their claim to fame is a weekend live band that does covers. The flyers say the band is doing Fall Out Boy songs tonight, and I think of the poster in Dakota's room. Prize money is listed for different categories of costumes, but I don't think anyone in our group is a running contestant. I might have had a chance if they had a 'non-fictional dead dudes' category, but Lincoln isn't exactly some super creative idea.

On the other side of the door is a bouncer checking IDs for at least eighteen and holding a handful of fluorescent wristbands for alcohol-legals like Jase's fake ID, a live band, fake fog, and the atmosphere that you can only find in a packed college hang out.

It's impossible to think when a band is playing loud enough that the bass lines vibrate your skull. You can't stand in a crowd of people dancing and not start to move. If you want to stick with your friends, you have to stay close, as the bunch of us do, but there is no talking; just occasional yelling over the noise to each other. It's camaraderie without any effort, and I feel like I'm surrounded by friends. I know it's an illusion, but I'm going to ignore that fact.

"I can't see past your damn hat," Jase says, and grabbing my elbow, he pulls me over to his side of the standing table we'd overtaken.

My back had been to the stage, and from my new angle, I have a view of it. From the first and only other time I've been here, the band's tacky banner on the wall has been replaced by 'Full Coverage' in purple neon lettering. The fake fog makes the letters hazy. Unaffected, the band finishes their song with a flourish of guitars.

"Woooooo," Alex hoots and slides a bucket of amber bottles onto the table, and Jase plucks one for himself before pushing the bucket onto me. I pass the bucket on because with my luck, one of the bouncers would catch me.

A singer leads the band off on another song to the kick drum's steady beat. I put my clear plastic cup of Pepsi to my lips, then slosh it all over the table when Jase buries his elbow between my ribs.

"What the hell?" I try to twist away from the pain, but the packed crowd prevents my escape.

"Dude, you didn't notice?" he yells. Shaking his head, he pulls his elbow out of my lungs and points at the stage. "There."

I wonder if he's talking about the changes to the stage since I was last here with him. The lead singer belts the verse, raising his hands above his head and clapping to the beat. Around me the crowd is getting tight, moving together as the bodies jump and scream the lyrics. Pulling his mic from the stand, the singer moves across the stage, and I see his black and yellow shirt.

"Batman shirt?" I yell at Jase.

I get a look that says I'm stupid.

"Not him. *Him,*" Jase screams as the music slows for the bridge. He's stabbing his finger at the stage, and when my eyes lock onto his focus, I'm shocked. The bassist stepping up to join the vocals is Dakota.

I know he is in the music program, but this wasn't what I pictured. Music kids I knew in high school played in orchestra and band and wore matching suits for seasonal concerts. I had imagined Dakota in the white shirt and tie, shiny dress shoes, plinking out Beethoven on a piano when he said music major. Dakota rocking a glossy black bass guitar, singing pop-rock in a college town hangout, isn't what I ever expected.

White fangs are screen printed on his black t-shirt, matching the thick white bracelets on his arms. I can see the purple neon reflection off his skin, highlighting the layer of sweat on his exposed flesh. Colored lighting above the stage flips, turning him a shade of blue then a warm red. The chorus comes again, and he's spinning and jumping and singing while playing simultaneously.

I'm not an expert, but he sounds good. The whole band sounds good, but I can't believe my suitemate is one of them rocking out on stage. I feel kind of guilty, watching him like a hawk for some sign that it's not really him, but I'm stupefied. A little alcohol in his drink makes him a pale puking seizure fest, but he can perform in front of people like this? That's the part that would make me puke and probably die.

I feel inadequate. When I first met Dakota, I had this idea of him just oozing confidence and cheek, but the blood and marks on his arms made him human and fragile like me. If we are alike, that means there's a chance for me. Now he isn't like me anymore. He is something so much better. I'm not jealous in that I want his life, but desperately envious of the way he's living it.

More than anything, I just feel sorry for myself. I feel stupid that I tried so hard to befriend him because I thought he needed me, and he so obviously doesn't. I've seen him around campus in his natural habitat, and he's the sun of his own solar system, his magnetism bringing everything around him into orbit. Like a sun flare, he's affecting everyone near him right now with his wild energy and bright soul.

Standing here, surrounded by the rest of the galaxy, I feel alone.

Chapter Six
November

I'm walking across campus when I get a text from Dakota.

I'm locked out of suite

> I reply: *Freshman problems. Where you at now?*

Small auditorium, Milford Hall.
Text me when you are going back
& I'll meet you

> *I'm coming right by, I'll come get you.*

I slide my phone back into my pocket and pick up the pace.

Milford Hall is a huge brick building, creepy enough at night that I wonder if the rumors of its being haunted are Dakota doesn't answer my next text, and it takes me awhile of wandering the halls until I hear music.

Following the notes of what sounds like two guitars,

one singing and the other screeching, I find my way to a tiny auditorium. Sitting on the edge of the stage is Dakota, his fingers slowly manipulating the guitar in his hands with exaggerated movements. A girl is sitting next to him, trying to mimic his movements. Their guitars are similar in color and shape as far as I can tell, but the flash on Dakota's guitar neck gives me the impression his is better.

When I get close to the stage, both stop playing.

"Hello," the girl says with a wide grin. Her bright smile is framed with choppy-cut dyed-black hair. "You must be the hot suitemate I was warned about."

"Ashley, this is Ian," Dakota nods in my direction. "Ian, this is Ashley, my fellow freshman that wants to learn guitar and owes me twenty bucks for her lesson last week and today."

Sara laughs and places her guitar in the black case sitting open beside her. "I'll give you fifty if you get me a date with your friend."

I'm flattered.

"Ian may mind if I start pimping him out, so let's go with twenty."

I chuckle and hold my hand out. The small-framed girl takes it and jumps off the stage. She gives me a wide grin and a wink while digging through her pockets. Finally handing a crumpled bill to Dakota, they talk over a time for next week, but I tune them out. Dakota's guitar has these shiny detailed inlays that keep reflecting the over-head lighting. I'm a guy, I like shiny stuff.

"What?" Dakota asks, and I realize he's talking to me. "You're making a weird face."

"Oh. Just thought it was funny." I shrug and point to the guitar's headstock where the word 'Taylor' is stamped. "My last name's on it."

"Coincidence or aliens?" Dakota whispers, his eyes

widening as he snaps his crumpled bill into full form. "Mine's on this."

"Twenty?"

"No, Jackson."

"First presidential assassination attempt was on Andrew Jackson," I blurt.

"Really?" Dakota asks, turning the bill around so he can see the woodcut portrait. "You said attempt, so how did he survive?"

The theater's steel door shuts behind Ashley, echoing across the auditorium seats. "The assassin couldn't get a shot off, so Jackson beat the shit out of the guy with his cane."

"He had some crazy hair too." Dakota's head tilts a little, his curious eyes looking over the bill to focus on mine. "Do you play guitar?"

"Uh, I haven't in a while." I stutter over my words a little, caught off guard by his change of subject.

"Here," Dakota says, pulling his strap over his head and holding the guitar out to me. "Got your name on it."

"Is this going to cost me twenty bucks?" I ask, taking the offered instrument. It feels foreign but familiar, holding a guitar again.

"First one's free."

I start strumming the guitar, fumbling out a few chords. "Wow I suck."

"I've heard worse," Dakota says, leaning back on his hands. "You've played a bit before."

"A lifetime ago."

"Shorter than that."

"I never really did it like hardcore or anything like you.

Saw you playing at Cover Ups on Halloween, by the way."

He shrugs like it's nothing.

"You're really good," I say.

"I just happened to know someone who knew their bassist was sick, and they didn't think I sucked too bad to be a fill-in. Luck. You used to play a lot though?" he asks.

"I haven't played since maybe sophomore year. I'm not that good at it." I watch my fingers, concentrating on the pattern of movements. It's not quite like riding a bike. My fingers know what I want; they're just slow to respond.

"You don't have to be an expert to enjoy doing something." Dakota frowns and folds his legs crisscross. "Why'd you quit?"

"I don't know." I frown and keep playing.

"That's Red Hot Chili Peppers. You have to have a reason to stop doing something you liked doing."

I stop playing, surprised he caught the song in just a few chords. "I got sick of listening to people riding my ass about it, I guess."

Dakota locks his two-colored eyes on me. "I'm not going to give you shit. Play."

"I really—"

"Swear it's okay," he coaxes. Sitting cross-legged on the edge of the stage, I can see how ragged his black chucks are, the white of his sock showing through a quarter-sized hole on the left one. "I'm not really the judgey ride-ass type."

I swallow my nerves and start playing again. I screw it up a few times and start over, but soon I'm relaxed, and the notes start flowing together, sounding like the song I had in mind. I can't help but smile.

I lose hours in that auditorium. The moon is high when

Dakota and I walk back to our dorm. My fingers ache, and my brain hurts with nerves waiting for Dakota to start questioning me—why'd I start playing guitar in the first place, why had I played the songs I'd played. Music is so personal, what we like and why we like it and what makes those certain songs speak to our soul. I kind of want to share that part of my soul, but I'm scared of rejection.

The third degree never comes, he just asks me about some new movie that had come out. Maybe he understands. He probably does, he's intuitive like that.

We meet Jase in the lobby, and my peaceful evening takes a steamy shit.

"Oh god no, Ian, you didn't bring that guitar back from the dead, did you?"

"This isn't mine," I grumble, tightening my grip on the black case I'm carrying.

"Don't give him musical instruments, Northie," Jase sighs. It's a big show, too, his shoulders rising and falling, his hands flopping at his sides as he makes a pained face. "What's wrong with you?"

"I'm a music major," Dakota answers.

"When I can't sleep because Ian's playing stupid shit in the middle of the night, it's your ass I'm coming after," he huffs. Turning his attention solely on me, his voice softens and asks, "I'm going down to Pete's. You want to come?"

I don't really have an excuse not to, and without thinking, my mouth answers, "Sure."

"Meet you at your Jeep," Jase nods. He brushes past, tapping a pack of cigarettes in his palm.

Glancing over, I see Dakota's smooth expression and wonder what he's thinking under that mask. Probably something about what an asshole Jase is and how I let Jase steamroll me. I feel like I need to excuse myself. "Someone has to babysit him in case he does something stupid. Tries to liquor up some unsuspecting freshman," I try to joke.

Dakota shrugs, but I can see his disapproval. There's a firm set to his lips and a stiffness in his body that exudes displeasure. "Ah. Well, if you ever want to hang out with Taylor..." He pauses to take the guitar case out of my grip. His voice is taut. "Just text me."

"Thanks." It doesn't sound as genuine as I feel it on the inside, and I have the overwhelming urge to apologize, but it will have to do. "Here, you can borrow my keys." I hand him my keyring, which he takes and quickly walks away.

Chapter Seven
November

Dakota's room becomes my sanctuary at some point. I don't know how it happened, but the only place I want to be is his room. It's quiet when I want to study, Dakota's conversational when I want companionship, and he lets me play one of his guitars whenever I want. Maybe it's that he doesn't need my attention every minute of the day—Dakota does his own thing whether I'm there or not—or maybe it's because he gives me his undivided attention when I need it.

I've made friends my entire life by jumping to attention for people. I'm loyal to a fault I guess, doing this or that, being here or there just because someone told me to. Like an accessory people put on when they need it but leave in the box when they don't. Dakota's the first person that has never asked me to jump.

It's so comfortable in Dakota's room that I only leave for class, food, or sleep. Surprise, Jase doesn't like it. He's constantly ragging me about neglecting my friends. One day he flat-out asks me if I have some sort of obsession with Dakota.

I tell Jase that's stupid, bcause I don't really know how to describe it to him. Not an obsession, but maybe an addiction? I need Dakota's companionship, like a daily dose of Xanax to keep me level. When I'm with Dakota, I can just be. It's like I finally tasted freedom, and the more I get, the more I want.

Yet, you can't always get what you want. Sometimes you owe people.

"Wow, you actually do still live here," Jase asks as he walks into our room and slams the door.

I grunt and pull my blue comforter tighter around my shoulders. Bad enough he just woke me up from a nap, but he's in a mood too.

"Name's still on the door," I reply.

"That doesn't mean much."

I want to argue with him, but at the same time, I see hurt in his expression. It's like a teeny tiny sliver of hurt hidden in his mask of bravado and asshole temperament. A layperson wouldn't see it, but I've known him long enough to notice. Guilt tickles the back of my throat, teasing my tissues with an invisible feather.

"Hey," I say, checking the time on my phone. "I've got study group later. Want to do dollar tacos after that?"

"I guess." Jase shrugs and flops down in his bed. "When are you done?"

"I'll be back here about 9:30. I'll even buy the tacos."

"You drive, and it's a deal."

I'm yawning through my study group when my phone

buzzes. It's a text message from Jase.

I NEED A RIDE TO HOSPITAL

"Excuse me." I shove everything into my backpack and leave the library at a run. I try calling Jase back, but he doesn't answer. My mind goes through a hundred different scenarios of what could have happened and why Jase wasn't calling an ambulance or Shelly. I try calling Dakota, but his phone is off.

When I enter my room, Jase jumps out of his chair with a towel pressed to his face. "Keys!"

"What the hell happened?" I ask, flinching when something crunches under my feet. Looking down, there's Jase's iPad on the floor, smashed. I sidestep it and ask, "Did you call Shelly?"

"I don't need Shelly, I need a fucking doctor." Jase pulls the towel away from his face, and I see a bloody nose and busted lip. "I need stitches. What the hell is Shelly going to do?"

"Hang on, let me look," I frown. When I'm close to him, I smell alcohol. "Are you drunk?"

"No, I don't get drunk." That's a lie. "That tool next door came over here and fucked me up."

"Wait, Dakota?" I hold the laugh in my throat, but my lips stretch into a smile. I try to imagine short and wiry Dakota taking hulking gym-fiend Jase down to the floor. I'll admit Dakota has the attitude, but I doubt the strength. Jase might be hindered with alcohol, but he's not falling-down drunk. I don't think *I* could take Jase out.

"Yes, Dakota. Who else, you idiot?"

I wipe the grin off my face. "If I call Shelly, she'll have

your ass for drinking on campus. I know it's bleeding and probably hurts like hell, but it doesn't look that bad. Come on," I grab his elbow. "Let's go to the bathroom and get it cleaned up."

"I want a fucking doctor!" he howls.

"Jase," I growl while shaking his elbow. "Shut up. You don't need a doctor. You've taken worse hits in sports. Let's get you cleaned up. If it's still bad in the morning, you can go to the walk-in clinic."

"I'm going to kick his ass, Ian. I'm going to kill him."

Rolling my eyes, I get him in the bathroom and start the water running. He's carrying on, but I get the blood off, get some painkillers and Benadryl in him, and put him to bed. Jase was capable of telling me every terrible thing he's going to do to our suitemate, but I didn't get a straight answer out of him as to what exactly happened.

Stepping out into our tiny hall, I knock on Dakota's door. After a long moment, I knock again, but there's no answer. When I try the door handle nothing happens. Going back to my dark room, I grab my phone and flip over to my messages. Nothing new from Dakota, so I start to type.

Hey what's going on? You okay?

After two unanswered texts to Dakota, I give up.

My phone buzzes in my pocket while my psychology teacher is lecturing. I slide it out and look at my messages.

Dakota finally answered my texts from last night.

> *Your roommate is an idiot*

> > *What happened?* I type back.

> *He wouldn't turn down his music*

> > *So you punched him in the face...*

> *He started it*

> > *He was drunk, you can't reason with him when he's like that.*
> > *You should have let it go.*

I really want to tell him I want him to stay away from Jase for his own safety, but that would probably be insulting and make me sound like a mother hen, and apparently he can fend for himself. I just worry that was a lucky shot, and I know Jase can hold a grudge and wait for his revenge.

I wait. When class ends I still haven't heard back from Dakota.

* * *

Thanksgiving break is something I'm looking forward to. The drive home, not so much. I plan my homework schedule so I can head out first thing Wednesday morning. Jase suckers me into spending my Tuesday cooped up in our room, helping him work on a big project he has due.

"I'm starving," I groan.

"Well," Jase muses. "How about those tacos you promised me two days ago? You can go get them while I finish this page."

"Tacos do sound good. Full order?"

"Order and a half. No sour cream, and hot sauce on the side. You should know that by now."

I'm off on a food errand, or a 'bitch run' as Dakota calls them. I frown when I think of him. It's been a few days since the Jase incident, but it feels like a year. I frown even harder when the elevator door dings open, and Dakota is already on it. He's scrunched into the corner near the controls, a camouflage baseball hat shading his eyes. The red W on his hat gives him away.

"Hey," I say with a forced smile and step onto the elevator.

He doesn't look away from the door panel. "Hello."

His voice is cool, but I keep mine bright. "You heading home?"

"What was your first clue? The suitcase?"

I exhale loudly as the doors groan to a close. I feel kind of stupid I didn't notice his suitcase. My frustration leaves my mouth. "You don't have to be a dick."

"Oh? I thought that's the way you liked people to treat each other."

"I get you don't like Jase, and you have completely valid reasons not to, but really? You just busted his face open over loud music, and you're going to act like he's the asshole after you stooped to his level?"

Dakota looks up at the ceiling and sighs, leaning against the trembling wall of the elevator car. "Ian..."

"What?" I prod. "What?"

He finally looks at me, dead square and steady, and I

see his wicked black eye. Like an eye-shadowed pirate, the darkness surrounds his right eye. The blue eye is a stormy lakefront surrounded by smudges of thunderclouds. For a long moment we're just staring at each other. The elevator dings cheerily, doors opening wide, but I can't look away. His eyes have an eerie hollow stare like the Grim Reaper doesn't want to be bothered by my mortal bullshit.

He doesn't have to say it-I know Jase threw the first punch.

"I'm sorry," I whisper.

Dakota pushes off the wall and enters the hall, dragging his rolling suitcase behind. When I follow him, he walks faster. "You don't have to apologize for other people," he clips.

I push through the security doors, quickening my steps. "I'm not. I'm sorry because I believed him."

"It doesn't matter," he says. There's something in his words, something that makes my blood chill and my intestines twist and crinkle.

"Hey, wait a minute," I say.

"I've got to go."

I chase him like a puppy, all the way to the parking lot. By the time he gets to a battered beige Chevy Colorado, I'm begging. "Hey. Wait a second, please?"

Dakota opens the driver's door and throws his suitcase into the truck's bed, then wheels around to face me. "What do you want Ian? My version of events? I had a headache and asked him to turn down his music. He said no. I threw his speaker on the floor, he threw the iPad at me and it hit the floor. He punched me and I hit him back." He takes a deep breath and swallows some of his irritation and continues, "That's what happened, and what's different now that I told you? Nothing. You're going to go about your day like you were, and he's still going to be an asshole." He throws his hands in the air and backs toward his truck. "You know what? This, this isn't even a blip on the radar of your life. Stop giving a shit. Just forget it."

"I-"

He turns his back on me and slides behind the wheel. I can tell he's mad; he slams the door, jams his keys into the ignition. He doesn't look at me as he drops the little truck into gear and backs out of the parking spot. His words are hanging around my neck as he drives out of the lot and disappears from view.

I'm scared. For a hundred different reasons, I'm scared, and it's pushing my insides through a meat grinder. I'm afraid of what he thinks of me. I'm afraid I'll never see him again. Afraid of what I'll become if he never comes back.

I'm petrified because he pushed me away. I'm ashamed I pushed him first.

Scrubbing my face, letting the skin on my palms burn my cheeks, I growl in frustration. I focus my eyes and notice something on the ground near my feet, a dusty black and brown leather check wallet battered well past retirement. I pick it up, and it flops open, several twenties and paper receipts falling out. I grab the money and turn the wallet so I can see the ID.

It's Dakota's.

Fingers trembling so bad my keys are jingling, I find my phone. My throat is stitching itself closed as my phone rings Dakota's number. Straight to voicemail. I open my mouth to leave a message, but nothing comes out.

* * *

Lack of sleep or Red Bull, I'm not sure which is to blame for being awake. It's after midnight when I finish packing and load up my Jeep. My brain just goes over and over the day as if I've missed some important clue I just need to find, and it will fix everything.

I've called Dakota several times, left a voicemail, and sent a text message. When I decide to try and get some sleep I check my phone; no phone call, no text message in reply. I unload my jacket pockets and find Dakota's wallet.

I rub my thumb over the worn leather as I sit down on my bed. The edges are a thick creased band of black surrounding a saddle-leather brown. It's smooth, almost slick beneath my thumb in some spots. Glancing over at Jase's empty bed assures me I'm alone. Grabbing my cell, I try again to call, and it goes to voicemail. Surely he is home by now and has charged his phone, right?

Frowning, I turn on my laptop. It's stalkerish, but I pull up Google and type in his home address. A map of nowhere, Wisconsin, pops up on the screen. I zoom out a little and see the closest town is called Sparta.

Even if he'd driven fifty the whole way, he'd be home by now. He should have charged his phone, should have checked his messages. He's ignoring me. Unless he never made it home. If something happened to him, it would be my fault this time—driving, distracted by his anger at my stupidity, at Jase.

Snapping the laptop closed, I flop backward into my pillows. According to Google, Sparta's only an hour and a half from home for me. I can take it to him. If I don't hear back from him, I can stop there on my way home. It's just a bit out of my way. Which sounds batshit crazy, but what if he did something stupid because of all this? He probably needs his wallet anyway. That sounds like a perfectly reasonable excuse for my unreasonable insanity.

Chapter Eight
November

The Midwest isn't that picturesque in late fall. The crop fields are just lined mounds of dirt, like fresh graves for the murdered crops. Trees are dropping their colored leaves, exposing their skeletons. I don't need my sunglasses; shortly after dawn, the sun disappears behind a gray blanket of clouds. My favorite playlist is all I have to drown out my thoughts, and the Jeep's speakers are way up.

I keep waiting for my phone to beep at me with a new message, for Dakota to respond, but it never does. Just after eleven o'clock, I pass a rusted once-black mailbox that says 'JACKSON' in white spray paint. You can tell it was a one-time attempt; the first half of the name is large, and the second half gets progressively smaller. It looks more like JACKson.

Turning past the mailbox puts me on a rutted gravel drive. Ruts run parallel, created by vehicles, and some perpendicular that were created by water washout. There's rusted wire fencing and long finger-like blades of brown thatched grass on either side of the driveway. I ease my black Cherokee along, avoiding the larger pits in the road. The lane ends in a parking area that's more mud than gravel, and I park between a greenish Oldsmobile Alero with a sagging headliner and Dakota's Colorado. There's a blue-and-rust Silverado that's seen better days, and a decrepit brown F-150 that looks like it hasn't moved in a decade.

Cutting the engine, I peer out the windshield at the ancient farmhouse watching me. It's old and tired-looking. The windows are dark. Once-white paint is curling off the siding, and the porch sags with age. It looks empty, but a mud-colored Labrador is lying at the foot of the porch stairs, knocking its tail on the ground in mild interest of my arrival.

This scene doesn't match Dakota. When all I knew about him was 'Seizure Freshman', I pictured him living in some immaculate suburban row house. One of those places with white carpet and crème furniture, and a worrisome overbearing mother that follows you around with a Swiffer in case you lost any skin dander. His dad was a scientist, too, in that version of him.

Then 'Wrist-Cutting Music Genius Freshman' changed my picture. Still suburban, but a five or six-bedroom colonial house with brick, the ones that always have an odd-shaped bedroom over the garage. It was on a tree-lined street near the local school, and Dakota had the odd-shaped room with black walls and tons of music equipment. I pictured his siblings living there, one big jock and one skinny goth kid, living with one of those super-powered business women mothers and a golfing father.

Sitting here, staring down an eighteen-hundreds farmhouse, I remember him saying something about a farm. That conjured ideas of hundreds-of-thousands-dollar tractors and implements and pristine metal buildings surrounding the brick colonial. Not this place. I'm ashamed of my assumptions.

I debate on starting the Jeep and making a run for the interstate, but I hear the loud putt-putt of a tractor coming. Someone's already seen me, so I sigh and get out, sliding Dakota's wallet into the pocket of my hoodie before shutting the door.

I can feel the brisk cold, and it embraces me in a firm hug. That same cold is fierce when I breathe in, sharp but fresh in my lungs. I smell mud and livestock; earthy scents garnished with the burnt-fuel aroma of the puttering tractor.

It's an open tractor with no cab to protect the driver. Red-faced and wearing duck canvas overalls, the driver raises a hand as he gets close. I do the same, and when the red metal beast lurches to a stop, I approach.

"Can I help you?" he yells over the tractor's rumbling motor. From far away I thought it would be Dakota's dad, but up close, I can see he's around my age. The bulky cold-weather clothing just accentuates that he's broad and built. I'm guessing he's Dakota's brother.

"I'm looking for Dakota."

The guy frowns, giving me an odd look as he cuts the tractor's engine. "Dakota, huh?" He shakes his head and starts climbing down off the tractor. "He's in the hay barn."

My eyes follow the direction he's pointing. A dilapidated old barn with a frayed blue tarp fastened to one of its walls is staring back at me. "The one with the tarp?"

"Yeah." He stares at me for a long moment but doesn't say anything. There's some kind of malice in his eyes, burning my soul. I feel like Dakota and his brother got the same superpowers, but Dakota uses his for good and his brother Overalls for evil.

"Thanks," I chirp and start across the yard. As I walk, I can feel him staring a hole in my back, and it's unsettling. When I glance back at the house, Overalls is smoking a cigarette, the lab at his feet as he watches me. I remember seeing some B-horror film that started something like this, and I wonder if the red-headed step kid is waiting in the barn to butcher me.

I enter the barn through a creaky half-door, and there's no killer. The smell of sweet grass and old wood is all there is. I listen and hear a thud-thudding of something against the dirt floor.

Following the sound, I walk around a pile of bales and see an aisle in the middle of the large barn with stacks of hay on the sides towering above it. There's a hay rack in the aisle, and I watch Dakota at the top of the hay pile sling a bale that lands on the hay rack. I'm relieved to see him alive.

I clear my throat. "Hey!"

"I'm loading it right now," Dakota calls back without looking. He throws another hay bale that hits the rack and bounces to the ground.

"Dakota!"

He turns and looks, realizing it's me. Wearing the same duck canvas overalls as his brother, a white t-shirt, and sweat, he's giving me a curious look. He scales down the mountain of hay bales, his curiosity melting into something else. Not angry, but not happy either. As he closes in, I shift my weight.

"How'd you wind up out in butt-fuck nowhere?" he asks and jumps the last few bales down to the ground.

"I tried calling you."

"I broke my phone."

"You left this in the parking lot," I say and pull his wallet out of my pocket.

"Oh. I thought I left it in my dorm. Well thanks," he smiles slightly. He looks exhausted. "You didn't have to drive it all the way out here."

"You're along my way home." I shrug and scratch my head. "Figured you might need it if you're going to be home for a week."

"Yeah, I might get off the farm," he snorts. "But thanks."

There's a silence because I don't know what to say, but I want to keep talking. I look at the hay rack. "You need help?"

"What?"

"You're loading up the hay, right? You need a hand?"

"I've still got an hour until the guy will be here to pick it up. I'll be fine."

"How many are you loading?"

"Two hundred."

I gape. "Screw that. Find me some gloves and I'll help you."

He lets me help him, and I enjoy it. Dakota's throwing the bales down, and I stack them in neat rows, fumbling with the heavy hay a bit. We work in silence, and I break a sweat despite the actual air temperature. The muscles in my arms and back are burning when the last bale is put in place.

"Thanks," Dakota says when I climb off the hayrack. I contemplate showing off and jumping to the ground, but when I think of my jelly legs giving away and me smashing face-first into the compact dirt floor, I err on the side of caution.

"No problem. It was actually fun the first five minutes before it started to feel like work."

He smiles a little at my joke, but it's a sad smile. A long

moment passes, each of us looking at the other, unsure of the next move. I don't want to, but I break the silence. "I've still got a couple of hours driving left. I guess I should let you get back to your thing."

"I'm done. Done until milking tonight anyway. I'll walk you back to your car. I'm heading up to the house." He pushes his hands into the pockets of his overalls as he speaks.

I can't completely wrap my head around the Dakota standing in front of me in his plain white t-shirt, brown duck overalls, and dejected look. His shoulders slump, making him look small. I can't mesh this image of him with the one of him rocking out on the stage of Cover Ups in a tight black t-shirt and jeans. Or the one of him standing tall, staring down Jase and not giving a shit. Or the one of him playing guitar in his room, his worn-out chucks tapping to his beat, expensive electronics all over his desk.

God, his black eye too. I'm not the one that put it there, but I might as well have. It hurts, and I want to apologize.

"Yeah, I think I parked in someone's spot," I say. "I think it was your brother that gave me the stink eye when I got out."

Dakota snorts loudly and leads the way through the entry door, grabbing a black Carhartt coat off the ground by the door. "Monty's a shithead. Just ignore him." I follow him across the farmyard, a hundred questions in my mind but too scared to ask them. Something about the vast, open space makes me nervous. The blowing wind might steal my words and carry them away to someone else.

My steps slow when we near my Jeep, and his do too. I follow his line of sight and see a dark figure at one of the windows, watching us. I can't make out any details, but I can feel their gaze boring into me.

"Drive safe," Dakota offers, his duo-colored eyes

turning to mine. Maybe it's my imagination, but I sense a hesitation in his voice like he doesn't want me to go. I wish we weren't here, that it was a week ago and we were in his room when everything was a perfect image. Before broken iPads and black eyes and broken down farmhouses.

"Always do," I reply, and fumble in my pocket for my keys. "Is there any good place to eat in town? I'm starving and don't think I can make it to Minnesota without gnawing my arm off."

"There are a couple little dive kitchens," Dakota trails off, looking in the direction of the figure in the window. Shrugging his shoulders, he turns back to me and says, "You helped me out; the least I can do is buy you lunch."

"I'll drive if you buy. Doesn't count as a bitch run if you come with me," I joke.

"Probably my only chance to get off this fucking farm anytime soon," he mutters and goes for my passenger door.

When I have the Jeep in gear and backing out of the parking spot, he speaks up in a mumbling voice, "I'm sorry. I would have invited you in, but my father's an asshole. You don't want to meet him."

I don't press the issue about his dad. I'm pretty sure I messed up a lot of things when I imagined his home life and family.

"Are your parents still married?" I ask.

"My mom died when I was in 7th grade."

"Sorry to hear that." I frown. I messed up a lot of things I assumed about him.

While I navigate the barren gravel farm roads back to town he exhales a few times between giving me directions. He's definitely upset, and I wonder if I pissed him off by showing up, or by bringing up his parents. Or maybe he's still mad about the whole Jase thing, which I can't blame him for.

We end up at some little restaurant with vinyl seats in faded colors and yellowed tile flooring. Dakota takes me straight to a back booth and slides in the first seat, leaving me to take the side against the wall. I have a view of the few other patrons in the diner, most of which are watching us. I must stick out since I'm not from around here; it seems like one of those small towns.

Three waitresses are loitering around the counter to the kitchen. One breaks off, grabbing some menus and bringing them to our table.

"Coffee okay or want something else?" the waitress asks, dropping two menus on the table. Her face is sour, which is a shame because without the pinched mouth and crinkled brows, she'd be pretty. She can't be much older than us.

"Coffee's fine," Dakota says, fiddling with his napkin-wrapped utensils.

"Water." I nod, and sour-face leaves. Raising an eyebrow, I take a menu as Dakota sighs and grabs the other one.

Curiosity gets the best of me, and I ask, "You okay?"

"When I'm on that farm, I feel like I'm dying. It's like a breath of fresh air to get away from there, but I have to get out of this town if I'm going to keep breathing." There's something about his words that makes me uncomfortable, and unease settles into my bones. I want to press him for more—it's unusual for him to talk about himself. Sour-face comes back with a carafe and glass of water, setting them in the middle of the table.

"What can I get you to eat?"

"Bacon cheeseburger, please," Dakota says, sliding the menu across the chipped Formica tabletop.

"I'll have the same," I say, putting my menu on his.

Sour-face grabs the menus and mutters under her

breath as she leaves.

"Did you hear what she said?" I whisper.

"She said isn't that cute. We went to high school together." Dakota looks out at the dreary afternoon sky, his expression melting into a blank void. "Any extended family coming in for Thanksgiving?"

I frown, knowing this game well by now. Deflect and refocus on me. "No. You?" I pass it back to him.

"No. What day are you driving back to school?"

"Sunday night. Why? Want me to bring your wallet?"

He smiles a little and shakes his head.

We banter a bit back and forth through our meal, ignoring everything that screamed out loud to be talked about, and it feels a little like before. Even though it feels okay, I still want to apologize. Finishing off my burger and fries, I realize he's barely touched his. I frown.

"I know I keep asking this, but are you okay?" I don't want to annoy him, but at the same time, I can feel something's wrong, and I don't want to think about the consequences of Dakota having a terrible day.

"I have a headache," he mutters, stirring his glass of water.

"If you're still pissed at me because of the whole Jase thing, I completely understand, I'm really-"

He lifts his gaze from his glass to me, shaking his head a little. "Ian, stop apologizing. Life is way too short to hold a grudge. Yeah, it pissed me off you believed him, but there are a lot worse things in life," he says, pushing his plate away. "I hate this town. I just want to get through this week and go back to school."

"Said no college student ever," I offer with a lopsided grin. "Is your family really nuts?"

Sour face comes back, dropping the check off on the table and leaving our dirty dishes and empty cups. Dakota pulls out his wallet and drops a twenty on the table, and starts whispering. "It's this town and all the people that only remember that one horrible thing you did in your life. Come on, let's get out of here."

He stands up and pulls his Carhartt jacket back on. I can't even begin to imagine what he could be referring to. What could he ever do that was so horrible? I can't think of anything except something stupid like playing his music too loud and pissing off the old farts staring at him. Maybe it was the new-fangled rock music of the devil he likes.

I stand too and notice that several people in the diner are whispering to each other. It creeps me out, all those pairs of eyes watching us leave and talking about him or me. We climb into the Jeep, and I start it, shivering in the chilly interior.

Two older men are sitting in a booth near the diner's window, staring at my black Cherokee as Dakota asks, "I don't suppose you've ever done anything that black-marked you in your town for the rest of your life, have you?" He exhales a heavy breath that sags his shoulders.

There's such a weight in his words and a tangible connection from the stares of the older men and Dakota's slouch. I really want to give them the finger, but my brain is flipping over Dakota's question. I open my mouth, then shut it with a click. I clear my throat instead of answering right away.

"Is this another one of those times when we talk about something serious, and I end up answering all the questions?" I ask gently.

"No." He says it so softly I barely hear it over the air blasting through the vents.

Cold air is still blowing through the vents, but I put the SUV in reverse and start driving. If we're going to talk about something like this, I need to be busy, I need something to focus on besides the creepy guys glaring.

"Jase and I were on the lacrosse team together, and we had a teammate named Evan. Jase had a huge graduation after-party down at the lake, with the whole team and everyone we knew. Jase was giving Evan a bunch of shit over his girlfriend."

I glance over at him and see the curiosity in his blue-green eyes. Shifting the Cherokee to drive, I look back to the road.

"One of those 'you wouldn't know her she goes to a different school' situations, so Jase was giving him a tough time about it." I swallow hard and skip to the important part. "He got ahold of Evan's phone."

"And?" Dakota prods.

"Evan didn't have a girlfriend; he had a boyfriend named Matt, who was also on the team." I look up at the unfamiliar street sign ahead. No idea where I'm going, but I put my signal on and turn left, letting fate decide where my tires take us. "Jase got the team together down by the dock, then called them out in front of everyone. He just humiliated them. Then he started hitting Matt."

"What did you do?" Dakota asks.

"Nothing," I sigh. "I stood there like a statue and just watched a few of my teammates beat the shit out of them." I glance at the speedometer, and back my foot off the gas pedal. "Jase and Matt ended up in the water. I thought Jase was going to drown him, and I still didn't do anything. Evan had broken ribs."

"You didn't hurt them."

I don't want him to justify my behavior. "That doesn't matter. I didn't step in, or speak up, so I might as well have hurt them. They were my teammates, my friends, and I didn't do shit to stop it. I don't care if they were dating each other. I was so mad I didn't speak to Jase all summer, like that meant anything. I'm a piece of shit nobody. That's what my town knows me as, just another POS nobody." I swallow hard. "What about you?"

He doesn't answer, and I wonder if I've blown him out of the water. Or if this is just our typical game where I spill my guts, and he holds his secrets. Leather creaks under my fist as I grip the steering wheel. I feel so exposed and bare.

"I…" Dakota's voice is strained. I glance at him, but his eyes are staring straight ahead at the rural view framed by my windshield. "When I was fourteen, I kissed my best friend. At our youth group's summer camping trip."

I don't get it. That sounds like a typical teenage rite of passage, unless he went to a super strict church or something. Which I can't imagine, but it wouldn't surprise me after all the other revelations of the day.

"And she?" I prompt him a little.

Dakota shakes his head and slumps against the door. "His name is Trevor."

The only noise is the rumble of the engine. I don't know what to say, but I should say something. "Oh," is all that comes out of my mouth. It feels like someone slathered Tabasco on my skin, making it prickle and burn. "So you're-"

"Don't call me gay."

"He kissed you?"

"No," he exhales in a soft growl. "See? I hate that that one action has me labeled, so everyone in this town gives me the stink eye and avoids me, so I don't give them the queer or whatever they're afraid of. One action, like two seconds of my life, and I get judgments slapped on me for the rest of my life. Which would be fine if they were right, but there isn't even a right option. It's either Dakota the Faggot or Dakota the Crazy Grief Kid, and those aren't right at all.”

I slow to take a turn down a loopy road. When the road straightens again, I look over at him, and the deepest kick of empathy hits me right in the gut. He’s rigid, bracing himself for whatever reaction I’m supposed to have. I don’t even have a reaction other than stopping that pain. “What is it then? I’ll listen.”

His expression softens, and I wonder if anyone without a doctorate’s ever said that to him before. He clears his throat a little and looks back at the road, as do I.

“It… Context. Trevor was my best friend. It sucked when my mom was going through her chemo and stuff so my parents put Pen and me in a bunch of after-school and weekend stuff, mostly at church. When I started seventh grade some of us in youth group started a band, and Trevor played drums. Yeah, start laughing at the idea of me in a Jesus worship band.” He flashes a small smile.

“When my mom got really sick, Trevor and I were inseparable. I stayed at his house for days sometimes.” Dakota pauses, swallowing hard. “We were at camp a few weeks after her funeral and snuck down to the lake after dark. Just talking, and I, I kissed him. And he flipped out.”

My brain registers the red octagon standing guard up ahead and puts my foot on the brake. As the Cherokee rolls to a stop, I ask, “Your dad freak out too?”

“He beat the shit out of me. Our pastor was a bit nicer about it, saying I was just messed up with all the grief with my mom. I wasn’t confused. I told him, I told my dad, tried to tell Trevor—it wasn’t anything sexual. I didn’t kiss him because I wanted to suck his dick; I did it because I cared about him, he was my best friend, and I tried to show it. If I was someplace other than rural America crazy church camp no one would have batted an eye, but here I got my ass beat and told I was crazy."

Dakota draws a breath, his voice rising as he continues, "It doesn't make any sense to me. If Trevor had been a girl and I showed any sort of physical affection it would be okay, but because we're both guys it was so wrong? After everything we'd been through together, if he was a girl I could have given him a hug, cried on his shoulder, held his hand while people paraded past my mother's dead body and said how sorry they were for me, but we're both guys, so I have to keep that all inside and pretend it doesn't hurt and just suffer alone? I didn't choose for Trevor to be a guy and not a girl, so why does it make such a fucking difference? It's not fair."

"I guess because a kiss is pretty meaningful?" I fumble.

"But what does it mean? You don't teach babies to only kiss their opposite-sex parent. You don't beat the shit out of kids under the age of five kissing each other. People encourage children to give kisses to loved ones. Some parents force their kids to give kisses to people. When does a kiss change from showing affection to someone you love to automatically being a sexual advance?"

His questions make my head hurt, like they're filling my brain and making more questions to push against the boundaries of my skull.

Dakota continues. "You should be able to express how you feel regardless of gender. Does a child love their parents differently because of their gender? No. Anyone in your family, you don't love them differently because of them being male or female. You just love them because they're your family. Why is it a different set of rules for everyone else in your life?"

"Normally, familial relationships don't blend with sexual ones. Everything gets more complicated when you start adding sex into it."

"Sex is an action and drive not an emotional bond."

"It's a pretty strong drive, though."

"Love is stronger, but for the sake of argument let's look at sex. There's sex for fun and sex with meaning. Sex for fun is with someone to get the chemical high, someone you're just physically attracted to. Sex with meaning is because you care so deeply about the other person, you want to share that with them, you want to please them, you want to express how much you care about them, not just to get the chemical high, and yes, you love that person, but it's an expression of love it isn't love," he sighs again in exasperation. "Love is completely different. Love is like this, this, bond, and it overcomes so many things like distance and tragedies and betrayals and so many things but what, it can't overcome something like gender? If you have a guy and a girl as your best friends, no sexuality involved, you love them the same, but you can't show it the same way. You can rough house or smack him on the ass to be funny, but if you did that to her you'd be a jerk and trying to get in her pants. You can hug her, you can kiss her on the cheek or the top of her head, you can do all that stuff and no one blinks, but if you did that to him you'd be a fag. That's not fair."

He's getting so flustered trying to explain himself all at once.

"I just, I don't think you should be labeled, have a set of rules as to who you're allowed to care about, to love, and how to show it. There's so much bullshit. Everyone is just themselves. Maybe if we weren't afraid to show each other how deeply we care there wouldn't be so much hate in the world."

The engine continues to purr, waiting for me to give it a direction. I keep my foot on the brake as my clogged brain soaks up the rest of the words hanging in the air.

"I'm lost." I breathe.

"I can't explain it all at once, I need like eight hours, I just—"

"No, I mean I'm lost. I don't know where we're at. Left or right?"

Dakota looks from me to the empty T intersection in front of us and back to me. He's fighting it, but I see the smile trying to break his lips as he collapses back in the seat. "Go left. Let you in on my deep dark thoughts, and you're worried about traffic."

I smile a little more and make the left turn. "I would say enlightening, not dark."

"Enlightening?"

"Your perspective. I've never thought of it like that."

Dakota tilts his head a little, and I can feel his eyes studying me. Probably trying to judge my sincerity. It's quiet for a few minutes, then Dakota asks, "You think I'm just mentally unstable and over-thinking homosexual tendencies that conflict with my religious upbringing?"

I chuckle. "No, that sounds like bullshit. I think—Well-" I stammer a little. Those curious two-toned eyes waiting for my answer make it hard to respond. People don't ask me for my opinion or moral stance on things. I don't want to mess up putting my thoughts into words; I care too much about his opinion of me. "I think I'm jealous. I wish I had the balls to stick up for myself like you do, to say the stuff I think about. Honestly, you just dumped a lot of questions on me that I really don't have answers to. But I don't think you're mental, crazy, or anything else. You have valid points. I don't care what label you get from anyone else. You're my friend. That's the only one I care about."

I drive a little farther, and Dakota points to another road to take. "Turn right. You sure you're not going to run away from me at school for letting my fag out of the bag?"

My nose crinkles at that F word. "Stop."

"You're not going to hide from me on campus because you're afraid I'll rape you, huh?"

"I could take you," I quip, but when he explodes in laughter, I feel my cheeks flushing again. "Oh god, not like that."

"Ooo," he teases, and I jerk the wheel a little to slam him into the door, which makes him laugh even harder. "Ouch, ouch, my elbow!"

"For the record, I'm not afraid of you trying to make out with me. Come at me singing those Jesus camp songs though, I will hit you."

"*A-B-C-D-E-F-G Jesus died for you and me*," Dakota belts out.

I tap the brakes as a warning and try to make an angry face. He stops singing, but I think it's because he can't breathe, not because I'm so scary.

Too soon, the exhausted mailbox comes into view, its flap door hanging down like a drooping lower lip. Clearing my throat, I slow the Jeep and turn for the driveway.

"Thanks for taking me away from this shithole for a while," Dakota says, unbuckling his seat belt as I navigate the pothole-ridden drive.

"Anytime."

"And not being a judgemental asshole to my face. Or with your eyes."

"Not doing it in my brain either."

Darker clouds are moving on the horizon, urging me to finish my drive home, but the closer I get to the farm-house, the less I want to leave. Not that I particularly want to stay, but I hate the idea of leaving Dakota behind. Selfishly because I want to pick his brain about everything he's dumped on me the last ten minutes, and unselfishly because I don't like the idea of parents that beat their kids for any reason.

Sure enough, there's a shadowed figure near the front window when I park the Cherokee. "Your dad or your brother?"

"Monty," Dakota says with a curled lip. "Just waiting to be an asshole. I better get going though so I can help him start chores." He pops the passenger door, and a black blur bolts off the porch.

"Someone's happy to see you," I comment when Dakota gets out and the black dog worries at his knee. Its oversized ears and crouched stance tell me it's a shepherd and young.

"This is my generically named dog Shadow." Dakota smiles a little, burying his fingers in the dog's ebony coat. "*My shadow's the only one who walks beside me.*"

"Green Day."

"You're getting better at that." Dakota chuckles and scrubs the dog's ruff.

"Practice." I frown and glance at the clock on my dash. I should get going.

"Drive safe," Dakota says, a small but sad-looking smile on his face. "Um, Pen's going to give me his old phone, and we're going to get it switched over tonight, so text me when you get home."

"I will." I can't help but frown when he puts his hand on the door to shut it. I force my hand to squeeze the shifter and pull the transmission into reverse. He starts to push the door, and I yell, "Hey, wait a sec."

"What's up?" He asks quietly, like he knows what I'm about to say is only for him to hear.

I'm not sure how to say this. I'm not good at talking to people, not about serious stuff. "Call me or text me if you get bored or something." I swallow and lower my voice. "Or if things get shitty for you, call me. I don't care if it's three in the morning or what it's about." Seeing uncertainty in his expression, I add, "I mean it."

"Alright. Swear." He holds up his pinky. I'm not sure if that means a promise or he's mocking me.

Chapter Nine
December

"Come on, Ian, time to get out of the house," Jase coos at me.

"Ouch," I growl when he kicks my chair. "I told you I'm busy."

"Dude, it's Friday. Get away from the studying, or the paper you're writing or whatever." He reaches over my shoulder and slaps my laptop screen down.

"You know, tantrums are supposed to stop during childhood." I scowl and push my screen back up. "I went out with you guys last weekend, so leave me alone for tonight."

"What crawled up your mood and died?"

"That doesn't even make sense."

"Fine, fuck," Jase huffs. He grabs his wallet, keys, and phone before leaving, making sure to slam the door just to make sure I know he's pissed.

I don't care. He's been riding my last nerve for a while now, and with the semester winding down, I have a lot on my plate. Finals to study for, term papers to write, and only one more week of classes before finals. My two scholarships do depend on my grades being decent, but it's more of a pride thing that I want to do well, and I'm having problems studying lately.

I'm wound tight, and I need to relax, but following Jase around some house party is not going to do it. I re-check my phone, making sure I didn't get canceled on—no new messages. I glance at the time, calculating how much time has passed and how far away Jase has gotten from our room.

It's early, but I don't care. I flip my books shut, close my laptop, leave my phone on the desk, and ditch my room. I cross the mini-hall to Dakota's door. I can hear him playing his violin, so I knock loudly.

"Come in!"

Relief relaxes me as I turn the knob and push into the dorm room. I don't know why he would reject me, but it is still a fear. Dakota's sitting at his computer desk, violin in his hands and headphones on. I have no idea what brand they are, but the shiny metal and etched black make me think they're expensive. He pulls them off, letting them rest on his neck, and points at his bed with his bow.

A guitar case is sitting there, opened and waiting for me.

"I look that stressed out?" I ask, sitting on his bed and taking the guitar out.

"You asked if I was going to be around tonight," Dakota shrugs a little and tosses me a pick. "I didn't think you were asking me on a date, so I assumed this was what you were looking for. Give me a minute to finish this, and I'll join you."

While he puts his violin away and closes down his computer, I pick at the strings, unable to choose a tune to play. My head feels so jumbled, and I don't know why. I stop playing when the bed bounces, Dakota and his guitar sitting down beside me.

"What'll it be tonight?" he smiles and strums. "Country? Rock? Pop? Death Metal?" he makes the guitar's strings complain, and me laugh.

"I get enough of that. I don't know, I always decide. You pick."

"Hmm," he muses. His notes and chords begin to string together, becoming something familiar.

"Crap. I know this one," I growl a little, my fingers repeating his strokes until we're playing in sync.

He keeps playing, giving me a chance to remember. *"We were merely freshmen,"* he sings.

"It's "The Freshman", Verve Pipe," I say quietly, recognizing lyrics and tune together. He keeps singing softly, and I keep playing.

I don't know what it is about playing that makes me centered again. It must be magic that draws the tension out of my body, ebbing through the strings and turning emotion into music. We play another and another until my hands hurt and my anxiety tank is empty.

I throw in the towel, putting the guitar away and flopping backwards on his bed. "I needed that."

"Hmm." Dakota mumbles, repeating the chorus of "Lips of an Angel". "Too bad I'm not studying music therapy; I could use you for a case study."

"I don't know how I managed to go without playing for the last two years."

"I'm sure you just found a different way to unwind," Dakota says, looking down at his fingers, flipping his red and white guitar pick across his knuckles and back.

"I drank a lot. Not the best solution to the problem, I guess."

"Alcoholism probably not the best, but it's probably

better than the one I've been using."

"Seeing how well you handle alcohol, though," I chuckle a bit.

"My arms beg to differ. You stressed about finals?"

"I don't know. No more than usual, I guess, but I'm edgy about something, and I don't know what. Like this horrible foreboding is hanging on my back, and I don't know what it's about. Am I going to flunk all my finals? Die in a car accident? What?"

"I don't know about any accidents, but I'm sure you'll pass your finals. You're smart. I might even pass History class thanks to you."

"Once I gave you the idea to do something about music during that time period, you were off and running. And like I told you, bring in your violin and play during your presentation, you'll get an A. Acklund loves stuff like that."

"Did I tell you he showed up at that gig last weekend?" Dakota flicks the pick in the direction of his desk and turns his attention on me. His eyes are bright, and I swear the blue one looks eager and the green one looks anxious. "I was filling in on guitar for the guy in my English class' band. Some dive honky tonk and Acklund showed up in jeans and a patterned shirt."

"Seriously?" I gape as Dakota gets off the bed and puts his guitar away. I've only ever seen Acklund in his solid-colored shirts and sport coats.

"Seriously. Cowboy hat, plaid shirt with pearl buttons, boots. He was all out."

"Did you take a picture? For blackmail in case you need it?"

"Nah. Just further proof we all have our secret side, I guess. Speaking of teachers," Dakota changes the subject, leaning his guitar case on the wall.

"Yes?" I ask warily.

"You." He flops backward onto the tiny bed, landing next to me with his legs hanging off the side. "Why do you want to be a teacher?"

"I don't know." I shrug. "I always liked history and didn't want to get a Ph.D. to be a professor. My guidance counselor said to be a history teacher for high school. So here I am. It's not really an epic adventure. I'm not even going to ask why you're a music major because it's painfully obvious. Did you ever think of pushing both beds together and having a decent-sized one?"

He laughs at my change of subject, making the mattress tremble. "I'm not a big guy, and I don't need that much space, I guess. I let a drunk girl crash here earlier this year, and I was glad she slept over there. She threw up everywhere."

It's my turn to laugh. "It ain't college life if there's no vomit."

"Hmm," he muses, rolling his head sideways to face me.

For a long moment I'm just staring at him; his jaw is straight and lightly scruffy. His skin has a permanent pink high in his cheeks, but what always draws me in are his eyes. Then I realize I must seem like some kind of creeper. I open my mouth and blurt the first thing that comes to mind, "Does the two-colored eyes run in your family?"

"No," he answers like it's not odd I'd just start asking dumb questions. He knows me too well. "I asked for mutant powers, and all I got was a genetic mutation."

"Alexander the Great had different colored eyes. One blue, one dark," I say.

"He was a bad ass, wasn't he?"

"Military genius. When he died, he was the King of

Macedonia, Persia, and the Pharoah of Egypt."

"Guess I know what I could be for Halloween." He turns away from me and springs to his feet. "Let's move the other bed over. I swear, though, if you let Jase bang a bunch of chicks on my bed when I'm gone, I'll kick both your asses."

Shaking my head, I roll off the mattress to help him.

* * *

I'm trying to go over my answers for my psych class final when the weather turns bad. Dark clouds storm into view outside the paned glass. Icy rain taps out an eerie melody. I pulled a late-nighter finishing my term paper and studying for this, but I can't seem to focus on the questions in front of me.

The closer it gets to winter break, the more my mind is on my suitemate. I've been crazy with studying, but in the spare moments I've caught with him, I've noticed his darkening mood. Dakota hasn't said anything, but I know it's the idea of five weeks at home.

Five weeks at home isn't settling well with me either. I want to see my family, but I don't want to miss… and that's when my thoughts start to get muddled and confusing. I can't bear the thought of Dakota heading home, spending the holidays in that desolate void of Wisconsin. Of him cutting his arms because of his pain, or anything else along that line, or—

Or leaving him behind.

The tip of my pen stops on the paper and I swallow hard. I'm afraid to say it, even in my head, but I don't want to leave without him. I can't even quantify how I'm scared of being without him, of being away from him. Part of me is scared he'll do something stupid. Part of it is selfish, that

I don't want to be without the companionship I'm used to. I need—

"Time's up," the professor announces, his graveled voice snapping me out of my thoughts. There's only a handful of us left in the room by then, and my professor eyes me a little as I approach his desk and turn in my paper. I mumble something, eyes down as I drop the paper on his desk and leave.

I head out of the building, but when I see the pelting ice rain outside the doors, my footsteps falter. My phone starts buzzing in my pocket, and when I fish it out, I see my mom's photo.

"Hey, Mom," I answer, forcing my voice to be upbeat.

"Hi honey, how'd your final go? You were supposed to call me when you finished."

"Sorry, I was talking to some people," I lie. "It went well, though."

"Are you hitting the road tomorrow after your last test? Or you going to stay and have one night to celebrate?"

Hearing her soft voice, I can't help but relax a bit. "I don't know yet. I'll know more tomorrow. Weather here's kind of crap right now."

"Well, be safe Ian. I don't know if your brother said anything to you yet, but he's bringing his new girlfriend over for lunch on Christmas Eve. Mia's bringing her friend Justin too."

"Justin, the not-a-boyfriend boyfriend?"

"That's him. He's a sweetheart. Once you meet him, you'll like him."

"Maybe I should get a dog so I can bring someone home with me too," I joke.

My mom laughs. "Honey, you're more than welcome

to bring any of your friends here. Even Jase."

"You hate his guts."

"But he's your friend, honey, and I'm sure you see some good in him. Oh, shit Ian, my dinner's burning, gotta go. I love you!"

"Love you too, mom," I chuckle and hang up the phone. Sliding it into my pocket, I smile as a crazy, and loud, thought comes to mind.

* * *

Jase must have sacrificed a goat or something to pass his finals; instead of studying for his next one, he decides to go out and celebrate the two he finished. Anticipation is making me antsy. I start folding some clothes, cleaning out my desk, and packing but don't finish one of them. Jase gives me an odd look and readies himself to go out.

He doesn't invite me to go with him. Not that I care, I have better things to do, but I take note of it.

"See you," Jase grumbles as he slides into his leather jacket.

"Later," I reply. Busying my hands with sorting through my backpack, I listen for Jase to leave our suite, the heavy door shutting behind him with a familiar click. The coast is clear.

I charge across the hall, barely knocking on Dakota's door before walking into a dark room. Some weak light from outside, refracted by the icy chunks splattered on his window, and nothing else. Dakota's lying on his bed, staring up at the ceiling. Embarrassment makes my stomach hurt.

He sighs and turns to look at me, mouth corner pinched in an attempt of a smile. "Hey Ian," he says.

"What's wrong?" It bothers me how clean his room is. He's never had a lot of stuff in it, but just about everything in it is packed. It didn't look like this the night before when I helped him study for his History final.

"Heading home tomorrow."

"Oh." I sit down on the edge of his two-into-one bed.

"My dog was the only reason I wanted to go," Dakota says, his hard voice a mismatch to the weakness in his features.

"What happened?" I ask tentatively.

"Shadow was too much trouble, so my dad dropped him off at the pound. Too much fucking work, couldn't wait two more days for me to come home and take care of him. God, I hate that man. I don't want to go."

I watch him push himself into a sitting position, his body now facing mine while his fingers pick at the stitching on his dilapidated black chucks. When I take a breath to say something, those two-toned eyes snap up and meet mine.

"Our emotional moment quota for the day has been filled now," he chuckles a little and sniffs. "What brings you over here?"

His smile is plastic—cheap and fake. I don't know how to comfort him about it exactly, so I follow his lead and change the subject. In light of the situation, maybe he'll be receptive to my thought.

"I had a question for you." I feel dumb now, and scratch the back of my head.

"Yes you can take a guitar home with you for break."

"No, that wasn't it."

"Both guitars?" He asks, tilting his head to the side.

My frustration comes out in a dumb little snort. "I don't want to take your guitars home with me. I want you to come home with me."

His eyes widen. I've surprised him, which I don't think

I've ever done before.

"You hate it in Wisconsin anyway," I start to ramble, "so why go there for five weeks of your life you'll never get back? No one wants to have a horrible holiday. Just come home with me."

"I..." His plastic smile breaks into a frown. "I don't want to be a bother to anyone."

"You wouldn't be a bother, my family will love you."

"Ian, it's Christmas, I'm not going to intrude on your—"

"I wouldn't have asked you if you were going to ruin Christmas." I roll my eyes. "Don't be stupid. There's plenty of room, you're not going to eat us out of house and home, and all those other bullshit excuses aren't going to work. I'm extending you an invitation, whenever you want for as long as you want. If you decide you hate me and my family, fine, you can leave after two minutes, but just, just, please come with me."

It's quiet. He's thinking. I'm waiting.

"Five weeks with me tagging along, huh?"

"If it were twelve I'd still ask."

"But..." he chews his bottom lip. He's never seemed so indecisive, so unsure of himself before. I want to grab him by the shoulders and shake him as hard as I can. This doesn't feel like a complex decision.

Lowering my voice, I lean in a little so our eyes meet. "You deserve better. You should not be spending Christmas alone because your family turned their back on you. I'm going to go crazy worrying about you if you're there and I'll have ulcers by the end of break. Look," I pause to draw a breath, but I can't tear my eyes away from his. "They don't care but I do, so come with me."

There's something different in the air, something electric that charges my nerves. My heart is hammering in my chest, the warmth in the room suffocating my skin. Senses are in hyper-awareness now, my breath catching in my throat as my stomach spasms.

"I don't want to make problems for you," he murmurs, looking down and breaking our eye contact.

"You're not a problem, Dakota. You're the best thing I've got." My hand moves on its own, closing the distance between us to touch his cheek. He doesn't shy, just looks back up into my eyes. I know I should move my hand, but the fingers I have against his skin are unwilling to break contact. Slamming against my ribs is my heart, pounding with so much force I'm sure its bony cage will crack any second.

"Ian," Dakota whispers.

A thought bubbles from the darkest corner of my mind. It builds inside me, a wave rising hard and fast, ready to crest and wash over me. I'm scared. Everything inside my body trembles, my mouth rejects the breath of air I try to drag in. I don't want to lose him, I want him safe and close. I want to convince him, I want him to see the truth.

I want to kiss him.

I'm terrified, but it doesn't stop me from pulling him closer or leaning in enough to feel his breath on my lips. I exhale, my shaky breath meeting his in the inch that separates our mouths. Closing my eyes, I can feel his warmth, how alive he is, and I want to feel more.

His peppermint Chapstick bites as my lips brush his. There's a millisecond of time for me to enjoy it before I hear a loud crashing and see light.

We jump apart, and I see Jase walking through the door I left open.

"Ian, I need you to come give me a jump."

"A what?" I try to rein back the panic in my voice. I can't look guilty, I can't sound like— if Jase had just—

"My battery is dead. Jumper cables, Einstein," Jase

huffs. "If you could tear yourself away from whatever the fuck you two talk about. Now I'm going to be late."

"I've got cables in my Cherokee," I say, hoping to every holy figure that my legs hold up when I stand.

I don't even grab a jacket, just follow Jase out to the frozen parking lot. He must not have seen anything, he would have said something, but I can't shake the feeling that stirs my guts as I retrieve my jumper cables.

"Are you sick or something?" Jase asks, eyes studying me as he pops the hood of his Yukon.

I stop dead in my tracks. He saw. He saw me kissing another guy, and I know exactly how he feels about gay guys. Would he listen to me if I explained it? I've never been attracted to guys, just Dakota, I'm afraid of losing him, he's too much to me now, and I was just trying to—

"Dude, Ian?" Jase tilts his head a little. "It's like twenty degrees out here and you're sweating. You getting sick? Because if you are stay away from me."

"I don't know," I mumble and hand him the jumper cables so I can pop my Cherokee's hood.

Chapter Ten
December

It sucks being home.

I'm laying flat in my bed, tossing an orange lacrosse ball into the air and catching it, kind of wishing the exposed timber beam on my ceiling will collapse on top of me. The odds are not in my favor though, my mom and step-dad's timber frame house isn't that old and it's well built. With a light slap the orange ball lands in my palm, and my phone whistles to let me know its done charging.

I look over at my pine nightstand, but can't reach for my phone. If I bring it to life it will just remind me what a stupid coward I am. It knows how I avoided going back to my dorm. How I was too scared to face Dakota and had just texted him.

I'm sorry about last night. I meant what I said though. Here's my address.

My phone would show me Dakota's response from

some god-awful hour this morning.

Did you mean what you did?

Narrowing my eyes, I chuck the ball at the beam. Maybe there is some factory fault in the rafter and if I hit it just right it will fail, extinguishing me and giving my parents a nice settlement to make up for the damage.

Just the rubber orb comes back down, and I swat it across the room in frustration. I've had all day to formulate a response, but I have nothing. I don't know what to say to him because I don't know what the right answer is. I don't know what the wrong answer is for that matter. The most complicated questions in life have yes or no answers, like some kind of sick paradox.

Groaning, I grab my comforter and roll, tightening myself into a blanket burrito. My mom thought I'd come upstairs to bed because I was exhausted from the drive. My sister teased me for avoiding Mom's new pot roast recipe. I came up here to hide from goddamn embarrassment and shame.

It reminds me of the first time my ex-girlfriend Sarah and I slept together, this strange mix of panic-excitement-shame. Back then I'd crossed some line, some marker in life that I couldn't backtrack from. A big step into adulthood, further away from innocence. Now I've trespassed into some dark, murky area of adulthood and I can't shake the feeling that at any moment everyone will be able to tell. Like something insignificant will give my secrets away; my mom will see the way my hair's parted or the telling shape of a zit on my face and be all like 'Ian Taylor what did you do?' and clutch her heart and gasp 'you kissed a boy?' and start asking too many personal questions and my dead grandmother's ghost will appear and tell me how I've dishonored my family.

Smothering my face into my pillow, I wish I could talk to Dakota. I need to hear him tell me how irrational this is and why it's not as big of a deal as I'm making it out to be. I wish I wasn't so much of a coward, that I could pick up my phone and call him. He'd just ask me the same question though, did I mean what I did? Did my actions reflect my words? I'd choke on air trying to answer that.

I meant it, I know I did. I felt too much at that moment not to have meant to kiss him. It played my heart and soul like a harp. God, it kills me to think about it—I meant it with all that I've got, I just don't know what it means.

"Ian?" a soft voice calls out, followed by a light knocking on my door.

"Mia?" I sit up. In comes my sister, wearing blue flannel pants and a pink tank-top against her amber topaz skin. Her braids tied up in pigtails make her look more like six than sixteen, but I won't say it. Her face scrunches a little as I untangle from my blankets and ask, "What's up?"

"Um, some friend of yours just came to the door asking for you. He looks like Barnstorm. Did you just fail to mention to me that you know him?" Her face is a strange mix of bewilderment that makes her brows slant, and wonder that makes her earthen eyes widen.

"Who?"

"Barnstorm. On YouTube?" When my face stays blank she throws her hands in the air and sighs dramatically. "Never mind, I'm not that lucky. Mom's in the kitchen trying to stuff food down his throat."

My stomach launches at the idea of the mystery friend being Dakota. I know it's highly unlikely someone I made a move on – and ditched – would show up at my door, but I'm stupid enough to have hope. Hope that squeezes my heart so tight it feels permanently misshapen.

Mia tags along behind me as I leave my room, cross the open loft area, and descend the stairs to the main floor. It has to be one of my friends from high school that heard I was back in town. One I haven't seen for a while or didn't hang out with me around the house if Mia doesn't know them. I want to ask her twenty questions about what they look like, but I silence them in my throat. I want to cling to the edge-of-the-Galaxy remote possibility I'm going to see Dakota.

"I'm sure Ben can take a look at it, he's a real gear-head." My mother's chipper voice echoes through the open living room. There's something in the acoustics of the house that amplifies her voice through the living room and up its two-story ceiling to collide with the exposed timber frame.

Gripping the newel post, I spin around the end of the staircase and dare to look at the breakfast bar separating the living room from the kitchen. Sitting there, second seat from the right, talking to my mother, is Dakota.

A plate of pot roast in front of him, that familiar camouflage Badgers hat on his head, and a smirk on his lips. His eyes are bright and eager, tempting me to run across the hardwood floor and crash right into him.

"You didn't leave after two minutes?" I ask, walking towards him at an agonizingly slow pace. I can't take my eyes off him, but I'm hyper-aware of every action I take. My mom and Mia are there, and if I slip up somehow they'll notice. Like the zit thing, but it'll be something about the way I walk or the pitch of my voice or the teeth-to-lip ratio of my smile.

"Your mom's too good of a cook," Dakota replies, nibbling a piece of potato off his fork.

"Excuse me," Mia pipes up, elbowing past me. "Not

to sound completely crazy and stalkerish, but, uh, are you Barnstorm from YouTube?"

I roll my eyes in a show of irritation and apology for my sister. They about roll out of my head when Dakota puts a finger to his lips and exhales.

"Shh, don't tell."

"Oh, my gosh. Oh my gosh. I've been following you for like over a year," Mia squeals and climbs onto the leather stool beside him.

"I thought you looked familiar," my mom adds, twirling her sandy-brown hair into a bun. "The cute guitar guy, right?"

"Mom," Mia hisses.

I have no idea what they are talking about, or why exactly my mother and sister who exist in a world states away from school would know something about Dakota that I don't. My eyes narrow in irritation as I take the remaining spot beside him.

"I just wish Ian told me you were coming," Mom says, swatting at my wrist while smiling at Dakota. "I would have had the roast warm. Ian, make sure you call Ben in the morning, he needs to get his car fixed. Mia, you have school in the morning so you get to bed."

Squabbling starts between my mother and sister, but I ignore it and take a moment to revel in the amazing realization that Dakota is right here in front of me. He'd taken my offer and was here, with me, in my house.

"I would have been here sooner," Dakota murmurs. "But I stopped in Wisconsin first. Then my truck started giving me problems."

"You could have texted me you were on your way," I chide him a little.

"You never answered my last text."

"Yes." I surprise myself by answering him with such

conviction.

I can see the smirk on his face when he turns back to his plate and stabs a chunk of meat. His voice murmurs at a volume meant for me as he asks, "You meant the first part, or the hiding in your room until you could sneak off campus without speaking part?"

"That was a knee-jerk reaction of self-preservation compounded by my natural stupidity. I meant the first part."

"Ian, you're not stupid."

My mom interrupts. "Did I hear you're from Wisconsin?"

My mom harasses him with questions until he finishes his plate, then she ushers us out of the kitchen and off to my room. There are only a couple of bags by the front door, so I grab them both and take Dakota to my room, feeling uncomfortable watching him rubberneck as we walk. My house is decorated pretty simple but it is a new timber frame and it is huge. His peeling white farmhouse could probably fit in my living room and kitchen. In this habitat, I look like a spoiled over-privileged kid.

We cross the upstairs landing and enter my oversized bedroom. There are two queen beds facing a wall of windows. A recliner is in one corner, covered in laundry, and two large desks stand back-to-back.

"Ben and I used to share this room, but he's not using that bed so call it yours," I say and gesture to the bed on the left.

Dakota launches himself onto the bed, bouncing across the mattress. "You weren't kidding about the whole slumber party thing were you?"

"Nope," I shake my head and grab the pillow. "Told you my house was awesome, Dakota," I say, smacking him in the chest with it. "Or should I even call you that,

Barnstormer?"

"First of all, it's Barnstorm. Second, it is my YouTube account. I do a bunch of guitar and violin lessons on it."

"Third?" I ask.

"*If you do not want to see me again, I would understand,*" he sings.

"Third Eye Blind." I name the band but smile at our game.

When I try to smack him again he grabs the pillow, ripping it out of my grasp and punching me in the bicep.

* * *

Dakota doesn't bring up the incident at school, and I don't either. For all the time I spent freaking out that he'd be mad, or what he was thinking, and to my surprise, it's like nothing happened. We fall right into the stride of our friendship despite the new scenery; we spend the weekend ice fishing with my step-dad, four-wheeling with my brother, and playing guitar with my sister.

There's a stolen moment here and there when I feel something different between us. When he touches my arm for a second, or when we're lying in my room talking about everything under the weak winter starlight peeking through the windows. Everything but 'the thing'. I don't want to bring it up, to burst the bubble of perfection I'm living in, so I keep pretending nothing happened. For the first time ever, I have a friend that accommodates me, and Dakota doesn't say a thing.

* * *

I wake from a dead sleep in the darkness of a winter night. A bitter wind is baying outside the windows, but it's not what woke me. I listen, and when the pounding of blood in my head slows, I hear Dakota moving in the other bed. The rustle of sheets, a creak from the bed frame. He tosses and turns for a few minutes, making me frown.

"Dakota?" I call out softly.

"Sorry. Didn't mean to wake you up," he answers in a weak voice that makes my frown deepen.

Pushing myself up on my elbows, I ask, "Can't sleep?"

"Headache," he croaks.

My heart goes out. I've never seen anyone get migraines like him. "Need me to get you some painkillers or a soda?"

Raspy, like the wind outside, he whispers, "No, it won't help."

I can tell by his voice he's on the verge of tears, and I sit up the rest of the way. "Do you need to go to the ER and get a pain shot or something?"

"No, I hate hospitals. I'll be okay."

Out of respect for his wishes, I lay back down and try to go back to sleep. It's pointless. I can't sleep when I can hear him tossing in his bed, and I know he's in pain.

"I'm going to have to do something, I can't just lay here while you're suffering." I'm frustrated, and I know it tells in my voice. I hope it sounds rough with desperation, but I have a feeling I just sound whiny. "Tell me something I can do."

Dakota doesn't answer. I can't see much in my dark bedroom, but I hear the creak of the box spring when Dakota gets up. His bare feet patter on the hardwood floor that I know is ice-cold. I can make out his features when he nears my bedside; Glassy-eyed, forehead crinkled and a tight jaw. He's hurting, and to my surprise, his request is, "Move over."

I scoot my body over a little, trading my warm spot on the mattress for a cold one. Dakota pulls back the comforter and crawls into my bed. I'm surprised, but even more so when he curls up against my chest. "It fucking hurts," he whispers, leaning his head into my shoulder.

I open my mouth to tell him I'm sorry but stop myself. "I know," I whisper instead. Pressing my fingertips against his temple, I start rubbing in small circles. "Close your eyes and relax."

He sighs, and as I keep massaging his body melts against mine.

"That helps," he whispers.

"The rubbing?

"And you're warm," he murmurs, nuzzling into my t-shirt.

I'm waiting for it but the feeling never comes—that overwhelming sensation when I'd kissed him, the rampant fire burning through my body. My heart is swelling, but on sympathy this time. I'm holding him close, but it doesn't feel wrong or even sexual.

I wonder if this is what he was talking about on that gravel backroad in my Jeep. Forget the labels and rules of what you should and shouldn't do, I don't care about them anymore. I just love him. That's what it is, when I peel away all the bullshit, the raw emotion I'm left with is love. I don't have to define it. I love him like a brother, like a friend, like a lover, whatever. I can just be, because he'll let me be.

I rest my cheek on the top of his head, breathing in the minty scent of his shampoo, and keep circling my fingers. "Sleep."

Sunlight wakes me. It's warm enough on my face I know it's bright, too bright to open my eyes more than a crack. I try to stretch, but I'm not tangled in my comforter like I thought I was. Something warm, breathing, and human is in my arms.

Blinking in the light allows memories of the night to return. Dakota's the body I'm curled against, the waist my arm's locked around. I can feel his breathing, the expanding and contracting of his rib cage against mine. I sigh peacefully, but my breath tickles the back of his neck and wakes him.

"Mmm," he murmurs. Stretching a little, he says a groggy "Morning."

"Headache?" I whisper.

"Manageable. Did I mention my neck, back, and feet hurt too?"

I chuckle. "I'm not touching your feet."

We lay there in quiet for a few minutes. I don't want to break away from him, and he doesn't move either. As the cobwebs clear out the questions start running through my head. Why are we lying here like this? Daylight has woken up some part of my brain that keeps telling me this is wrong, but it doesn't feel wrong. It feels like the most natural thing in the world, holding my little Dakota spoon.

"We should probably get up, figure out what we're doing today," I say.

"Comfy here."

Before I can argue there's a brisk knock at my bedroom door. I jump back and push him forward harder than I need to. When Mia walks into my room I'm half-sitting in my bed and Dakota is sitting on the floor. I'm pretty sure they can both see my heart seizing in my throat.

"Ian, are you going to sleep the day away or what? Ben and Nikki are here with the snowmobiles. Justin should be here any minute, you guys want to come with?" She's just standing there with one hand on her hip, waiting for an answer. As if she sees people sitting on my bedroom floor frequently. I rub my arm as if she could somehow tell Dakota's skin had been touching that exact spot.

"Dakota?" My voice sounds steady and sure, somehow. "You want to go?"

"We have enough for everyone," Mia adds with a smile for him.

"I've never done it before. Can I just ride?"

"You can ride with someone," Mia says.

I clamber off the bed and head over to my dresser. "You're kidding me, right? You grew up in Wisconsin, and you've never gone snowmobiling?"

"We didn't have one and none of my friends let me drive theirs," Dakota shrugs a little.

"You have no idea what you're missing," Mia squeals. "Come on, get dressed."

When I'm sure she's out the door and not coming back, I turn away from my dresser and back to Dakota. Guilt hugs me hard, seeing him sitting there on the floor in his white t-shirt and blue flannel pants. He's looking up at me with this curious look, his dark hair awry, and the blanket half-draped over his shoulder like a toga.

"Sorry about that, I-"

"Zzzzz." Dakota makes the letter hum in his mouth like a pissed-off bee. "Don't apologize for stupid stuff."

"Okay. Um, you sure you're okay with snowmobiling? Your headache-"

"I'm fine," he snaps a little. As if to prove his point he jumps to his feet and throws the bedding back in its place. "Are you worried about my skull, or you just feel threatened because your sister totally has the hots for me?"

"Shut up." I turn back to my dresser.

Chapter Eleven
December

When I bring up going to the twin cities for the day and Mia invites herself along, I'm wishing Dakota wasn't so likable. I object, making Dakota laugh and Mia pout.

"I still have Christmas shopping to do, too," Mia argues. "I'm done with classes, why can't I come with you?"

"Because you're going to buy a whole bunch of stuff we're going to end up carrying around the Mall of America for you, and it's all going to be heavy."

"I want to take pictures in the city too."

"Mia, Ian's probably got some of his own plans." My mom steps in, and I give her a look of thanks. "You and I can go on another day."

"But Mom—"

"Dakota didn't come up here to be tied to your hip. He was Ian's friend first," she says with a wink. "You have to share, Mia."

I get my wish, and it's just Dakota and me that head into the city for the day. The weather is kind of iffy, but I hardly notice past the radio blaring and us laughing. We sight-see and do some shopping until dark. The flakes are fatter and blowing hard, but I don't think much about it. Snow and wind are the last things on my mind when we find a nice Japanese restaurant for dinner.

It's shopping season so the place is packed, the service slow, but the hostess tucks us into a small private booth. I don't notice the time it takes for our petite waitress to take our orders or bring us drinks, and neither does Dakota.

Maybe it's because we've been talking nonstop today, or because we're away from everything and everyone else, but I'm feeling bold. Questions that I've been wanting to ask, but too afraid to, I feel brave enough for.

The waitress brings bowls of soup to the table, and I wrap my hands around mine. After Dakota takes a sip of his I clear my throat. "Can I ask you something? A personal question."

"Well, yeah," he smiles a little and sets his bowl down.

"Why." I pause for a drink of water. "Why did you cut yourself that night at school?" I can tell by the way his mouth twists he's going to blow me off and try to make me laugh. "I'm being serious. Why?"

Dakota sighs. "Ian, it's not really," he stumbles over the words. I don't press, just wait until he lifts his eyes to look into mine. "It was a moment of weakness. In the past..." He leans across the table, forcing the cuff of his flannel shirt up his forearm. Lowering his voice, "I used to cut myself. I hadn't in a long time, trying to be strong and optimistic and everything, but it hadn't been working. I'd missed two days of class with a migraine, I was sick of hurting, I wasn't settling in at school and I didn't see the point of even being there. I went in the bathroom and started cutting. Then this thought came to mind." He looks down at his miso soup and stirs it with his chopsticks. "After I accidentally gouged the hell out of myself I was watching the blood going down the shower drain, and I thought, what would it matter if it ended then? What would I be missing out on? Who would I even affect, or who would care?"

It bothers me, thinking of the emptiness inside a person who would think such thoughts. "Dakota," I murmur, but he smiles slightly and shakes his head.

"I may not be a religious person but I believe there is a God, entity, Flying Spaghetti Monster or whatever, and it works in ways we can't understand. I was thinking that I had no reason to stay. The next thing I saw was you."

The waitress returns to fill our glasses. I wait until she's out of earshot before asking my next question.

"Do you still think like that? I mean, you don't feel the need to do that anymore?"

He shakes his head. "No." That smirk of his spreads on his face. "You make me a little happy."

"I'm getting a little fond of you," I chuckle a little and look down at the glass I'm reaching for. When my hand closes around the sweating glass I see Dakota's fingers brush my knuckles. I release the glass, but stop myself from grasping his hand. Raising my eyes, his bi-colored orbs are staring deep into mine.

Dakota murmurs, "I need you. That's why I'm here. I'm not going to make it anywhere else. I don't want to be anywhere else. I need you."

It's my heart smashing my lungs, making it hard to breathe. If he asked me to jump into lava I'd do it right now and not feel the burn.

Plates of sushi rolls slide across the table between us. I answer the waitress' ten questions of how it looks and do we need anything routine while Dakota grabs the first bite, shoving the whole piece in his mouth.

I shake my head and laugh a little, picking up my chopsticks. "With all that, you've definitely usurped Jase for the best friend world title." I snag a piece closest to me.

"He's just going to argue with me on that," Dakota rolls his eyes. "He'll say he's the heavyweight champion and I'm the featherweight, we're going to have to get giant leather belts bedazzled or something to prove it, it's just going to be a mess."

"There's no competition between you, honestly."

Dakota watches me pop the sushi in my mouth, smirking as he reaches for another piece. "I know. I'm the only one you've had in your mouth."

I try not to spit my food out, eyeing him like the devil as I choke. My skin turns to fire, and as I grab for my water I'm remembering that barely-a-kiss kiss.

"Do I taste good?"

I gulp down water, swallowing the rest before replying. "There was no tongue action that night that I remember."

Dakota snorts a little and taps the tip of his chopsticks on the serving dish between us, on the vacant spot from the sushi piece I'd taken. I look from the plate to him then back before I realize it. He starts chuckling and I roll my eyes.

"Dakota Roll. Really?" He tries to smother his laughter while I glare and snatch another piece. "That was dumb."

"You still didn't answer my question," he says around a laugh. I reach under the table and flick him in the knee as hard as I can. "Ouch! Ouch," he gasps.

"I think this one reminds me more of you," I hold up my new piece. "Big Mouth Roll." I mock anger, but it only makes him laugh harder.

"Because it's spicy?" he hisses between laughs.

"Shut your face."

"Will you do it for me?"

"You are a bad, bad—" I stab my chopsticks at him, but freeze when I see, no joke, a blonde, brunette, and a redhead approaching our table.

"What?" Dakota asks, craning his neck to see what I'm looking at. When I groan he looks back at me, arching an eyebrow as I plaster on a smile.

"Ian Taylor, I knew it was you from across the room," the pale girl with cropped walnut-colored hair says through a cool smile.

"Hey Shelby." I clear my throat and stand to give her one of those formality hugs, the ones where you put your arms around each other but your touch is light as feather dust. "Tyler." I nod to the redhead and hold my hand out to the blonde. "Cameron, how're you doing?"

"Home on break." Cameron shrugs, shaking my hand then sliding his into the right pocket of his elbow-patched sport coat.

"You should have said you were coming into the city, we could have done lunch," Shelby chastises me. Maybe it's the length of time since I've seen her last, but I can taste the fake in her voice.

"It was spur-of-the-moment," I smile stupidly.

"Are you still doing that teacher thing?" Tyler asks, pulling at the Rolex on his left wrist.

I try not to roll my eyes. "Yeah, still doing the teacher thing."

"Too bad you're just here for the day," Tyler nudges my shoulder. "I'd invite you down to the shop, we're having an open event tonight."

"Speaking of," Cameron clears his throat. "I think our dinner arrived, and we've just an hour until then. It was great to see you again, Ian."

"That's right." Tyler glances at his watch and frowns. "Let me know next time you're in town."

"Tell your parents I said hello," Shelby smiles wide,

giving me a wave as she heads back across the restaurant.

I exhale the breath I didn't realize I was holding, and Dakota nudges my shin under the table.

"No introductions?"

"They probably didn't even notice you," I huff a bit. "People from high school."

"Your friends?"

"I guess you could call them that." I grab a piece of sushi, but I feel him staring at me. Setting the chopsticks down, I draw a deep breath and summarize it as well as I can. "Shelby was the girl, last I knew she's studying painting or something. If you couldn't tell, she's more into the image of an artist than actual art. Tyler and Cameron, I was on the lacrosse team with them. Cameron is going to some fancy college for Engineering. Tyler's family owns restaurants, and the shop he mentioned is this coffee shop nightspot he's helping manage. Coffee by day, kind of a bar at night. It's weird, but it's been open for a year now so it must be working out for him."

"Sounded like he was having an open house or something. Want to go?"

"They do open mic nights and stuff." When I look up and see his expression I shake my head. "No. No way."

"Oh, come on, it might be fun. Those are more entertaining than karaoke."

"But you won't just sit there and watch, you'll want to get in on it, and with my luck, you'll drag me into it. No."

"But they're your friends," Dakota starts but I cut him off.

"Not a one of them gave me the time of day when we moved into town. After my mom married a doctor, and we lived in a nice house, they decided Ben and I were okay to be seen with. They're not friends."

Dakota raises an eyebrow. "They didn't ask about your

brother, did they?"

"Ben made it clear he wanted nothing to do with any of them. I was in lacrosse, so it was just easier to go along with them than to make a big deal out of how they treated me before."

Dakota is chewing thoughtfully, eyeing me. I just know I'm not going to like whatever is going through his head. When his thoughtful look turns mischievous I frown. Flicking his aspen-wood sticks, he picks up another roll and shoves it in my face.

"Eat, we have somewhere to go tonight."

"No, we are not going." I pinch his arm with my sticks.

"Yes we are. I'm the guest," he hisses and jabs the roll at me again.

"Absolutely not," I grumble and snatch the roll.

"Oh, hell no," I shake my head vehemently.

I let him drag me down to Tyler's shop, but I'm certainly not participating. It's bad enough just being in the trendy industrial building when we stick out something horrible. The dress code seems to be cocktail attire, but we're in jeans and flannels. Tyler came over when we first arrived, I'm sure to ask us to leave, but when he recognized me he plastered on a smile and welcomed us. I was hoping to linger in the back of the room, but Dakota bullied us up to the front of the stage.

I'm embarrassed, but Dakota's unfazed. Unfazed enough that when he returns from the bathroom he informs me he signed up for the stupid ass open mic contest. Which

I should have seen coming.

"What?" he asks innocently.

"You don't even have an instrument."

"Tyler said your buddy Cameron would lend us guitars."

I feel my appendages numbing. "Us?"

"Well, yeah."

Leaning close, I croak in his ear, "I can't get up in front of these people. I don't play in public."

"It's not that bad," Dakota rolls his eyes. "Come on, most of these people so far have sucked balls. Cameron's band is on next, then it's our turn."

"No, Dakota." I'm whining, I know I am but I don't care. "I can't do this."

"Why? What's the worst that can happen?" God his eyes are so intense for the dark atmosphere. "You completely bomb it and so what? These peoples' opinions aren't going to affect the rest of your life. Come on," he takes my hand in his and squeezes. "You're not doing it alone."

I let him lead me out of the crowd, but when I see Tyler watching us approach I pull my hand out of his. Tyler fakes a smile as we near him. "I had no idea you were into music, Ian," Tyler greets us. "Or in a band."

"Kind of," I gulp. The guy on stage finishes, and Cameron leads his bandmates on.

"I should stop letting Cameron come down here for this," Tyler says. "We give out twenty-dollar gift cards to everyone who participates, but the winner gets a hundred dollars cash. Whenever he comes down he wins."

"You should just hand him the money up front then instead," I joke. I'm sweating. Dakota isn't nearby, and I swear if he set me up to go up there alone, I'm going to kill him. Slowly too, like drag him behind my Jeep all the way back to Rochester.

"This is more fun, and I make a shit load off people buying drinks," Tyler says.

Cameron leads his band off on a popular song, and I watch them perform. There's a tug on my elbow, and I find Dakota standing beside me, his eyes on Cameron as he holds out two shot glasses.

"You don't drink," I object.

"They're both for you. Suck 'em down."

I knock both back, grimacing against the burn in the throat. I'm grateful because Cameron's song is winding down, and I'm sure I'd faint if it weren't for the pain in my throat. Pretty sure the burning is what's keeping it from closing up completely.

Dakota drags me by the elbow over to the stage, and I take the glossy blue guitar Cameron hands me. The place is loud, but I swear I hear Cameron laughing as he leaves me to stand with Tyler. Steeling my expression, I adjust the guitar strap and Dakota offers me a pick.

"I could punch you so hard right now," I grumble and snatch the pick.

He smirks, standing on his tiptoes to reach my ear. "No one else matters here, let them go and just play. You'll live."

I catch his elbow and bow my head to reach his ear. "You owe me so fucking big for this."

"You'll thank me later. "Wonderwall"?"

"Whatever," I sigh.

He steps back with the biggest grin on his face and bounds up the stairs to the stage.

"Shit, what the hell happened?" I can't tell if I'm

screaming or not, but half a second ago I was sound asleep and now I'm staring at white.

"Ice. Ice, I didn't see it," Dakota replies, his voice hoarse. He has a death grip on the Jeep's steering wheel, but I can see the shake in his arms.

I take a few breaths, taking in my surroundings. "Are we in the ditch?"

"Y-yeah. I didn't see it, the ice and we just slid right off the road." There's not much outside but darkness and snow glowing from the headlights. We are definitely in a snowdrift. "I'm sorry. I'm so sorry."

I unbuckle my seatbelt as I look at Dakota. "Hey, it was an accident." He's shaking, and not just in his arms. "Hey." I squeeze his forearm, finally getting him to look at me. "Accident. I'm not mad, we're both alive. Relax, okay?"

He swallows a gulp of air and nods.

"Calm down. Seriously, we're okay," I smile a little. "Let's see if we can get out with the four-wheel drive then we'll see about panicking."

Four-wheel drive isn't any help, the snow is too deep and the incline too steep. The sky is dumping more snow on top of us, and we're both covered when we get back in the Jeep after surveying the situation.

"Now we panic?" Dakota asks quietly, huddling in the passenger seat as I slide into the driver's seat.

"Not yet." I shake my head and grab my phone. "What was the last city you passed?"

"Pine Island, I think."

I dial Ben's number and flinch when he answers the phone.

"Ian, it's three in the fucking morning this better be good."

"Love you too Ben. I need a tow, the Jeep is in a snowdrift."

"Are you in it?"

"No, Ben." I roll my eyes. "I walked home first then I called you. Yes I'm in it. On fifty-two, between Pine Island and Oronocco somewhere."

"Didn't you notice this whole blizzard thing?" His voice sounds gruff, but I hear rustling in the background as he gets dressed.

"On my way back from the cities and didn't realize it was this bad. Jeep seems fine, I just need to get pulled out."

"Alright, I'll grab the truck and head out that way. I better get a nice Christmas present out of this is all I can say."

I'm laughing when I hang up the phone. "He'll be here before you know it."

Dakota exhales and flops back in his seat. "I'll pay for it."

"Seriously, it's not that big of a deal."

"No, it was my fault."

I frown at his sudden mood. When I fell asleep we were trading stories of being in boy scouts when we were younger. He was cheerful. The accident must have freaked him out, but why so much? It wasn't much of an accident, more of an inconvenience. "Dakota, really, it's okay."

He sighs again, and turns his back to me, leaning his head against the passenger window. He doesn't say another word to me until Ben shows up to the rescue.

* * *

"Where's your friend?" Ben asks, sliding into the passenger side of my Cherokee.

"Dakota? He's at home with Mia, helping her with some photography project. Why? Can't a guy go to lunch with just his brother?"

Ben frowns sheepishly. "I kind of told, well," he trails off.

"Your girlfriend is meeting us isn't she?"

"I thought you were bringing him with."

"He's my friend, not my date. Jeez." I pull out into traffic and head down the street to the small diner. "You're lucky I like Nikki."

We're quiet on the rest of the drive there. It's only a few minutes but they make me nervous. Ben's never quiet without a reason, and I don't like the way he's looking at me.

When I swing into a parking spot I ask, "What?"

"I don't know, something just seems different about you." When I roll my eyes he continues, "I'm serious."

"What's different about me? And don't say I gained weight either."

"No," Ben muses, unlatching his seat belt. "You're more you. More relaxed, more yourself. I don't know how to explain it, but you just seem so chill now. Usually you're so guarded, keeping in tune with whoever's around. I can tell you're not hanging around Jase as much."

"Yeah, not so much anymore."

"It's Dakota, isn't it?"

I avoid looking Ben in the eye. I'm afraid of what he'd think if he knew the strange thoughts that live in my mind. I'm not ready to face them, much less him after dragging them out of me. "Yeah, he's a good influence."

"Well don't lose him anytime soon."

Chapter Twelve
December

"What's the deal with him?" Mia whispers in my ear. It's hard to hear her over the cacophony of Christmas Eve. My aunts and cousins are there, and some of Troy's family too. Chattering adults and screeching children running wild are making a racket that echoes in my skull.

"I don't know, Mia," I sigh and glance at Dakota. He hadn't spoken unless spoken to at dinner, and now with the socializing happening, he's hung back, helping my mom in the kitchen. "He's been in a mood since the accident."

"That was three days ago."

"I know."

"Well? Go figure out what's wrong then. People shouldn't be unhappy on Christmas Eve."

"You go talk to him."

"Ian," she scolds me. "He looks like a kicked puppy over there, go talk to him."

Looking across the room, I certainly don't see a kicked puppy. More of a lone wolf with the world on its back, stalking for the staircase. Sighing, I take a sip of my eggnog.

"Go after him," Mia hisses and shoves me in the back.

As badly as I don't want to, I go. I'm not good at approaching people, I never have been, and the vibe I've been getting from Dakota is to leave him alone. I drain my eggnog and leave the glass in the kitchen before scurrying to catch him at the top of the stairs.

The landing overlooks the party, but it's quieter up here. The lights are off, but the twinkling glow from the massive tree below makes it serene. It's not having the same effect on Dakota though, who is giving me his dark glare. I slow my step, not sure if he's going to cuss at me or start crying.

"Had enough festivities?" I ask as I crest the staircase. He ambles away from me, leaning on the railing overlooking the living room. I follow, leaning against the rail beside him. Below us, the tree sparkles, some of my young cousins are playing video games, and I can hear the opening lines of "Rocking Around the Christmas Tree". "Or are you missing your family?"

"Family that I have now? Not so much. Family in the past, yes," he says quietly.

"Well, I get kind of sick of them sometimes, you can have my family," I joke.

He looks at me, smiling sadly as he shakes his head. "This is just my luck, get a glimpse of something like this before it gets taken from me."

"No one's taking anything from you."

"Never mind," he sighs and rubs a palm across his face. "I guess I'm not used to all these people caring about each other."

"What happened to your idea that if everyone showed more love and compassion the world would be a better place? Best time of the year for it now."

"I do believe that, I just," he stammers. "I don't fit in with it, I'm not, I don't know how to just—" He steps back from the railing, but I grab him by the elbow before he can get away. I'm not used to this, to him looking so lost and running away. Those are my jobs.

"You don't know how to take it?" I ask. His eyes light in surprise. "You're not used to people making it easy for you, or being kind without wanting something in return."

"That, and..." He bites his lip.

"You're scared it's all going to disappear."

"Or I'm going to destroy it. Ian, I've fucked up so many things in my life, I'm afraid I'm going to ruin this too. I don't deserve—" His argument dies when I pull him into my chest, holding him in a firm hug.

"Shut up." I take a deep breath, feeling his body relax against mine a little. The mint scent of his shampoo teases my nose when I lean into his ear. "You're being irrational. And a hypocrite."

He chuckles, a deep note that tickles my ribs. "Sorry."

"You're apologizing now?" I smile, loosening my hold to end our embrace.

I can't let go to really end it. Maybe I drank too much during the party, making my body disobey me. My hands should fall back to my side, I should take a step back to make an appropriate amount of space between our bodies. I don't take that step back, and my fingers never let go of the red cotton on his shoulders.

I say, "We must have switched roles."

His eyes, one blue one green, stare deep into mine when he lifts his chin. "Then this is where you do something bold and don't apologize for it later."

Something breaks inside me, something I'd stretched so far it finally snapped. Repercussion vibrates my skeleton, shaking my fingers that rake over his t-shirt and press the fabric into my palms. Dakota's gaze falls, leading my eyes to his lips. My mouth waters, remembering their peppermint taste.

I lean down, his name escaping me in a tattered breath. "Kota."

Dakota looks up, and I touch my lips to his. He'll push me away, stop me somehow, but I have to feel it again.

He doesn't stop me. Pressing his mouth into mine isn't the chaste whisper of lips in his dorm room. I feel him now, his mouth soft but the force behind it strong. I push into his shoulders, pinning him against the wall hard enough he groans, parting his lips enough to let me in. God, he tastes like the peppermints he's been sucking on all night, drawing me back for a second and third taste.

My hand cradles his jaw, breaking the tangle of our mouths for a breath. Stubble tickles my palm, and I wish I knew where this was coming from. I want to make him feel it too, to feel the sparks, and I want to feel him. I try to catch my breath, impossible when stealing kisses in between pants. I can't stop myself. I'm drunk, but not on the alcohol. On him.

"Ian," he croaks, catching me around the waist. "You don't." He leans into my kiss, tongue tasting mine as he death-grips my flanks. "Somebody sees you, they—"

I force him to look at me, for our eyes to meet. I want him to read the emotion in mine and I want to see his. "I don't care about anyone else, just you." I really don't care about anyone else in the world, just him, and with that thought warm in my mind I kiss the top of his head. If I kiss his lips again I'll be gone for sure.

Taking a deep breath, I calm my pounding heart and inhale the scent of his shampoo. "Go climb in bed, and I'll be up when the festivities are over."

He nods and mumbles, "Just say I have a headache. I don't want to be rude."

"You're not being rude." I linger, nudging his scalp with my nose. "Just need to recharge those social batteries."

* * *

I swear I hear my bedroom door click shut, but when I open my eyes no one's there. No light in the hallway, no intruder in my room. Clouds are pinking outside my window, a Christmas dawn. I don't really see the point in getting out of bed yet. I don't hear anyone up and moving.

Dakota grumbles a bit, so I know he's awake. When he sighs, my arm around his waist rises and falls. I give him a little squeeze, a reminder that I'm there, and hope he doesn't pull away. As if he can read my insecurities, he scoots back against my chest, pulling the blanket up then resting his arm over top of mine. I wish we weren't wearing our shirts. I can feel the warmth of his back against my chest, but it's filtered. I want purity. I twine my fingers in his, and can't help but smile at the feeling as he sighs again.

"How much longer?" he whispers.

"An hour, two if we're lucky until Mia wakes everyone up," I answer, nuzzling the back of his neck. His skin is surprisingly soft in this spot, and warm when I press my lips against it.

"Your mom might come looking for you," he chuckles. My body stiffens at the thought, and he squeezes my hand. "I'm not going to say anything unless you want me to."

I hadn't thought that far yet. I hadn't thought at all. Living in my little bubble of perfection, I keep forgetting that people can look in. "It's nothing against you, I just-"

He rolls over, facing me now and sharing my pillow. "You don't want to tell your mom you were making out with a guy at Jesus' birthday party? You horrible, horrible son."

"I don't want to offend you, or make you think I don't care," I huff a little. "It's just complicated."

"Oh trust me, I know it's complicated." Dakota wiggles up a little to kiss my forehead. "And you're not offending me." He scoots down, eyes meeting mine. "Do you think your mom would be mad?"

"No," I answer honestly. "I don't think Troy would be mad or anything. My brother, I don't know."

"Well as far as I'm concerned this is between me and you." He pokes me in the chest. "Whatever you want it to be."

I don't know how I would explain it anyway, really. He's closer than a friend, but what exactly did that mean? When along the way had I gone from revering him to being attracted to him? The drive inside me, the one that makes me want for his lips and touch, isn't all sexual attraction either; it's an overwhelming desire to be close to this person in front of me. I want to be close to him in every way possible, including the ways I have no idea how to describe. And no idea how to act on.

"I can't really define it, this is all new territory." It's new to me, and not for the obvious reason that he's a guy. It's new because I've never loved anything as deeply as I love him, I've never needed or cared for anything as much as I do him.

"No harm in a little secret then," Dakota smiles.

We're quiet for a few minutes before I ask him, "What would your mom think if she were alive? Would she be mad?"

Dakota chews his lip for a minute before answering. "I don't know. I think because of her I ended up with such an open view of the world, but at the same time, she used to drag us to church every Sunday. I really don't know."

"She'd still love you. For being brave, unafraid, how you believe in yourself. One of the things about you that I'm in awe of."

"I'm not that brave," he scoffs.

"You are."

"Ian, you have no idea. I'm not brave."

"Prove it."

He has a curious look in his eyes, like he's dredging up a painful memory that's stuck in his throat. I try not to pry, as badly as I want to. When he starts and stops, I take his hand in mine again.

A loud banging on my bedroom door startles us both.

"Ian! Presents and breakfast!" My sister crows. "Dakota you sexy beast get up!"

"Mia!" I scream.

"Don't make me come in there, I don't care if you're sleeping naked."

"Go away, we'll be down in a few minutes. Ugh," I growl. "What were you going to say?"

Dakota shakes his head with a smile. "Never mind, let's get ready." Before I can object he's rolling out from under the covers and going to his suitcase. I know my moment's gone, and I grudgingly leave my warm bed and head into the attached bathroom. I brush my teeth and scrub my face, catching my reflection in the mirror.

Same Ian staring back at me. I'm surprised, but I don't know why. For some reason, I thought my reflection would change, that something about me would be visible like a tattoo on my forehead. It just goes to show you have no idea what could be hiding beneath the surface; so much has changed on the inside for me, but my outside stayed the same.

I leave the bathroom, and Dakota is sitting criss-cross on my bed. He's wearing one of my flannel shirts over his t-shirt, and it comforts me somehow.

"Want me to wait for you?" I ask.

"No, go stake me out some food before your brother eats my share," he replies, bouncing off the bed and heading to the bathroom. Grinning, I head downstairs to see what kind of goodies my mom cooked up.

Chapter Thirteen
New Year's Eve

I feel like a kid with a high school crush again; the looks exchanged in the car or across the dinner table, a stray touch while we're fishing with my step-dad. The secret makes me giddy. The temptation I'm dancing with is far more adult.

I should say something to my parents, to my siblings, but I put it off, because what am I supposed to say? 'Hey Mom, just so you know, I love this guy so I guess that makes me bi? I think I'm bi'? I don't know if that's even the right name for it. I'm not gay because girls still turn me on, but am I really bisexual? I can't think of any other dudes I want to make out with. Is there a name for that? Uno-homo-sexual or something?

Maybe I don't have to say anything. We'll be heading back to school in two weeks, and what I'm doing at school isn't really their business. I'm not sure if I can hide something like this from Jase though, not when I'm sharing a tiny living space with him.

Dakota doesn't push me about it, but I wish he would. I need his opinionated voice to tell me what I'm supposed to do. I'm used to people telling me what to do and think, but Dakota gives me the freedom to find my own opinions. I'm afraid to ask him, to rock the boat when I'm enjoying the ride.

He's in a mood when we drive into Rochester for dinner on New Year's Eve, bursting my bubble of perfection. When we find a table at the grill side of a bar, I order an icy Pepsi from the waiter and Dakota asks for just water.

"What are you having?" I ask while skimming the menu. The adjacent bar is raucous.

"Nothing," Dakota sighs and pushes his menu aside. Bowing his head, he runs his fingers through his hair. It's pretty shaggy, not like the close-crop he showed up at school with. I like the choppy length, it suits him better.

"You had me drive you all the way into Rochester on a holiday so you could order water?" I raise an eyebrow. Out of habit, I glance around to see if I recognize anyone before I reach out and touch the back of his hand. His skin is cold against my fingertips, turning to ice when he pulls away. "D-"

"I'm fine," he sighs and picks at a cocktail napkin. "Just have a lot on my mind."

"Okay." I draw the word out so he knows I'm not taking that for an answer.

"School and everything. Realize there's four months until the end of the semester?"

That wasn't the answer I was expecting. I'm not sure if he's being for real or throwing me off his trail.

"It seems like a long time but it will go by fast," I say.

He exhales in a frustrated growl. "I don't want it to go by fast. Two weeks from today I'll be in class. Where did winter break go? I don't want summer to be here."

Only Dakota would be dreading summer when it's below zero outside. I can't help but half-smile. "You don't want to come back to Minnesota for the summer?"

"You can pawn me off as a wayward freshman for winter break, but your family isn't going to buy it for the summer."

"I'd hang out with you in Wisconsin, but I don't think your family likes me," I say.

He leans back, kicking his chair onto its back feet and stretching his arms above his head. The blue wording on his dark grey shirt is legible now, 'Charientism'. "Ugh," he grunts and slams his chair back down on all fours. "It doesn't matter anyway. So, New Year. What's your resolution going to be?"

"I'm going to figure you out," I answer without thinking.

"Figure me out?" he laughs. "I'm not that complicated."

"I still don't know what you've done to me."

"I just accept you the way you are," he shrugs with one shoulder, winking with his green eye.

"That doesn't explain—" I stop mid-sentence. The waiter returns with our drinks, and asks for our order. I mutter something about being indecisive, shooing him from the table. Taking a long pull off my Pepsi, I wait for the waiter to move onto another table before leaning in toward Dakota. "Doesn't explain why I want to kiss you."

Smirking, Dakota leans forward as well. "It's because you're comfortable with me. You can be affectionate and I'm not going to call you a fag and punch you in the face. And I'm fucking adorable."

There was no argument there. "Even if he swore not to punch me I still wouldn't make out with Jase."

"That's because you realize he's an asshole and doesn't really give two shits about you. Not adorable in the looks or personality departments either."

I think he's going to kiss me, and the thought sends two sparks through my spine; one of excited anticipation, and one of fear. When he slowly sits back in his seat my stomach drops in disappointment. There's mischief in his smile though, and I wonder if he knows just how crazy he's made me in that one moment.

"So?" I clear my throat. "Your resolution?"

"I don't make resolutions. I can't keep them. I could challenge myself though, like 'this semester I will attempt to irritate your roommate more than last semester'."

"That's not going to be hard. He's a homophobe, you could easily set him off."

"He's not my type."

I roll my eyes. "That's not what I meant."

"I wasn't going to say anything to him. Were you?"

My throat constricts, holding breath in my lungs. He's giving me an out, a way to avoid dealing with Jase. If we keep it a secret I won't have to explain myself, or make excuses, or try to make sense of whatever's happening, but his suggestion feels like rejection, not relief.

"I hadn't thought about it," I lie.

"It'd just be easier. If you didn't tell him."

"Maybe." I don't think it will be easier. I'll have to stay in my room, Dakota will have to stay in his. I'll have to watch what I say and do. I'll have to hide. It'd be easier if I could just be myself, and everyone in my life would let me do it in peace or get out of my life.

"It wouldn't be any different than here."

I nod, agreeing with him on the outside but screaming on the inside. It will be different, it'll be hard and it will push us away from each other. It scares me that he's okay with that.

Snow is falling as we walk down the street back to the parking garage. There's a satisfying crunch under our feet from the accumulation of powder. The cold air is sharp after the warm restaurant, but the fire in my veins keeps the chill from reaching my insides. Dakota stops in front of a bar's large windows, nodding at the people crammed inside.

Throngs of people who've been partying for hours by now fill my view. A big screen above the bar is showing the lighted ball in New York City. "We could have stayed at the restaurant if you wanted to watch the drop."

"This is better," he replies.

"It's snowing out here."

There's thick glass between us and the crowd, but I can still hear the roar of people beginning to countdown. Dakota and I are silent, watching the glowing orb sink as the mass inside chants. A new year is born to a kaleidoscope of fireworks on the screen. Inside the bar, confetti starts falling and people are cheering. Out here, snow falls down the collar of my coat.

I look at Dakota and am surprised at the sadness in his features. It bothers me it's there and bothers me more that I don't know why it's there. Maybe Dakota doesn't keep resolutions, but I'm going to. I changed my mind. Scratch the old resolution, because I don't care if I figure Dakota out; I just don't want to lose him.

"Hey," I say. He turns his head, looking up at me. The streetlight and the snow make his skin a pale tone of blue. Leaning down, I mean to kiss him, but a loud noise startles me.

I spin around to see drunks falling out of the bar's entrance to the off-key singing of "Auld Lang Syne". One of them, a girl with oversized glasses, beckons us to join them.

I look over my shoulder at Dakota. Singing randomly in the middle of a snowstorm sounds right up his alley, but not tonight. The blank expression on his face, and his stare, tell me so. I open my mouth to speak, but he beats me to it.

"Let's get going." Cramming his hands into the pockets of his Carhartt, he starts walking again.

Maybe it's the thought of all the changes I'm going to be making in the new year, or maybe it's my brain on fire, but I can't wait to get home. I fidget the entire drive back, Dakota asking me a few times if I'm okay, but I tell him I'm fine. There isn't anything wrong with me anyway, just incredible impatience.

To my surprise and dismay, my mom and Troy are still awake, curled up on the couch in the den. I try to sneak past them, but my mom asks us how our evening went. A brief summary is all I give her but Dakota starts chatting. We exchanged maybe twenty sentences the entire drive home, and now he wants to talk.

I shift my weight, wanting to scream at them both to shut up.

"Mia's still up with her friends in the game room, I'm sure she wouldn't mind some extra company."

"Mom, we're not going to hang out with a bunch of high schoolers. We're old and going to bed." I ignore the look Dakota gives me. "Night mom, night Troy."

I hear Troy asking my mom, "What are we then, ancient?" but I don't slow down my rush to the stairs. Dakota trots to keep up with me.

"Ian? What's up?" he asks, following me across the landing. I just need to get to my room. "Ian?"

I exhale when I reach the safety of my room. Spinning around, I grab Dakota by his shirt, pulling him across the threshold and into a hard kiss. I've caught him off guard;

he doesn't yield to me. Confusion fills his eyes when I break the kiss to drag a breath. Letting go of his shirt, I reach past him and push the door closed.

He opens his mouth, and I know he's going to ask me what the fuck is going on. God, his mouth— just another thing I'm addicted to. He'll taste like the peppermints he's always sucking on, and damn it he's a good kisser. I've kissed him plenty of times by now, stolen ones in daylight and meaningful ones in the dark, but the one I use to silence him is different. The urgency driving me is different. The touch of his hand on my jaw is different.

I want the safety of my world staying predictable, but I want this more. Coward Ian could go back to school and pretend we're just friends, but I don't want to be him anymore. I can't pretend all of this, the feelings tearing me apart and squeezing me together, don't exist. I need to know if these are the feelings that will make me happy, and the only way to find out is to give in.

Dakota's mouth is meeting mine, but I scrape my fingers across his neck, pulling him deeper. I feel him resist me for a moment, surprised probably by my action. Ignoring his hesitation, I grab at his flank and pull on his button-down to reach the grey t-shirt beneath it. I'm being rough, but I don't want him to feel the nervous shake in my fingers as I slide them under thin cotton and across skin. I'm surprised how soft his skin is against mine, but thumbing at his hip I can feel the miniature peaks and valleys of hard muscle. I push my hand up, following the lines of his body, but his fitted shirt stops me.

"Why did you button that thing?" I growl, breaking our kiss and freeing my other hand to pull at the buttons.

"I was cold," he replies with words so simple.

Ignoring my struggle with his shirt, he leans up, nipping

my neck.

"That doesn't help," I argue, but find myself leaning into the sensation.

"Yes it does," he whispers, flicking his tongue across my earlobe then pulling the sensitive skin into his mouth. Some brain chemical is tingling through my veins, starting at my ear and going straight down. Sparks fly when his fingers push up my henley for his palms to press against my abdomen.

This is new. My skin has met his before, chest to chest or chest to back at night, but never has this craving taken over me because of it. My hands are clawing at his shirt as I try to decapitate the stubborn buttons.

Dakota shoves me hard, separating our bodies. I suck in a breath of air, but it's not enough. He squirms his shirts off and over his head. For all the want in my body, I can't help but feel self-conscious seeing his. I'm not built like him. I can see his muscles working under his skin as he yanks the shirts off and throws them down on the ground.

"Off," he growls, stepping back to me and pulling at my shirt.

I can't resist him when his fingers sliding up my chest send tremors through my nerves. I don't have a chance to feel sheepish, he pushes me into bed and follows, tangling our mouths in an urgent kiss. There are lightning bolts throughout my body; kissing Dakota is ten times better skin-to-skin, the sensation setting every nerve off.

His mouth finds my throat again, and the words "Holy fuck" escape my mouth.

Dakota laughs, the vibration against my throat making me moan. Digging my fingers into the muscle of his back, I try to pull him closer and he nips my collar bone. I close my eyes as a tremble shakes me from shoulders to toes, my hands gripping at his hot skin.

Sharp pain pierces my skin, like a knife sinking into my collarbone.

"Ouch!" I gasp, pulling back to look him in the eyes. "What the fuck? Did you bite me?"

Dakota raises an eyebrow, judging my outburst as his left hand thumbs at the sore spot on my collarbone.

"You bit me," I hiss.

"You owe me more than sixty seconds."

He's smirking, his mouth curling in a way that tells me he's amused by me and awfully proud of himself. One eyebrow twitches, waiting for me to answer. Dim light from the bathroom plays against his skin, throwing his shadow and mine against the wall.

"I wasn't even close," I reply, but I'm not sure I believe it.

He's right though, if I keep at this dizzying pace I'm going to be gone before I know what happens. I want him, but not in some rushed fuck way. He deserves better than that.

Moving slow, purposefully, I circle his waist with one hand and my other guides his mouth back to mine. It presses our bodies together, and I make sure to feel it completely, like the warm pressure of his smooth chest against mine. I can feel the tightness of his abdomen, feel fingernails rake against my side. His mouth moves, leaving a trail down my throat as he slinks backward, dragging his body across mine.

Every muscle in my body is a tightened rubber band, humming with tension and ready to snap. I can't even control my body, it's twitching and arching on its own as he tongue-flicks my skin. I bite back the need to call out, literally biting into my bottom lip as my head presses back into the mattress while Dakota's delightfully warm and wet tongue marks territory on my skin. My hand finds his scalp, grabbing his sweaty brown hair, knotting the strands with my fingers.

Dakota's fingers slide under the waistband of my jeans, jolting me back into control. Cursing, I sit up halfway. He freezes, eyes wide and his other hand on my belt.

"What are—?" I pant. I can't finish my question. Air won't stay in my lungs long enough. His knuckles are pressing against my abdomen, fingers hiding in my waistband. Fingers I can feel against my skin, hot and tempting me.

"You don't want me to?" he asks. I can't read his eyes, but I feel the quiver in his body and hear it in his voice.

"I…" I shouldn't want to. Some part of my brain is whispering it's wrong, but my heart is screaming that it's right, and my body is demanding it now. That's a two out of three vote.

Sounding uncharacteristically unsure, he locks gaze with me and whispers, "Do you want me to just…" He releases my belt, moving his hand lower and teasing me through the denim. I wish the bulky fabric was gone. "Or I can stop. If you want me to, I'll stop."

His whisper could shatter the windows. The pressure of his fingers disappears, and I'm aching instantly. My body shrieks internally, but my heart is the one screaming the loudest.

"No," I growl, louder than I meant to. He flinches, and I grab his wrist. "I'm sorry, don't. Don't go. I've never done something like this before. I just, I want you, you have no fucking idea how bad."

Dakota's expression changes, over-cautiousness replaced with trouble. He leans forward, pressing his mouth against my ear and his hard-on against my hip. Kneeing my legs apart, a laugh claws out of his throat. "Yeah, I do."

Chapter Fourteen
January

When I get out of the shower Dakota is still curled up in my bed. His dark hair is wild, and when I approach my dresser he pulls the chocolate sherpa comforter over his bare shoulder. I don't think there's anything that can pry the smile off my face.

"You could still get out of bed and come with me," I offer. Being shy for some reason, I face the mirror but stare at a dresser drawer handle while wrestling a grey t-shirt over my damp skin.

"Mm, I could get dressed and come with you to see some friend of yours." He yawns and makes a big production of burrowing deeper into my pillow. "Or I could stay in this warm bed and go back to sleep. Tough choice."

I pull on a pair of jeans and start threading my belt. "Or we could trade places, you go see Jamie and I'll go back to sleep."

"Nope."

"Fine, I'll face the world without you. But put some pants on, if Mia comes in here she'll be all over you."

My phone goes off as I buckle, and Dakota grabs it

off my nightstand. "It's your mom. Hello?" He taps the speaker button.

"I wanted to make sure Ian was up, I know he had plans this morning."

"I'm up," I growl a little. I'm a nineteen-year-old adult and my mother is wake-up calling me the morning after. Embarrassing.

"Dakota, are you going with him?" my mother asks.

"Hadn't planned on it."

"Well come downstairs, I'm cooking."

"Thanks, Mom." I take the phone from him and end the call. "Now you do have to get out of bed."

"Your mom's cooking is worth it. I think. I don't know, this bed is really comfy."

"Get up and put your pants on." I roll my eyes and slide my phone into my pocket, but jump when my mom's voice comes to life.

"Hello? Ian, your phone's still on."

Heat burns my cheeks as I pull the phone out and hang up for sure this time. "I'm glad you think it's funny," I hiss.

"I wish I'd been saying something about how badly I want to put my mouth on—Ow! Ouch!" Dakota tries to wiggle away as I attempt this horrible wrestling move and pile-drive him into the mattress and start beating his face with the pillow. "Stop! Ouch," he laughs.

I hit him once more over the head. "That would be the best way to tell my mom, let her listen to you coming on to me," I huff and toss the pillow.

"It would be better if you came on to me." I make a face and he says, "Unless you had a better idea."

"I don't have any ideas actually." Realizing there's just the comforter separating me from his blissfully naked body gives me other ideas though. Seeing a wicked purple mark on his collarbone, my fingertips brush against it, and

I have this overwhelming urge to make another mark.

"Just put 'it's complicated with Dakota Jackson' on Facebook and be done with it." Dakota shrugs. "Then your entire family can be shocked at once."

"I'm not informing family of my life choices via social media." I tug the blanket up over his shoulders.

"She like Boston? You could sing to her. *I closed my eyes and I slipped away.*" My expression is blank. He rolls his eyes, then belts out "*It's more than a feeeeeeling.*"

"*When I hear that old song they used to play,*" I add. More of a wounded animal's death shriek than singing, but I get a smile. "Now I'm *walking away,* to the garage to leave." I drag myself off the bed and away from him.

There's a second of hesitation at the door to my room. This isn't the first time I've left him behind, but I feel like I owe him more than a simple 'later' before I leave the room. Is there some kind of secret handshake for guys you swapped spit with that I can use? Because 'see you later' sounds impersonal, but I'm not going to give him an intimate kiss on the cheek and say 'I'll be home later honey'. I don't feel like he's the type to need that kind of reassurance.

"You forget something?" Dakota asks. God, maybe he does want some weird goodbye kiss thing, which doesn't seem like him but things are different now, right? We had sex last night, sex changes everything. "You're just standing there staring into space. You forget your wallet or phone?"

"Huh? Oh, uh, no." My hand brushes my back pocket out of habit. Wallet is there.

"Okay. Have fun then," he says and rolls over. "Later

Ian."

* * *

I jump when my phone buzzes in my pocket. Expecting to see Dakota's name on caller ID, I fish it out to answer it and frown when my step-dad's picture greets me. It's not unusual for Troy to call me, but at the same time, I get a sinking feeling. My stomach squeezes as I swipe my finger across the screen and bring the phone to my ear.

"Hello?" I ask.

"Ian, I need you to come down to the emergency room. Dakota was in an accident."

I can feel the blood draining from my extremities and pooling in my gut. Plugging my ear, I bow out of Jamie's living room, straining to hear Troy clearly. "What happened?"

"I don't know yet, they're not telling us anything, but it was a car accident. He was driving my truck."

"What?"

"Ben called and his Colorado was done. I told him he could take my truck in, it needs ball joints, just swap them at the shop."

"Where is he?"

"Saint Mary's. Are you okay to drive?"

"Yeah, I'm fine." I nod even though he can't see me. He sounds so calm, I'm embarrassed when my voice shakes.

"Be careful Ian." Grabbing my keys off the counter, I hang up my phone and slide it back into my pocket. I feel eyes watching me as I pull my coat on.

"Ian? Everything alright?" Jamie asks.

I mumble, "I've gotta go," and bolt for the door.

Driving to the hospital is a blur of cars and urban scenery. Pulling into the parking garage, I park next to a white Honda. Throwing it in park, I lock the Jeep and dash for the entrance to the emergency room with my heart in my throat.

It is bright outside, sunlight glinting off the snow, and it takes my eyes a moment to adjust when I enter the building. My mother is sitting in a chair next to Troy, and she jumps up to give me a hug. Her embrace soothes me for a second—nothing could be that bad when I feel so safe.

"What happened?" I ask while grudgingly releasing her. She motions for me to take her place, but I shake my head and perch on the edge of the coffee table littered with outdated magazines.

"Your brother's boss towed the truck back to his shop," Troy sighs and looks me in the eye. The firmness in his grey eyes is unsettling. "Ben said it's totaled. Went into the ditch and rolled in a one-car accident."

"One car accident? No one hit him?" I frown. How on earth did Dakota end up in a ditch on a bright, sunny day with dry pavement? There's only one way I can think of, and it closes my throat.

"One of the witnesses told your brother," my mom pauses to swallow. "The truck braked hard, went off the road, and rolled down the embankment. It could have been an animal or debris in the road or something and he swerved and lost control."

Oh God. He did it on purpose. He doesn't swerve for squirrels. He wouldn't lose control of the truck, he drives a damn truck. My eyes sting, but the knife in my heart stabs with each beat. I said something, or what I did, made him try to hurt himself. I'd pushed myself on him. I'd made him —I've screwed up. Again.

My mother's voice interrupts, "Why don't you tell them at the desk you're here, maybe he'd feel better if he saw you? He is probably afraid to see us right now, but you know we're not upset, just worried. The truck is replaceable."

I nod meekly and go to the reception desk. Give the nurse my name and Dakota's, wait as she makes a phone call. Braked hard and went off the road… he did it on purpose but why? I thought he was happy now, I thought he was happy with me. I changed things last night though, I took them too far. I'd been too forceful or didn't give him a chance or it wasn't what he wanted he just owed me or, or—

"Follow me on back," the nurse breaks my thoughts. She stands and heads for the double doors, tapping the sensor with her ID badge. I follow her into the white and grey hallway. Doors to small rooms are off to my left, some closed and some open. A child is crying in one of them, screaming that he doesn't want stitches.

At the end of the hallway, the nurse pushes a cracked door half-open. She stands aside and I squeeze past her, entering a dark room. It smells like a hospital, the air heavy with detergent and antiseptic, the scent and cold temperature raising the hair on my arms. Holding my breath, I slowly push the curtain aside.

Dakota's head is propped up on the gurney, his skin a shade darker than the sheets. Tubes and wires snake out of his blue gown, joining to beeping machines and IV bags. There's dried blood on his gown, on the sheets, on his skin. Two butterfly bandages hold his temple together. I must have exhaled, because his body twitches like he's been startled.

I fall back a step, thinking of turning my back and running away. I don't want to see him like this, and I don't want to hear him say it was because of me. He struggles to sit up and I'm frozen in place when his two-toned eyes meet mine.

I don't see the pained emptiness or blank disregard that I'd expected. None of the emotions I thought I'd see were there. Instead, there's the same fear I know he sees in mine.

He hadn't done it on purpose, he was as scared as I was. Something had happened, something that had almost taken him away from me. A genuine stroke of bad luck, not a calculated action. It squeezes my heart, compacting the muscle until it hurts to breathe. The stinging in my eyes sharpens as I cross the room, tears slipping out when I put my arms around him. I don't care if he sees me cry, or if anyone sees me holding him. As long as I'm holding him I can't lose him. He gets a handful of my shirt in his grip, easing my self-doubt.

Bowing my head, I press my cheek to his. "Don't ever fucking scare me like that," I choke around the knot in my throat.

"No promises," he whispers.

"You're going to give me a heart attack at this rate." Loosening my grip on him, I scan him again for injuries. "But you're okay, right?"

"Busted up, but in one piece."

"What happened?" I'm as bad as one of those hover-parents, barraging him with questions while gently touching his body to check him over. I feel a pinch in the bridge of my nose, then the sensation of snot threatening to drip out; I wipe my eyes and sniff hard.

Dakota scoots over, moving cords and tubes. "Sit with me." Part of me feels like I shouldn't, but my wrenched heart wants to be near him. I carefully swing into the bed.

It's a snug fit with both of us, but I don't mind his head on my shoulder, his body pressed tight into my side. His arm rests across my abdomen, IV line taped to the back of his hand. The machine whirrs and clicks, still audible when I turn on the television to drown it out.

How long we lay there watching PBS I don't know. I hear footsteps approaching, making us both tense. A light knock on the door is a warning that someone's coming; Dakota releases my shirt and pulls back from me.

I don't know why I'm surprised by the action, it's the game we've been playing. So close, but far apart if someone can see us.

Gentle as I can with his battered body, I pull him back into me. His eyes tell me he's surprised. I haven't shown anything toward him in public like this. The door handle turns with a metallic clunk as he rests his head on my chest, and I kiss the top of his head. I don't care anymore, I don't care if a doctor or a nurse sees me with him.

A hand slides the curtain back a bit, but it's not a doctor or even a nurse that appears. It's my mother.

My hands are choking a cup of coffee I have no intention of drinking when my mom slides into the hospital cafeteria's small booth. She pushes a grey plastic tray between us, but my empty stomach doesn't even react to the pastries.

There's another coffee cup on the tray. "Troy coming?" I ask.

"No, he got called in for a consultation. When he left the nurse told me I could check on you two."

I can't help but cringe. This is not the way I'd imagined

it all coming out. Not that it couldn't be worse, but that isn't much comfort. I start talking but keep staring holes into my coffee. "I'm sorry Mom, you're going to be disappointed in me."

"Ian, you're not a disappointment to me. I don't think you're going to start now either." Her small fingers pry mine apart so she can take my hand. Even though it takes two of hers to envelope one of mine, I feel like a kid again, safe and guided. "You're not hurting anyone or breaking the law, are you?"

"I'm probably breaking your heart."

"Only because you don't feel like you can tell me whatever's on your mind."

"Mom." I shake my head a little. I can't look her in the eye when mine start to sting, so I focus on the nearby window. "I don't know how it happened, I really don't, but he, he and I," I stutter. How exactly do I explain this? What was an acquaintance three months ago was now, what? "I don't know what to call him. It sounds really gay to call him my boyfriend," I snort a little and shake my head. "It's not even that. He's my best friend but he's more than that. I don't know." Shoulders sagging in defeat, I sigh loudly.

Squeezing my hand, she asks, "Has this been going on a while? Wanting to be with men, I mean."

"I haven't been gay and hiding it. I wasn't gay and met him, I met him and this, this whole thing happened. I'm probably more confused than you are right now." I lift my eyes to meet hers, and I'm surprised to see that ever-patient love in her gaze like she always has. "I know I shouldn't, but I can't help it. I love him and I don't know how it happened."

"Honey, that's the way love works. I don't think we're supposed to understand it." She smiles gently as her thumb traces a circle on the back of my hand. "You know I love you no matter what. I just want you to be happy, and if Dakota makes you happy, then I'm happy."

"I am happy. Other than being scared shitless having to come here," I laugh a little, making her smile. "I could have done without that."

"We all could have." One last squeeze and she releases my hand, trading it for her cup of coffee. I take a sip of my own, surprised how light my shoulders feel. "If it's not too personal, what's going on with his family? We found out about the accident when Ben called, and when we got here they said Dakota had refused an emergency contact. You mentioned his dad before, why wouldn't he want to tell his mother?"

"His mom died a few years ago. He doesn't get along with his dad, that's why I asked him to come here for winter break."

"You said that." My mom's features turn cheerless and she asks, "That bad?"

"Really bad."

I'm trying to decide how much to elaborate when my phone makes a cheerful chirp. I pull out my phone and see a strange local number. Frowning, I answer it. "Hello?"

Dakota's groggy voice replies, "They're letting me out."

Relief floods my veins. "I'll be right there."

I just know he's going to say something to deflect me, so I hang up. "They're discharging him."

"That's a relief." My mom smiles as I stand up. She catches my hand as I reach for the tray. "I love you, Ian, I'm always going to."

I'm the luckiest guy in the world; twenty minutes ago

I was sure my entire world crashed out of the stars.

* * *

"You sure you don't want something to eat?" I ask again as Dakota slides under the covers of my bed.

"I'm fine." His voice is still raspy, and his eyelids heavy from the painkillers he's taken. I flip off the lights and lay down beside him; him under the covers and I on top. I can't stop myself from touching his cheek, his jaw, his shaggy hair.

He relaxes when my fingers comb through his hair, and I ask, "What did the doctors tell you? Other than the bruised organs?" That was all he'd said on the way home. A result of the crash, not the cause of it. I hadn't pushed it in front of my mother, but now I feel an overwhelming need to know.

"Probably a seizure. Fan-fucking-tastic," he grumbles.

"Do you need to see a neurologist now or something?"

"Do we have to talk about it right this second?"

"I want to know you're okay." I scowl a little.

As if he knows I'm making a face, he opens his eyes to meet mine. "It was probably just a fluke thing. They'll take my driver's license away for six months or something, I don't know." He sighs and winces when the movement causes pain. Growling under his breath, he scoots in closer to me, muttering against my chest, "The whole thing is embarrassing."

"There's insurance, Troy's not going to kill you. Everyone's just glad you're okay, since you scared the shit out of us." I chuckle and kiss his forehead. "Besides I took the focus off by telling my mom I love a guy, that news will keep everyone preoccupied."

His body tenses for a second, and I catch my slip-up.

Now is not the time to say that, how can I be so stupid? My heartbeat slows, my stomach clenching a fist when he pulls away from me slightly.

"I don't deserve that from you," he says quietly.

"You don't have to say anything, this just caught me off-guard." I try to cover my tracks, but I wonder if it's too late. I just take-backsies admitting my feelings. What was worse; blurting it out, or blurting it out and being such a coward I rejected it?

"It's not that, it's," he exhales in a whoosh. "You deserve better, not this."

"Well I happen to like 'this'," I argue. "I don't know where that self-assured spunky bastard is hiding, but I know he's in there." I tap his chest lightly. "What's with all the mopey emo shit all of a sudden?"

"Because I don't want to see things be hard for you."

"What's going to be hard? I told my mom and she isn't disowning me. Anyone in my family who decides to do that, fine let them. So what if you lose your license, I'd be happy to drive you around. Jase will have a shitfit I'm sure, but hey I can move into your room. Listen, quit being an ass and just let things be, okay?"

Dakota mumbles, "Okay," and reaches out, taking my hand in his.

"Go to sleep and rest up so spunky comes back." I squeeze his hand when our fingers entwine. His hand's smaller than mine, but for some reason, it always seems stronger to me.

Watching his eyes close I start thinking about school.

How different things are going to be when we go back.
    "Ian?"
    "Hmm?" I look down and his eyes are still closed.
    "I love you."

* * *

Someone is blasting the radio downstairs, and it's what wakes me up. I'm alone in bed, so I get up and dress quickly. I find my mother in the kitchen, who just smiles and points to the game room.

It's not the radio, it's Mia singing her heart out. I recognize the tune, and the lyrics shaped by her voice sound haunting. Stepping into the room I see Mia with her back to me, strumming her pink Epiphone. Dakota's sitting catty-corner from her with his violin, and gives me a wink then looks back at Mia when she starts on the chorus.

Mia was good before, but with his help the last few weeks she is playing like a pro. Their voices blend notes and words into a harmony that gives me goosebumps. I'm not even jealous, I just feel lucky to hear it.

"That felt really good," Mia squeals after finishing the song.

Dakota points his bow at me and asks, "What was it?"

Mia spins around, her expression pure mortification. I can't help but raise an eyebrow and smile at her. "Easy. "If I Die Young". Mia, since when did you listen to country music?"

"What, I can't listen to country because I'm black?" she teases. "I listen to all sorts of stuff." Seeing the embarrassment in her eyes I decide not to tease her about it. Instead, I give one of her dark braids a little tug.

"Sounded really good Mia. Really, really good."

"He makes me sound good," she mutters.

"It wasn't his voice that lured me down here, it was yours."

"Whatever," she grumbles and strums once. "I was just trying to practice before Justin gets here."

"I get to see the little punk again?"

"Ian, quit pretending to be a badass. You're not going to be here anyway, Mom said you were going with her and Ben to Faribault. It's the third."

I hadn't really forgotten, I never will, but it had slipped my mind with everything else going on. "Mom's letting you hang out with Justin unattended? Not sure if I approve."

"Your boyfriend is going to babysit us." Mia shrugs with one shoulder, and I see Dakota stifle a laugh when my skin starts to burn.

"Is that so?" I fold my arms in defense.

"Mom told me last night. Because I asked. Because I already knew." She looks over her shoulder at me, smirking with her pink lips. "Aw, you're blushing Ian!"

"Shut up, I'm going to get breakfast," I grumble and turn my back on both musicians who start laughing at my expense. I'm not really mad, but it's still an odd feeling knowing that people know. I feel like I lucked out with the reaction my mom and sister have had, and I pray it holds out for my brother and step-dad.

* * *

My mom didn't tell Ben, but I don't want to bring it up on the drive to our grandmother's grave. Mom stays pretty neutral and I try to guide the conversation away from it, but Ben bullies the accident to the topic of conversation.

For all of his roughness, he's just as sensitive as I am and can tell there's something he's missing.

"Did anyone figure out what happened with that accident yet? Troy stopped on his way to work to take pictures, and that truck is fucked up."

"Ben," Mom barks.

"Jacked up." He rolls his eyes. "Was there something wrong other than just being a Wisconsin driver?" When neither of us laughs he scowls.

"They think he had a seizure, he doesn't remember the accident," I reply curtly.

"A seizure? Out of nowhere?"

"He had one at school earlier this year. I guess he's pre-disposed to it." I feel someone looking at me, and I glance up to see my mom staring at me through the rear-view mirror. Haven't told her that story yet. Don't think I will either. "Does it matter? Insurance is going to pay for it."

"Well yeah they are, I was just wondering if he was an idiot Wisconsin driver or there was something wrong with him."

"There's nothing wrong with him. Are you just not happy unless you're being a prick?"

"Christian," my mom snaps from the front seat.

"Put the claws back in Ian, fuck."

"Benjamin. You are grown men stop squabbling like children, and clean up the language."

Ben huffs. "I was just asking a question."

I scoff. "You don't have to ask it like an asshole."

"What are you so protective about?" Ben raises an eyebrow. "The way he sticks to your side and you can't take a joke I'm about to start calling him your boyfriend."

I know it was meant to be a jab, something to piss me off and make me retaliate. He's been instigating with me for twenty years if you count in-utero, and he's good at it.

I know what he's doing and I know how I'm supposed to react, but I can't process it fast enough.

A pregnant silence swells in the car. I swallow and I swear it echoes. I try to think of a response, but my mind is blank. When I see Ben's expression change I know it's too late.

Ben's eyebrows inch up as his eyes widen. He sits up straighter, his head brushing the sedan's ceiling. "Ian, you are not going to tell me you're a faggot."

"Benjamin Taylor!" Our mom shouts from behind the wheel. The car jerks when she brakes hard and turns for an exit ramp. "You watch your mouth in this car."

"Don't tell me you're a fucking queer," Ben snarls.

"If I do, what are you going to do to me? Beat me up?"

"My brother is not a fucking faggot." He spits the words with so much contempt, I'm not quite sure where he was hiding that much hate. In spite of or because of him being my brother, I jump right into the argument.

"Grow up, Christ you don't have to be a backward-thinking idiot."

"I'd rather be that than an ass-fucker."

The car stops abruptly but I don't even notice. Anger is pumping through my veins, and I can't hear my mom yelling at us. I only see my brother's face twisted in anger and disgust, and it fills me with hatred. He's always been better than me, and now I'm sick of it and gonna stand up to him.

"You don't care if I found someone that makes me happy? That doesn't even matter to you, I'm just vile and disgusting for being different than you? And for someone who pounds it in their girlfriend's ass more than her pussy, you're calling me an ass-fucker?"

Our mom's scream stops us both. "Enough!" She pulls on her seatbelt to twist, facing both of us. "I am not going to listen to you two fighting. You're both adults, so if you can't talk to each other in a civilized manner, keep your mouths shut. We're going to your grandmother's grave, so out of respect to her, both of you shut up."

Her words are angry, but there are tears in her eyes. She turns and unclips her seatbelt before leaving the car, slamming the door behind her with enough force the body rocks in place. We're at a rest area. I climb out of the backseat, leaving Ben behind. I walk in the opposite direction as my mom, hoping the icy air will temper the fire inside me.

* * *

The sky turned to grey, a perfect match to the somber mood. When Rochester's city limits come into view the snow starts to fall, pristine white against the grey afternoon. There was silence in Faribault, silence the drive back. Tradition dictated we have lunch together, reminiscing and trading stories about grandma, but it was thrown by the wayside this year.

I don't think I relax until Ben is out of the car. I flashback to being fourteen again; dropping Ben off at the mall so my mom can console me for his dickish behavior toward me. I'm not in middle school anymore though. My mom saying he'll come around or whatever doesn't ease the hurt I'm feeling. I didn't expect Ben to be excited for me or anything, but I didn't expect him to hate me either.

She must have told Troy our lunch plans were off, because when we walk in he's chopping vegetables in the kitchen. He smiles and hugs my mom, but his expression turns a little cool when he looks at me. I'm ready for this day to be over.

"Need any help?" I ask as my mom starts digging in the fridge. My appetite's long gone now, replaced by dead weight in my stomach as I sit at the counter.

"Oh, we can manage. Justin's car's not here, is Mia home?"

"Uh, no," Troy says with a frown. "She sent me a text a little while ago saying she was going to Target with Justin. House was empty when I got here maybe fifteen minutes ago."

"Snow's getting thick," my mom murmurs when she glances out the window. "I'm going to call Mia."

The front door opens, and I lean back to see Mia come in. I can't help but smile when I see the blush on her cheeks. Instinct tells me it's not the temperature that put it there.

"Hey," she grins and enters the kitchen, dusting the floor with snowflakes as she unwinds her scarf. "I thought we were having Chinese for early dinner?"

"They're home early so we're cooking." Troy goes back to chopping.

"Everything go okay?" Mia asks hesitantly, looking at Mom then me as she climbs onto the stool beside me. No one answers her right away and she frowns. "Or did something else not go well? I noticed the truck's gone. Unless you put it in the garage?"

"What truck honey?" Mom asks as she sets a pot in the sink and starts to fill it.

"Dakota's truck."

"It's still at Ben's work," Troy answers.

"We brought it back earlier." Mia frowns and the kitchen stops. Troy's knife rests on the block, Mom cuts the water off and turns to face us. "What?"

"Who's we?" Mom asks.

"Justin drove me and Dakota up to the shop, and I drove it back. What? Dakota was in the truck with me, and Justin followed us back here."

That solid knot in my stomach is choking my throat.

Troy and mom exchange a look, and I lose it. Spinning out of my chair I bolt for the stairs, taking them three at a time to the landing. I am hoping, but part of me knows what I'm going to find.

I crash into my room and it's empty. My things are all where I left them, but both beds are made and Dakota's things are gone. His suitcase, his backpack, the book he was reading, all gone. I look in the bathroom and it's clean and orderly.

Stunned, I walk back into my room. There's nothing left, like he erased himself completely from existence. I scrub my face, wondering why he left me behind.

"Ian?" I look up and see Mia leaning against my door jamb, wide-eyed as me. "Ian, what happened?" She looks around my room, shaking her head. "He was here when I left, it didn't look like this. I wasn't gone that long."

"When did you leave?" If I'm blunt my voice doesn't quiver. If I sound angry, it masks the confusion and hurt tearing me apart.

Mia glances at the alarm clock on my nightstand. "Maybe two hours ago? Ian!" she gasps when I brush past her. "Ian, what's going on?"

I don't answer her and head back down the stairs.

I bet all my chips on Dakota taking the highway, and that he is heading to Wisconsin. Full of fear and adrenaline, I tear up pavement, pushing my Cherokee faster than is probably safe. The weather betters when I put tires on I-90, but my bravado wanes.

I don't know why he left, so how the hell can I know for sure where he went? I'm guessing Wisconsin because it's the only place I know, and the thought brings the rest of my foundation crumbling down. I have no idea where else he would go because I don't really know him.

Easing off the speed of the Jeep lets my mind go faster. Miles go by as I remember every detail of the last four months, dredging my mind for some kind of clue only to find nothing new. What has changed from this morning? I remember saying I'd see him later, and his lopsided smile when he said he'd be there. The last thing he said to me was that he'd see me tonight.

No note. No call. No warning. I dial his number once more, but it goes straight to his voicemail message. No answer.

He's not even supposed to be driving, what would possess him to go out at night, in snow? Tightening my grip on the wheel, I try not to think of him in his Colorado, rolled into a snowy ditch I'd already driven past. Wherever he's going is worth dying for.

Or what he's leaving.

It has to be me. If he left without me he doesn't want me to follow him. He doesn't want me with him. I'm the variable.

I've felt rejection before, but I don't remember it hurting so much. Like my chest was cracked open, and everything inside me ripped out and thrown away until there's nothing left to be put back. Logic tells me I'm pathetic; abandoned and I'm driving on to chase down my abandoner. Still the same old Ian, left behind and trying to catch up. My father. Sarah. Now Dakota.

In reality I should turn back. Chasing something I want has never worked before, what fool am I to believe it would work now? But the idea pulls at me from darkness, and some light of hope inside me drives me on. I need to keep going. I need to find him, I need to see him in one piece to tell me why.

I can't concentrate when my mind is tearing itself in two. A blue sign glows in the beam of my headlights, promising a rest area ahead. Forcing everything else out of my mind, I stare out into the darkness and snow. Another reflective blue sign, with its institutional arrow pointing me off the interstate.

The ramp turns one way then another before I see parking lot lights and a small building. The snow seems to be falling lighter here, taking its time to dance under the amber streetlights. A plow truck hasn't been here yet though, and a white blanket crunches under the Jeep's tires.

My blood turns to ice as I slam on the brakes, cussing loudly. In my headlights, dusted with snow, is the tailgate of a beige Colorado. My tires slide a foot or so before getting traction, but I can't look away. Is this the cruelest joke of the divine or can I actually be this lucky?

Cursing, I goose the Cherokee into the curb and throw it in park. Leaving the door open and the engine running, I bail out and go for the front of the Colorado. There's no one inside it, and I crouch at its nose. I don't even feel the icy cold as I put fingers to the license plate and wipe the snow away.

Red letters at the top spell out Wisconsin. Heart in my throat, I wipe the rest off with my palm. Bold block letters read 'NDAKOTA'.

I scramble up on shaky feet. He's here.

Scanning the surroundings I see nothing but emptiness. Trees and snow, the rest area building, and a few idling semis in the other parking lot is it. Forcing myself steady, I turn off the Cherokee, pocketing the keys after pulling on my coat.

Resisting the urge to run, I walk the sidewalk up to the building. No sign of life in the outdoor area, not even footprints. Stepping inside I'm met with a blast of hot air and the hum of fluorescent bulbs. The door slamming behind me echoes. No one in the bathroom. I listen at the door before taking a glance through the women's bathroom even, and find nothing. The maps and brochures are neatly stacked and organized, the vending machines are stocked.

Did he slip past me?

Forging out into the cold night, I jog down the walkway to the parking lot. The Colorado's still sitting there, undisturbed. No new cars, not even remains of tire tracks. Frustrated, I start pacing. Through the building once more. Down the rest of the sidewalk, to the end of the parking lot. A raccoon is all I see in the picnic area.

I go back to the vehicles, making sure his hasn't moved. I wonder if I should call my mom, tell her I'm not dead in a ditch or anything, and I see it. Another walkway, one I hadn't seen when I drove in. Forgetting the phone call, I head for the walkway. There's no footprints other than the ones I'm leaving behind me as I follow the path, but when it leads me around a stand of trees I see Dakota.

Still as stone, he's sitting on the top of a picnic table, staring into nothing. He's as pale as the snow that's accumulated on his clothes. It stops me in my tracks, stealing my breath. In one moment I'm relieved to find him, my heart aches to hold him, I want to turn from him, I want to shake him as hard as I can, I want to kiss him and curse him in the same breath.

The emotions pouring inside gives me a head rush, and I do none of those things. I stand, frozen, as I growl his name. "Dakota."

He doesn't startle. His head hangs a little, acknowledging he heard me.

"Dakota!" No one else is there to hear me choke on his

name.

Slowly, he turns his head, and there's nothing that I expected. His face is distraught, and eyes red from shedding frozen tears. He doesn't answer me, but tightens his jaw as his eyes well.

"What the hell is going on?" Anger makes my voice strong, when on the inside I feel ready to collapse. I move closer and he shrinks back into himself.

"Go home, Ian," he whispers, making the words shake.

"Why?" I demand, and when he doesn't answer I'm slamming a fist into the table, making him flinch. "Tell me!"

"Ian, you have to let me go—"

"Why are you running from me? What did I do?" I can't control the anger in my voice, or the tears pooling in my eyes. "Tell me!" When he shakes his head I grab him by the upper arms. "God damn it, tell me something."

Tears are streaming down his face as he shakes his head vehemently. "Ian, just walk away. Walk away and it'll be easier."

"Easier? How is this easier? You, you're my," I let go of him to slam my fists into my temples. As if my hands can hold me together when I feel all my seams separating.

"This isn't a joke!" he yells. "I'm doing this for you. Go home. Your family is all you told, your friends don't know anything, everything will go back to normal."

"I won't be normal! I'm never going to be the same, how can you think that?"

He slams his fists into the table and doubles over. "I can't be there for you Ian."

"Yes you can, you've been here—"

"I can't. I don't want you to lose everyone. I don't want you to be alone. I can't do that to you."

I'm grabbing his wrists, squeezing until he winces and

looks at me. "If they can't accept me for me then I don't need them. I'm not going to be alone if I have you."

"I can't!" Pulling out of my grasp, he slides off the picnic table, a steel expression on his face hiding the sorrow I swear is there. "I have to go, before I mess up your life."

"Before you mess me up? Make me fall in love with you, then disappearing behind my back isn't going to mess me up?"

Stomping his feet in the snow, he pushes past me, barking. "Go away Ian."

"Why are you turning your back on me?"

The crunching stops, he looks up but won't face me. White smoke leaves his mouth, but no words.

I know I'm hurt, a deep wound down to the bone, but all I feel is anger. Thick and wicked, twisting through my body and choking back the sadness. "If you can't face me then go! Turn your back and walk away, you lying piece of shit." He flinches and I kick at the snow, screaming "Go!"

No reaction, and I scoop up wet snow and throw it at him. Immature, but if he's leaving I want him to disappear. I can't bear watching him stand there, teasing me with the hope of changing the situation. My snowball hits him square in the back. Hunching over, he walks on. Panting, my breath leaves in puff clouds. I watch his back until he disappears around the clump of trees.

Dakota's gone, and my anger I've used as a coat of armor is gone, leaving me vulnerable to the realization I've lost him. Without him I don't know what's left. I don't want to be alone when I don't understand myself.

Sitting on the picnic table, I wait. I can't watch him drive away, so I try to think of anything else. It doesn't work. Close my eyes and I see my bleeding heart in my mind's eye. Open my eyes and I see the cold, empty scenery. I want to go home, hide in bed with the covers pulled over my head. My stomach sinks when I think of returning, trying to explain to my mom, Mia. All the questions everyone will have for me, and no real answer to give them. And when I go back to school?

What if, without him, I become what I was again?

I can't face it. I can't. Trudging through the snow I follow the path back to the parking lot. He has to be gone by now, and the thought stings my eyes. Scowling, I try to bring back the anger; I can't curl into a sobbing ball if I'm angry.

Rounding a thick pine, I see his Colorado. The little truck is running, its headlights on, with Dakota standing in front of it. A dark-colored sedan is in the parking spot next to him, bass rumbling the car's plastic body panels. Stopping in my tracks, I watch a passenger door open. Dakota doesn't notice me, he's watching the car.

A slender guy with dyed-black hair exits the car, speaking to the driver, then shuts the door. Slender isn't dressed for the cold; high-tops, skinny jeans, and a black band sweatshirt. As the sedan backs out of the parking spot he meets my gaze and holds it. I see facial piercings reflect the glow from the streetlight.

I don't know what I'm seeing, but Dakota follows Slender's eye and sees me. He twists and goes for the passenger door of his truck. When the new guy doesn't move, just stares at me, Dakota barks, "Get in the truck."

Slender pulls his earbuds out, looking from Dakota to me and back. "What the hell did I walk into?"

"Get in the truck and stop asking questions."

Anger is back, giving me strength. I've been played, played for the biggest idiot. Stepping forward I ask, "What's going on?"

"Get in the," Dakota's voice breaks as he yanks the truck's door open. "Get in the fucking truck!" When I get closer and Slender doesn't move Dakota screams, "Pen! Get in the fucking truck if you're driving or I'll leave you here." Pen pops the driver's door, but he's still looking at me. Realization sinks in that I'm staring at Dakota's younger brother.

"Wait, wait a minute." My feet slip on the sidewalk, but I grab the Colorado's grill for balance. "Don't leave yet. Dakota! What's going on?"

Sitting in the passenger seat, eyes on mine, he shakes his head fervently. "Ian, go home," he croaks and pulls his door shut.

"You. Don't get in the car." I look at Pen's blue eyes, hoping my desperation isn't showing. Forcing my voice to be firm, I ask, "Why did he call you?"

The teenager's face reflects confusion, and he looks to his older brother. "What's going on?"

"Get in the truck, Pen. Please."

I'm surprised when Dakota starts crying. I don't understand and it's driving me mad; why is he hurting? Why is he hurting me? Why is this even happening?

Pen looks at me, and he looks just as surprised by Dakota's reaction. His expression softens a little, and I wonder what he's seeing in mine. "Did he," Pen starts and stops. "Did he tell you?"

My voice chokes as I ask, "Tell me what?"

"Pen!" Dakota starts screaming, but neither of us look at him. "Pen, shut up! Shut up and get in the truck!"

"Tell me what? Please, tell me what?" A moment passes, Pen biting his bottom lip. There's something inside him trying to escape, and it's the answer. The reason my life flipped upside down in the last three hours. "Please."

"You're Ian?" Pen asks. I nod, and Pen frowns hard.

Looking down, he hikes a leg into the truck.

"Wait, Pen—"

"It's not you," he shakes his head a little.

"What?" I'm not sure I heard him right, with the pounding in my head and Dakota screaming obscenities. He apologizes and drops into the driver's seat. I scramble for the door, but it closes before I can stop it. "Wait!"

My words aren't strong enough to stop them. The truck backs out of the parking spot and drives away, leaving me in an empty parking lot with my breaking heart and Pen's words echoing in the air.

***

I'm exhausted when I park the Jeep and enter the house. The drive was long enough when I didn't want to make it, but I had driven the whole way with those four words bashing around in my head. 'Did he tell you?' Tell me what? And why? If it's not me then what else could it possibly be?

It's late and the house is pretty much dark. To my surprise I find Troy sitting at the kitchen counter with his laptop. I want to slink off to hide in my room, but out of politeness I say, "I'm home."

"Ian?" I freeze, watch him turn his chair to face me. He frowns. "You alone?"

"Yeah, I'm alone." As badly as I want to be indifferent, I know I'm wearing my heart on my sleeve. Troy's looking at me with pity, and it makes me feel even worse.

"You okay? You look…"

"No, not really." What's the point in lying about it? "I don't really want to talk about it right now."

Chapter Fifteen
January

Mia enters my room, gliding across the floor to perch on the spare bed. I ignore her and shake out a t-shirt. She sits silently, and I take my time folding the navy cloth.

Clearing her throat, she speaks first. "Dinner's ready."

"I'm not hungry."

"Ben's here."

"I don't care." Smoothing the creases with my thumb and index finger, I add, "If he wants to say something to me he can walk up here."

Sighing, she jumps off the bed. I hope her footsteps are taking her out of my room, but she's beside me in a moment. Pushing my suitcase out of the way, she takes its spot and forces me to meet her deep gaze.

"Really Ian? It's been a week and you're still pouting? Just call him."

"Mia, you don't understand. You weren't there."

"I don't, but I doubt you do either. Have you even tried to talk to him?" she asks, head tilting to the side as her umber eyes stare right through me.

"No, Mia," I snarl and grab for my suitcase. "He's not

interested in talking to me."

"You haven't even tried, how do you know?"

"Mia! He left, I'm not going to chase after him."

Her dark eyes begin to smolder. "You're just going to go back to school like this then? You're not even going to try to talk to him? Don't you share a suite with him? Are you going to ignore him if you see him? Did it ever occur to you that he's just trying to protect you?"

Her words hurt my brain, and thinking about Dakota hurts my heart.

"Protect me from what, Mia? What?"

She flinches.

"Mia, shut up and get out of my room," I snap.

She's surprised. I've never talked to her like that before. I expect her to scream back, maybe throw a punch. I deserve it. Instead she stands and leaves my room without a word.

Picking up another t-shirt, I keep folding.

* * *

It's the longest drive back to school. I can't bear to take the highway like I'd done that night. I hate thinking of that drive, finding his truck only to watch him leave. I'm dreading the new semester. I don't want to see Jase. I don't want to see Dakota either, but at the same time I know I'm hoping I'll see him. That stupid foolish part of me is hoping if my life can go wrong in a moment, it can fix itself just as fast.

I'm an hour into Illinois when my phone rings, and Ben shows up on caller ID. I debate on answering, and finally do. Could be something important.

"Hello?" I say as evenly as possible, which is hard when I feel so many emotions rising in my throat. Anger for the last words we shared. Embarrassment for what happened between Dakota and I.

"Hey Ian." There's a long pause as he draws a deep breath. "Look, I'm sorry for blowing up on you the other day. Mom told me what happened."

My hands tighten on the steering wheel. "Okay."

Silence.

"Now that you're away from him have you changed your mind?"

"About what?" I ask. I'm not following him.

"The whole, you know. Deciding you like guys or whatever."

I can't deal with this right now. He doesn't understand, and I can't explain it. Brother or not, I don't think he'll ever understand; Ben has never loved anyone on a deeper level.

"I didn't know if this was some weird phase or something," he mumbles.

I hang up on him and toss my phone in the passenger seat.

I'm relieved when I get back to campus and Dakota's Colorado is nowhere to be found. A second later I'm disappointed. Loading up my bags I head to my room to find Jase, sour-faced as I left him. He says hello but not much else. There's an awkward silence in the room as I unpack and he sits at his computer desk. He has to feel the silence too, he cranks his music up.

Halfway through my unpacking I'm wondering if I should even try repairing our damaged friendship. Things were so simple back then, my life was predictable and easy. Easy, but I wasn't happy. Scowling, I push the memories aside and pull open my dresser drawers.

With a flurry of slamming noises and grumbling, Jase gets up and goes out our door before I can ask what's wrong. A few seconds later he comes back in, cussing as he reaches for his jacket.

"Jase?"

"He kept me up all night, I fucking swear I'm going to put him out of his misery."

"Who?"

He snorts and rolls his eyes. "Your pet Northie. You're here now, you can deal with it, I'm going over to Alex's."

"What's going on?" I know the confusion is plain on my face, but it doesn't stop him. Jase stomps out, leaving our door open and letting the suite door slam behind him.

I hear someone getting sick.

Leaving my dresser, I gravitate to the door, listening but trying not to at the same time as I hear heaving. Standing at the bathroom door I listen, and find my own stomach rolling when I recognize Dakota's panting. I can't stop myself. I can't go back to my room, knowing he's right there and there's something wrong. Maybe he won't give me an answer why, but I can see him and know he's okay. Hurt and anger and worry are sharp in my heart as I grab the door handle and push the door in.

Crumpled against the wall is Dakota, with black track pants and a grey Badgers t-shirt on. I expect him to start screaming like that night, to make me leave. Instead he curls further into himself, his eyes on the floor. His hair is a sweaty mess, and his skin a shade of ghost.

I can't feel my anger anymore. Grabbing a washcloth off the rack I soak it in the sink and grab my bottle of mouthwash off the counter. "You look like shit," I choke. Unsure of myself, I crouch beside him and offer the mouthwash.

Dakota takes the mouthwash, but doesn't look at me.

I wait for him to spit before pressing the washcloth to his forehead. He slumps against the wall, murmuring a quiet "Thank you." Now that he's here in front of me I can't stop myself from touching; my fingertips on his forearm, my thumb wiping away the water dripping down his temple.

When I speak my voice is raw, a reflection of how I feel on the inside. "What's wrong, Kota?"

Some part of me must have been hoping it was a mistake, a cruel joke, something, because devastation fills me when I see his mouth tighten in a frown and his chin begin to quiver. Whispering, as if speaking will make it too real, too true, he croaks, "I'm sick."

"That's why you left?" I ask as the word 'sick' flies around my brain.

Taking a shaky breath, he pulls the cloth off his forehead. His eyes fall to the floor as he murmurs. "I'm sorry, Ian. I never meant, I didn't mean to drag you into this." He starts trembling, and I take his hand in mine. "Years of wanting someone to understand me." Finally his bi-colored eyes look up to meet my gaze. "The one thing I wanted was someone perfect for me. Can you blame me for falling for it so hard? For not wanting to let you go?"

I shake my head a little, confused as I push back his damp hair. "Are you talking about me? Because you didn't let me go, you pushed me away." His skin is hot against mine, too hot. Choking on the knot in my throat, I ask the question that has been haunting me. "Why? Even if you're sick, I still love you, I'll be here for you, I'll take care of you."

His eyes well with tears, and I wish I could take it back. "Because," he sucks a shaky breath. "Because it's, it's," he hiccups. A sob tears from his chest, and I catch his crumpling body in my arms. Holding him close I try to soothe him, but he only shakes harder. "Because it's killing me Ian.

The tumor in my brain's killing me, and I don't want to die. I don't want to leave you."

"No, no, no." I shake my head and squeeze his shoulders. "You're not leaving me, and I'm not leaving you. We'll be okay. Troy can help you." My words rush as I process this bomb detonation. "Troy's a freaking brain doctor, he knows other doctors and stuff, he works at the Mayo Clinic for piss' sakes, you're not going anywhere."

He whispers, "Ian, he can't save me."

By now he's shaking hard, but I feel numb. I want to argue with him, to dredge his mind for every detail he hasn't told me, but I refrain. Instead I hold him and sit on the bathroom floor where this all started.

* * *

The world is pitch-black outside, but the inside of Dakota's room is lit by the television. It's some show neither of us were really watching anyway. I glance at my phone to see the time, then look down beside me. Dakota is sound asleep, and his body relaxed for the first time today.

Grabbing his tablet off the nightstand, I watch him while I start it. There's the rhythmic rise and fall of his chest, wrinkling his black t-shirt the slightest bit as it does so. He doesn't stir, so I stare at the Google search bar. I don't want to wait for him to tell me, I want to know what I'm up against. Tapping at the letter key icons I type the two-word answer he had given me; glioblastoma multiforme.

Seconds, minutes, and hours pass. I can't stop reading, can't stop ingesting every piece of information I find. I don't like what I'm reading so I keep going, desperate to find something, anything that changes. Instead of what I want, I keep seeing the same words over and over again. Malignant. Stage IV. Surgery, radiation, chemotherapy, craniotomy. They fill my head and weigh me down, making me sick.

I hate statistics, I always have, but the one staring back at me is the worst. Median survival is twelve months.

Setting aside the tablet, I try to catch my breath. The words have moved out of my head and sit on my chest. I clench my jaw when my chin quivers. With the tablet off the words are gone, it's safe in the small dorm room. Closing my eyes I try to breathe, to force the weight off my chest.

I'm okay again. Opening my eyes I see the familiar walls, and a dumb reality show on the television. Like it didn't happen. Dropping my gaze I see Dakota, peaceful in his sleep. He's curled against my flank, a limp grip on the edge of the blanket. All at once the words come back, the weight, the fear clamping on to me as I slide down under the blankets.

One year?

I choke on the sob swelling in my throat when he stirs. He doesn't wake, just sidles closer to me and sighs softly. Struggling, I hold back the sobs, but I'm useless against the shake in my hands as I brush his hair back. My body trembles at the effort to keep silent, and the only outlet for my emotions are the hot tears pouring from my eyes.

One year.

One. Year.

* * *

"The headaches. They'd tried migraine medication and it didn't touch the pain," Dakota says quietly, his words almost swallowed by the ruckus of the busy coffee shop, and stirs his cup of hot chocolate. "One night it was so bad Monty ended up taking me to the emergency room. There they did the CT scan."

I swallow, letting the bitter coffee burn my throat as I sit down across from him. The coffee shop's tall tables have uncomfortable chairs, but the booths are all taken.

Dakota twines his fingers around his paper cup, squeezing and deforming the paper. "They sent me to Madison, to the University hospital. I remember thinking how insane it was, how things changed in a minute. I was working on a project for my social studies class, for my finals when the headache came on. When my classmates were walking to get their diplomas I was getting my skull cut open." He's relaying it so lightly, not giving a clue to the weight of his situation. "See?" he asks, leaning forward and parting his hair to show a white scar line on his scalp. "At least my hair grew enough to be evened out before I started school."

"Why here? I mean, why come here for school, why are you—" I frown when the words catch in my brain. One year, one year, one year.

"Why would I bother going to college if I'm probably not going to graduate?" His factualness saddens me, but I suppose he's had a lot longer to get used to the idea than I have. He must have seen the look on my face, how hard it is for me to take his indifference. His voice softens, and he continues, "Because it was something I always wanted to do. I wanted to go to college, get an education, and get away from the farm. I'm not going to just sit around and wait for my brain bomb to go off."

"But they already did surgery on it?" I ask.

"The craniotomy last May. They got 90-95% of it.

That's why it's so bad; it's not just a lump in there, it has all these tentacles coming out of it and embedding in my brain. They can't get everything out without me losing my brains or bleeding to death."

He sounds so indifferent about it, his hands clasped together as he relays these facts as if he was reciting a case study, not telling me his story.

"How," I start and stop, choking on the words. It's easier to speak when I'm staring down into my coffee. "How are you so nonchalant about it?"

"Because getting upset at this moment isn't going to help anything. I already did that. It's unchangeable. There is nothing I can do."

"There has to be something."

Dakota murmurs, stirring his hot chocolate again. "Um, I did one round of radiation over the summer, but once it was over I stopped all the treatments. There isn't much left to do. The drugs, they can only buy me time. That's why…" his voice trails off, and he hunches over his cup. For the first time today he looks vulnerable. He'd woken up in his usual fighting form, but now his armor is cracking. "That's why I pushed you away, Ian, I—" he sucks a breath through his unsteady mouth before looking up and meeting my eyes. "I love you. I love you and I don't want you to feel sorry for me, I don't want you to watch me die. I'm, I'm going to become something that's not me, and that's what you're going to remember me as. I've changed so much in your life already, I can't make irreconcilable changes and then abandon you. It's not fair to you."

There's a deep sadness in his blue and green eyes, a depth I know I can't possibly reach, but it doesn't shake my faith. "I like the changes in my life, and as far as making me do things or feeling sorry for you or whatever, don't you think it's my decision? I fell in love with you."

"You didn't know I was a ticking time bomb either," Dakota interrupts. "I don't want you to feel trapped because I didn't tell you first."

"Dakota, shut up for a minute and listen." I cut him off. "You don't get to decide how I think or feel about this, I do. The only thing you get to decide is if you want me, and how you want me. Do you want me to disappear and leave you alone? Do you want me as your friend, or are you going to let me be with you?" I don't know when I got so brash, so sure of myself. It's not like me at all, but then I've never been faced with something like this. "Not what you think you need, what you think I need, what do you want?"

His phone is possessed with life, buzzing and chirping as it scoots across the lacquered table top. Scowling, he picks up the device and taps it into submission. He slides off his chair, picking his backpack off the floor. "I have to go or I'll be late for class."

I want to grab him by the shoulders, force him to look me in the eye and give me an answer. This is more important than school, than anything else. But I don't. I watch him shoulder his backpack and mumble a goodbye as he walks past me. He starts to leave, but his step falters. I look over my shoulder, he half-turns, and neither of us closes the few feet between us.

"Ian, I want to be with you," he whispers hoarsely. "Not a month, not a year, not ten years. I want forever, but I never get what I want." He turns on his heel and clips out of the coffee shop, leaving me alone and just as lost as before. I sit there, alone with my coffee. Almost as lost.

Six months ago I would have let this pass me by, but not now. Not him. Scared Ian would have taken the out he offered and gone with it. I would let him walk away and never speak again, but that's not me anymore. I scramble my things together and leave the coffee shop, heading straight for my dorm.

* * *

I forgot about floor social, but Shelly reminds me when she pokes her head in the open suite door.

"Are you coming tonight?" she asks. One hand on the doorframe, she watches me cart an overflowing laundry basket across the suite hallway. I kick it into Dakota's room—our room now—and stop to flash a smile. She laughs, "You finally figure out Jase is more trouble than he's worth? Dakota seems like he'd be a better roommate."

"Something like that." I don't want to tell her the truth, or not the whole truth anyway. Guilt though, like I should be screaming it to everyone I know without being ashamed. It's still so new to me and I'm afraid of it, afraid of everyone's reaction. Shelly offers to help, but I wave her off. "I've got a few more things then I'm done. Maybe see you tonight."

"Okay. Don't forget a flak jacket when you tell Jase you moved out. I'd text him if I were you."

"Thanks." I might typically avoid confrontation but I'll tell Jase to his face. Eventually.

Shelly leaves, and I finish making my move. With my things gone what is now solely Jase's room is still an overflowing shitpit. My things added to Dakota's room makes it feel complete. Maybe I'm being poetic or something but it feels more like home.

Tossing my pillow on the two-became-one dorm bed, I slide my phone out of my pocket. I flop down, careful to avoid the seam between the two mattresses butted against each other. Tapping through to the home screen, I smile a little at the time. Dakota's out of class, he should be here any minute.

Waiting makes me about burst at the seams with so many emotions growing inside me at once. I've known in my heart what I want, but this is making a very public statement about my allegiances and a private statement about my intentions. I've always had intentions, but to make them a priority? This is crazy, and it makes me light-headed. My body twitches when I hear keys in the door. I quickly sit up as Dakota slips into the room, dropping his keys on his desk.

"Hey," he nods, dropping his backpack on the chair. When he sees the look on my face he tilts his head a little, that unsure half-smile forming his lips. "What?"

I raise an eyebrow, holding back from screaming the words out. It's worth it, watching his eyes take in the rest of the room he hadn't noticed, and seeing his expression change. His eyes widen, his jaw loosens and he meets my eyes with some mixture of awe and disbelief. He doesn't say anything, and I start to panic. He's going to tell me he changed his mind, make me move out, it's going to be that night in Minnesota all over again.

Pushing myself to my feet I open my mouth to start explaining, to defend myself, and Dakota charges me. Laughing, he tackles me into the double-mattress bed.

"You're crazy," he breathes, eyes searching mine. "Absolutely crazy."

When I chuckle it's a deep-stomach laugh. His fingers tickle my jaw, his thumb finding my earlobe to stroke. His eyes are searching mine as he chews his lip as if he's struggling with his words. "What are you thinking?"

"I'm thinking *I love you, always forever, near and far, closer together, everywhere I will be with you.*"

His eyes glimmer at our little game, emotion in his smile cracking his face. His lips brush mine, and he's murmuring against my mouth, "Donna Lewis."

The electricity in his fingers against my skin, and the way he deepens the kiss sends me to the past. Before I knew about brain cancers, before the accident, just us and the quiet in my room. I want that again, but as his mouth moves to my neck I fight back the memory. If I touch him too hard, or if I'm rough? I won't allow it, I can't.

"Ian," he says. There's a thickness to his voice that makes it harder to resist him. "Ian." His hand on my cheek forces my eyes open, meeting one blue and one green staring deep into me. "You're not going to break me."

"What?"

"You're not going to hurt me if you touch me. Unless that's all you've got."

Grabbing him by the waist I flip us over.

Still no Jase by the time Dakota and I leave for floor social. I'm eyeing Jase's door, and Dakota laughs.

"You didn't tell him yet, did you?"

"Well he hasn't been back yet." My defense sounds good. "I don't want to just send him a text message."

There's a long pause, me frowning and Dakota smirking. "He's going to be pissed," Dakota says, stepping into the hallway and holding the door for me. I know he's gleefully imagining the explosion when Jase finds out.

"He should be happy he'll have a room to himself. Isn't

that what he hounded you about from day one?"

"That's not what I meant." Pushing his hands into his pockets he starts for the lounge as I fall in step beside him.

Maybe half the floor is already milling around when we get there. Dakota's steps slow, waiting for my lead. A steaming buffet of catered Mexican food is sitting out but I go past it, knowing he won't eat any of it because his stomach is off today. I spot Shelly entertaining Drew and a handful of others I know, so I hone in on the familiar group gathered on the leather couches.

I'm grateful Shelly doesn't say anything when we join the group. It's going to be bad enough to tell Jase without him hearing it second-hand from Drew or someone else. I flash her a smile and get a knowing, soft smile back.

As we talk, time slips past and I forget about my Jase problem. Dakota leaves to get drinks and I'm grilling Drew about his Sociology project when Shelly jumps from the couch. Our conversation has an instant death, and the rumble of voices in the lounge dies out.

Apprehension squeezes my chest as I turn around. Shelly is halfway across the lounge already, heading straight for the long counter where Jase has cornered Dakota. I spring off the couch, hearing Shelly's booming voice echoing off the walls.

I know everyone's staring, watching and wondering, but I don't feel their eyes. My only focus is Jase and Dakota. Both are tense and locked in an argument that neither look ready to back down from. Jase takes a step closer and leans over Dakota, spewing some line of bullshit I can't hear. He looks like a vulture; dark hair and clothing, drawn up to his full height but bending his neck over Dakota's shorter height.

Dakota isn't easy prey. He's never been bullied by Jase like I was, and he stares down Jase's predator stance without giving an inch. Shelly reaches them before I do, pushing Jase back to put space between them.

"What is going on, Jason?" Shelly growls in her authoritative voice, her glare going straight to Jase. "Are you having a problem?"

"This little shit is my problem. Oh, hey, Christian," he spits my full name and turns his angry black eyes to me. "Thanks for giving me a heads up, buddy. Awesome you moved out. You move in with fucking Northie?"

"Jason," Shelly snaps.

"You hate my guts anymore anyway, what do you care if I move out? You wanted a room to yourself, you've got it. What are you so pissed off for?" I ask.

"Because you were fine until he moved in." Jase reaches around Shelly and strikes at Dakota, grazing his shoulder. "Stop smirking at me you little shit!"

I grab Dakota's upper arm, stopping him from retaliating like he wants to, like I want to. Instead of going after Jase I hold my ground, pulling Dakota behind me to protect him. Shelly moves in front of Jase, pushing him back a few more feet to separate us, but I can't stop glaring at him. It's hard to hold back with his challenge staring back at me.

Shelly is muttering at him in harsh whispers, something about cooling off and talking things over. He can't be listening, his angry eyes are still boring into mine. Staring back as calmly as I can, I loosen my grip on Dakota's bicep. There's tension in his body, vibrating against mine as my hand slides down his arm.

I haven't forgotten about my peers in the room, every one of them are watching the exchange. I'm perfectly aware my friends are there, that my volatile once-best friend is staring down my soul. My palm glides over Dakota's forearm, and reaching his palm, I let him go.

"Fuck you, Ian. Both of you can go to hell," Jase spits

in my direction before spinning past Shelly and leaving the room.

* * *

"I'm heading to Wal-Mart, do you guys need anything?" Shelly asks, poking her head into our room. I still can't get over how natural it sounds, our room.

"What?" Dakota asks, taking off his headphones and pushing back from his desk.

"I'm going to Wal-Mart, do you guys need anything?" she repeats.

"A couple things. Do you need company?" Dakota asks. Without waiting for her response, he puts his headphones down on his desk and goes for his shoes. Shelly's mouth turns up in a pleasant smile.

Setting my textbook aside, I wonder how Dakota does that. He just seems to know what to say or do to be friendly. It must be something you're born with, because I've always been awkward and self-conscious. Finding my black and blue Nikes, I stomp my feet into the shoes and grab my coat.

"I'll drive," Shelly offers, brushing the string and pom-pom of her hat over her shoulder. I've never ridden with Shelly, or actually done anything with Shelly outside of floor social events. It's not that I don't like her, but Jase never wanted to be seen with her. I feel like an ass for it.

We head down to the parking lot, and I let Dakota take the front seat. I know he gets nauseated easily, and I hate that I know that.

"Jase hasn't been giving you guys any trouble has he?" Shelly asks, settling into the front seat and starting the car.

"He calls me names, but sticks and stones," Dakota

shrugs.

"He's giving me the silent treatment," I say. "Which is fine, it makes him a lot easier to deal with when I can just ignore him."

"Let me know if he causes any problems, but I hope he can behave himself," Shelly sighs. She pokes at the radio button and starts to back-up, but stops dead when "Love Is An Open Door" starts blasting through the speakers. "Sorry!" she apologizes, turning the volume all the way down and wincing.

"Sorry for what?" Dakota asks. Reaching over he hits the back button to restart the song, then pushes her fingers away from the volume button so he can turn it back up. "Who cares what music you like, it's your music and your car?"

Shelly smiles at him, a little look of awe in her eye at his acceptance. I realize I'm seeing myself not so long ago, being thrown for a loop because someone just told me to be myself. I love how Dakota can go anywhere and make anyone around him feel better about themselves, that acceptance he has for truth.

Dakota reminds me of a good family dog. He doesn't hold back affection, he cares no matter what, and is loyal, loyal, loyal. But he can sense things so much deeper than the average human like me. He sensed Jase, he sensed Mia, he senses Shelly. He's something so much better than me, something I aspire to be like with all my soul.

Dakota starts belting out the male line of the song. Laughing, Shelly joins him for the duet line. She can't sing like Dakota can, but it doesn't matter for an impromptu car concert. Looking in the mirror of the passenger visor, I catch Dakota's gaze and see his green eye wink.

God, I love him.

* * *

"What's in the bag?" I ask while shrugging out of my backpack. Dakota is sitting at his desk reading, and there is a huge white paper bag on the desk, plopped down on top of his iPad.

"Drugs." Dakota grumbles. He flips a page and sighs.

"No, seriously."

Dakota marks his page and sets the thick book on the desk, turning his attention onto me. "Seriously, it's drugs."

Not really believing him, I open the bag. A bunch of prescription and non-prescription pill bottles. And a box of condoms. Grabbing the box of Trojans, I pull it out of the bag and ask, "You afraid you're gonna knock me up or something?"

Dakota smiles, shaking his head a little. "No you dork." He takes the box from me and throws it in the direction of the nightstand, "So I don't kill you."

"Kill me?"

He busies himself with taking the pill bottles out of the bag. "I'm going back on the drugs, buy me some time hopefully."

I can't help but feel an overwhelming sadness at his situation, but it's wrapped up in a strange blanket of affection because he wants more time with me. It's sickly flattering. I sit down in the other desk chair and watch him arrange the bottles.

"The downside is I'll be basically poisoning my entire body. So, you should probably avoid touching me as much as possible," he sighs.

I can sense his disconcertion with the matter. Reaching

over to touch his knee, I try to lighten the mood. "There's worse things than wearing a rubber."

"Yeah, now I'm going to be a biohazard."

"So what if you have risky spit," I shrug. "Maybe I'll get mutant powers or something."

"Ian, this is serious," he almost whines. "Look, if I do this yeah it buys me time but it also means I'm a fucking patient now, and there's certain things about it."

I roll my eyes at his insecurities, but for once I can outdo him. "Tendar, right? Probably a 5/28 schedule, so those five days I really shouldn't kiss you unless I want mutant powers, but it does have a half life and I'm all about calculated risks. I have no problems playing with a condom if it makes you happy while you feel like absolute shit like that stuff is probably going to make you. This," I grab one of the orange pill bottles. "Should help with the nausea you're going to have, meaning we can still hit up Santori's. This," I pick up another bottle and read the script. "Is the seizure med you were already on, so still no drinking. I'm going to take a wild guess that this Rx bottle is Dex, and the rest are other awesome cheerleaders to keep you healthy. I'm not an idiot Kota, I know what I'm in for and I'm still here and not going anywhere."

He looks at me in startled awe.

"I love you, you're not scaring me away," I say with the deepest of conviction.

Dakota's dual-colored eyes measure me up, his mouth softening into a sweet smile. "Ian, you're something else you know that?"

I am something else, something different than what I was before I met him. I'm something braver, stronger, better. He says it was in me all along but I don't think I believe him. Either way I couldn't have become this without him. "Likewise," I say, setting the bottle of Dex back down.

Chapter Sixteen
February

"So, whether you like it or not we're coming down to see you next weekend for a visit," Mia's voice chirps through my phone as I glance out the coffee shop's front window, bright sunshine stabbing my eyes as I do. "All of us."

"You, Mom, and Troy?" I ask, dragging my highlighter across a slick textbook page. The line is crooked. My eyes are seeing spots from the sun blindness.

"Ben and Nikki are coming. Mom will make him behave."

Mia's voice sounds so sure, but it doesn't convince me. I haven't talked to my brother since that phone call when I'd driven back to school, the one where he basically asked me if I was done being a faggot yet so he could speak to me.

Wrinkling my nose, I reply, "Right. Well, I'll look forward to seeing you I guess."

"I want to see your school too, and tell Dakota I want to see all the music stuff."

"Are you already shopping colleges Mia?" I ask.

"Never too early," she answers. "So text Mom and tell

her what hotel we should stay at."

"I will. Love you Mia."

She returns the sentiment and hangs up. I'm not sure how I feel about my family invading for the weekend. Ben worries me; not just that he'll be an asshole, but that he'll say something damning. I haven't told anyone at school about Dakota and I, especially not Jase or anyone in my former friend group. I don't know what would happen, and I don't want to find out either. I don't mind losing friends or being ostracized, sticks and stones and all, but punches could really hurt us. I need to protect Dakota.

Other than Mia wanting to see the campus, maybe I can focus the rest of this family invasion off-campus.

* * *

I leave the bathroom with a towel around my waist and enter our room to find Dakota already dressed. He's sitting on the edge of our bed, dark wash jeans and his black chucks on, wearing a slate grey button-down and a sick expression.

"Do you feel okay?" I ask, feeling my stomach flip inside itself. A possessed squirrel has been residing in it recently, seizing and contorting and flipping my guts around.

"Nervous," he answers honestly, his smile taut.

"Don't be," I smile softly and pad over to my dresser. "My family likes you more than they like me, you know that."

"Your brother doesn't."

I pull the top drawer open, but my fingers stay on the rounded knobs. "Ben won't say anything," I lie. I don't know what he's going to say or do.

"He's your brother Ian, you shouldn't be fighting."

"We're not fighting." We aren't speaking over a

difference of opinion. There is no argument. "You don't disagree with your brothers?"

"That's different. I shouldn't be some kind of wedge between you, I…" he trails off when I give him a look that plainly says to shut up.

"Kota, don't." I shut the drawer and move to sit next to him on the edge of the bed. "You're not some kind of wedge, you're not tearing apart my family or anything else like that. You're the best thing that's ever happened to me," I murmur, drinking in his surprise expression when he snaps his neck to meet my gaze. "Ben is probably just going to be really gross and handsy with his girlfriend to try and show me what I'm supposedly missing out on, and he's just going to look like a dumbass because I've got you."

"But," he pouts, his lower lip puckering the slightest bit. I know what he's thinking, what he's always thinking about. After.

"Now," I remind him. I kiss his temple, inhaling his scent before turning away and going back to my dresser. Later it is going to matter, the tumor in his brain, but it doesn't have to matter tonight.

"Where are we going again?" Dakota asks as I pull my jeans up my hips.

"Luciano's, so food coma later," I answer.

Luciano's is a local Italian restaurant, as upper crust as you can get in the middle of Illinois. The parking lot is pretty packed, and the inside is comfortably cozy. Everything is candlelight; the tabletop hurricane glasses, the wall fixtures, the chandeliers. It's very medieval-rustic with modern updates in crystal drinkware, stamped silverware, and expensive white linens.

"May I help you?" A petite blonde hostess asks as we shuck out of our coats and hang them.

"Taylor, please," I reply. She smiles politely and leads us back to an oversized booth. My mother, Troy, and Ben are seated on one side and Mia on the other. Mia sees us coming and jumps out of the booth, her dark eyes shining bright in the dim interior. She's wearing a cute cream sweater dress, but it's her smile that lights up the room as she smothers Dakota in an overbearing hug.

I can hear my parents chuckle, and I glance over to see Ben looking down at his menu. I wonder where Nikki is, but decide not to ask.

"I'm happy to see you too," Mia insists and gives me a hug.

"Mm, not obvious you have favorites," I grumble playfully, hugging her back before shooing her then Dakota into the booth.

My mom starts asking Dakota about classes and his music, Troy asks me about school, and conversation fills the table, erasing my worry.

I was afraid of a lot of different things ruining the evening, but I'm relieved that the only one really left out is Ben. He sits in the booth corner, quiet, until I start to feel bad. He's my twin; I don't mind making him mad but hurt pulls a special string in my heart.

"Hey Ben," I dare to break the ice. "Nikki couldn't make it?"

"We broke up a few days ago," Ben answers curtly.

I can't decide if I should press on, but an approaching waiter saves me from making an ass of myself. I sit back and smirk as the waiter brings an oversized crystal goblet to the table, filled with scoops of white and pink ice cream conquered by two red and white striped peppermint sticks.

One is straight and tall and the other in the festive hooked shape, somewhat resembling the number 19.

"A birthday to celebrate this evening?" the waiter asks with a broad smile.

I can't help but grin, watching Dakota's expression when he realizes everyone at the table is staring expectantly at him. Taking the hint, the waiter places the goblet of ice cream in front of Dakota.

My mother reaches across the table and squeezes his hand, her smile gentle as she says, "Happy Birthday Dakota."

Dakota turns to me, bewildered. I love the surprise on his face, but at the same time I feel sad. He had agreed to go to this dinner with me and never mentioned it was his birthday. He had no intention of celebrating the holiday. Reaching over a bit, I squeeze his thigh and give him a sheepish smile.

"I know you're not a fan of vanilla so I brought in peppermint instead." He whips his head back to the over-sized dessert, staring at the red flecks of peppermint bits. "Happy Birthday."

* * *

It's nice having my family in town. Saturday we go out to see the local sights, catch a movie, eat at a few of the better local restaurants. My mom and Troy practically adopted Dakota as their own, and it makes me wish for spring break. In the restaurants or at the movie theater, away from campus or possible spying eyes, I can slip my hand around Dakota's or startle him with a kiss but it's not the same as the little world we'd had in Minnesota.

As I'm getting dressed for dinner Saturday night, Dakota is getting dressed for work. I have to be a presentable looking son for Excelsis Steakhouse, and he has to look his part filling in at Cover Ups. I'm khakis and he's jeans, I'm black button-down and he's fun yellow t-shirt. I don't like being apart from him, but it soothes my nerves to see him lace up the pristine grey chucks I'd given him yesterday.

"Who are you guys doing tonight?" I ask and fasten my watch.

"Shinedown," he says and threads a shiny black belt through his jeans.

There's something off in his demeanor. I wonder what's wrong, if he's feeling well.

"You could cancel," I suggest, watching his face for any clues in his expression.

"It's cash," he says with a shrug, not looking up at me. Something is bothering him. "Besides, you should have some time with your family without me tagging along."

"I like it better when you're with me," I murmur.

Looking up and meeting my eyes, I see his familiar spunk again. "You'll survive. If you don't get going you'll be late, too."

I step over to him, and give his shirt hem a tug. It's his birthday gift from Mia, a bright yellow t-shirt with a bold black lettering that says 'agathokakological'. "I can make it a good reason to be late."

"I'd love to see you tell your mom the reason for missing the first course," Dakota purrs, then leans up to kiss me. I can't help but deepen this kiss, wanting him to stay with me. "Mm, remember that later when I get back."

"I won't forget it while you're gone," I answer, then sigh wistfully as he grabs his wallet.

"Oscar is picking me up downstairs. I'll see you later." He smiles at me, looking so freaking adorable I hate to let him go, and he ducks out our door. A moment later I hear the suite door open and close, and finally force myself to finish getting ready.

When I leave our room Jase is coming back, both of us meeting in the small hallway between rooms. His eyes are pure fire, boring into mine, and I feel the urge to cower. Old habits really do die hard.

"Hey, Jase." I say.

"Go to hell Ian," he snarls, twirling his keys around his finger.

I'm surprised by the words slipping out of my mouth. "Fuck off Jase, what do you have to be pissed about? You finally got your own room didn't you? Wasn't that the most important thing?"

"My best friend shouldn't have betrayed me in the process. You'd rather hang out, rather live, with-that weird ass guy than me, that's betrayal."

"Jase, you never gave two shits about me. Replace me with some other gutless kid with no self esteem and you'd never know the difference." I can't wrap my head around the possibility of him being genuinely hurt by me moving out. I can understand him being upset it makes him look bad, or now it's a pain because he has to find someone else to be his little bitch, but truly hurt?

Jase sighs, hanging his head and leaning back against the wall. His fingers fidget with his keys. "Look, I'm sorry alright. I know I get on your case a lot, and probably give you too much shit sometimes." He looks up, eyes meeting mine. "Sorry."

I'm utterly stunned. Seriously? Jase is not only apologizing, but actually apologizing to me? "Oh."

"Look, it's stupid to give each other shit over where we live." He takes a deep breath and exhales. "Can we just be cool?"

"Uh," I stammer. "Yeah, we're cool." Weren't we just cussing at eachother a moment ago? God, I hate stepping back into old habits but it's just easier to go with it. I can't think.

"Fine," Jase nods and keys himself into the room that used to be ours.

I think this is a truce, but it feels like I might be staring down the reincarnation of Charles the Bad and I'm Charles de la Cerda.

The steakhouse is top-notch and makes me uncomfortable as soon as I step through the glass doors. My family is waiting, my mother greeting me with a hug before the waiter takes us to a round table for six. My parents order a bottle of wine.

"Where's Dakota?" Mia asks as soon as the waiter leaves. There's an intensity in her gaze I'm not quite used to.

"Working. He's filling in for someone he knows in a cover band." When her mouth opens I know exactly what words will fall out, so I answer, "No we can't go bother him."

"Mia," our mom corrects her. "It's rude to pester people at work."

"But he's like the best player ever," Mia whines a little. I can't help but smile at her obsession. Truth is I know Dakota's good, but don't realize how good he is. Mia studies guitar, I know she can appreciate his skills more than I can. It still makes my chest puff with a little pride, then deflate when I see Ben rolling his eyes.

"I thought we might run into Dakota's family down here," Troy mentions as a different waiter appears with the beverages. "Being his birthday and all."

"He," I pause. "Doesn't get along with most of his

family."

"Because he's gay?" Ben asks. Our entire table freezes. Wine glasses clink with water glasses, and the waiter ducks his head. Ben's eyes scan the table, he shrugs his left shoulder and asks, "What?"

My jaw tightens, but I force my words to be calm. It was a crude but genuine question. "His mom's dead, his dad and older brother are backwards-thinking homophobes and his younger brother is in high school and can't drive out this far." Ben's mask of indifference cracks a little, and I can't resist the urge to hit for home. "He's lucky one of his brothers isn't a dick to him."

"Christian," my mom murmurs, touching my arm as she uses my full name.

The rest of dinner is mostly me talking to my mom and Troy. Mia and Ben are quiet, Mia unusually so. I'm absolutely floored when we get ready to leave, and Ben asks if I want to go out for a bit.

"You two go on," Mom encourages with a smile. "We're heading back to the hotel. Ben, you have your key?"

"Yeah."

Ben glances up at me then down at his phone. My mom smiles at me expectantly, and I realize they're both waiting for me to respond.

"Uh, sure. I can just drop you off there later."

Ben follows me out of the restaurant, nose in his phone, and then it's the two of us alone in my Jeep. Two of us and some thick awkward silence.

"Where did you want to go?" I ask.

"I don't care."

I put the SUV on the main road and start driving. I really don't know what to say to my brother, and it's an odd feeling. Throughout our lives there were plenty of times I didn't want to say anything to him, but to not know what to say?

"I didn't want to come down here," Ben says softly, glancing over at me. "But I'm glad I did. Don't get mad because I know this is going to sound really shitty, okay?"

"Okay."

"I thought I was going to come down here and you'd be different. I mean, you are different, but a different different," he rambles. I raise an eyebrow and he sighs. "I don't know, I thought you'd be wearing different clothes, changing your hair, talking with that lisp and stuff."

"Because why exactly?"

"You know," he prompted, squirming in his seat. "Being gay."

"I think I'm bi. I think. I still find women attractive, but I just, with Dakota... It's complicated." I am not getting into the specifics of my sexuality with my brother. I haven't really figured it out myself. "But Ben, seriously? I never thought you'd be so narrow-minded."

"I've never really known anyone gay or bi or whatever you are."

"You just didn't notice because they weren't wearing their rainbow jumpsuits." I glance over and feel a little sorry for him, the frustration is clear on his face. I didn't meet his expectation and he doesn't know what to do with that. "Look, forget about everyone else in the world, I'm not on a crusade to mold your opinions on sexual freedoms. Hate everything else to your heart's content, but can you just be okay with me? I'm still your brother."

"I know Ian, and I am okay with you. I am trying to tell you, I expected all these things about you to change, but they didn't. You're still you. Even more you. You're happy. I'm glad you're happy, Ian, you deserve it. It's just weird, I can tell you're smitten with him but you really don't act like it."

"I don't act like it?" I ask.

"You don't hold hands or touch each other in public and stuff. You act like straight people together. Like you could be brothers or something." Ben gives me a sideways glance as I stop the Jeep for a red light. "Are you like, in the closet or something here?"

His words hang in the air, and make my heart hang with a weighted shame. Dakota left it up to me, and I pulled us both into the closet and slammed the doors because it was easier. Easier, but it isn't really right, is it? Which is really worse, Ben giving me shit for my homoerotic tendencies, or me hiding those tendencies? Ben should feel ashamed of his behavior but I am acting ashamed of mine, aren't I?

Ben's voice interrupts my guilt, his words quiet and genuine with concern. "Ian, what are you going to do when he gets sicker?"

My head whips around. "How do you know?"

"I overheard mom talking to Troy. You called Troy."

I don't need a reminder of that phone call that didn't go my way.

"Ian, what are you going to do?"

"Still be right there with him," I answer surely. God, it's from one hard topic to another with him.

"But he is going to die isn't he?"

The light turns green, and my stomach turns over itself. Pressing my foot to the gas pedal, I answer honestly, "I try not to think about it."

"How?"

Up ahead I see the sign for Cover Ups. "I'll show you." Changing lanes, I cut through traffic and pull into the parking lot. It's busy, so I park at the back of the lot.

"Is this a bar?" Ben asks, exiting the Jeep.

"Yeah, kind of." I lock the doors and start walking.

"You drink it away?" he asks, his nose wrinkling in confusion.

"No," I sigh and roll my eyes. "Just come on."

I lead him to the main entrance, and into the crowded atmosphere. A loud instrumental intro is blasting from the speakers by the stage. Pushing through the crowd as the song starts, I can't help but smile.

Stopping near the stage, I lean over and yell at Ben, "This is how I can ignore it."

Up on the stage Dakota is front and center, an electric green Ibanez in his hands. He's sweaty but doesn't look tired, his fingers moving nimbly over strings as he sings. It's powerful as he belts out the lyrics. He's so full of energy and life, no one would believe me if I said he's sick, and said he's dying.

"He's so alive, Ben, and he makes me alive. It's easy to ignore it when it's like this."

* * *

"Hi!" Mia greets us both as she slides into the backseat of the Jeep.

As I drive across town to Small Town Bakery, Mia makes music conversation with Dakota. I'm glad they get along so well, but at the same time I can't help but feel like she's ignoring me. When I park in front of the brick building with a wood and teal sign, I catch her eye and she looks away.

Sighing inwardly, I open the front entrance door for both of them. "What is everyone else doing for breakfast?"

Mia shrugs. "Don't know. After breakfast I can come

see the school, right?"

"Yes," I answer and Dakota chuckles.

"Just the important stuff, like the music department," Dakota adds. "I want eggs," he states and heads over to the bathrooms.

Folding her arms over her chest, Mia steps up to the display case of quiches, muffins, scones, and breakfast sandwiches. A large woman in a teal apron greets me from behind the register, a bright smile creasing her face. I give her my order and Dakota's, then pull bills from my wallet as Mia orders.

When the woman moves off to fill our order, I lock eyes on Mia's and plainly ask, "Did I say something to piss you off?"

Pursing her lips, she yanks a handful of napkins off the dispenser atop the display case. "No."

"Then why are you giving me the silent treatment?" I ask.

"Because you're acting like a douche." She lowers her brow and her voice. "You're lucky Dakota puts up with you."

Taken aback, I feel my eyebrows pinching together. "What are you talking about?" My first thing is that she's jealous. I know she has a crush on him. I'd be blind not to see it. But it doesn't quite fit.

"You don't treat him like your boyfriend."

I mentally cringe at the word boyfriend. It just doesn't sound right for so many reasons, not all of them stupid ones. Even when I had girlfriends I thought 'girlfriend' sounded dumb. What else can I call him though? My bed brother? My amicus? Boyfriend will just have to do.

"If you like him that much you shouldn't hide it. Don't you get tired of being scared, Ian?" she asks, propping her fist on her hip. "You are always worried about pleasing everyone else, well guess what? You can't make everyone happy, so you better choose who to make happy."

"I'm not scared, Mia, it's complicated," I say, but I'm not sure if it's the truth. Time to hide my guilt and confusion with a tough facade. "We have our own rules, Mia, which don't concern you to begin with, but we made them."

"Doesn't mean he's happy with them."

"*We* made the rules."

"He'd go along with anything to make you happy." Mia snorts and lowers her voice to a whisper, her eyes darting over to the bathroom doors. "You're hurting him."

I open my mouth to respond, but nothing comes out. The woman in teal pushes a tray across the counter, and Mia grabs it before I can. Mia's scowl fades instantly, giving Dakota a cheerful smile as she asks, "Where do you want to sit?"

"Over there by the window?" Dakota suggests, pointing to a booth by the window as he joins us.

Mia's words are swirling in my head, mixing with Ben's from last night. Am I really doing something wrong, hurting Dakota's feelings? It'd be easy to take his happy demeanor and run with it, but the answer is nibbling my heart. I'm the asshole, aren't I?

I slide in next to Dakota, and try not to meet Mia's eyes as she takes her food off the tray. It's not that I don't want to admit she's right, I just don't want the reminder that I'm wrong. Really wrong. Taking a sip of my coffee, I reach over beneath the table and find Dakota's knee. Resting my hand there comforts me, an assurance that right now things are okay. It bothers me when he doesn't react to the touch, not even flicking his eyes in my direction.

As the two of them start chattering about some band I've never heard of, I sip my coffee and focus on the feel of Dakota's worn denim under my fingers. It's soft and familiar, but I wonder if I've turned Dakota into those jeans. He's become my favorite thing, so familiar and comforting, but I'm wearing holes into him. Before I know it he'll be worn out and used up, and I won't even have him anymore.

Biting the inside of my cheek, I glance sidelong at him. The sunlight streaming through the window makes him look like some kind of angel with his black hoodie and halo of light. The light in his eye is brighter though, talking about music.

He's not an angel, he's a saint. He's never pushed anything on me about our relationship because he said he didn't want to change my life. He wants my life to be easy, and it would be easier in my world if I didn't have any controversial labels.

I know all about labels. I'd been so happy to get one in high school; Jock, Preppy, In-Crowd. I'd played lacrosse for 4 years to get a label because it was easier to exist in high school with one. When I came to Milford I'd sewn together my tattered friendship with Jase because it made my life easier. I got the Cool Guy or the Party Guy label if I was with Jase, giving me a circle of friends and a social life. I know Dakota thinks if I hide from new labels — gay, bi, queer, whatever— I can go back to my ordered life from before, I can live easier without those labels.

A label never made me happy though, and I wasn't happy with my old life. I don't want my old life, I want my new life. And god, I can't replace Dakota like a worn out pair of jeans. I can't keep him like a dirty little secret, I have to change this.

Swallowing a mouthful of hot coffee, I feel resolute. Things should be different. Things will be different.

Chapter Seventeen
February

Valentine's Day is problematic. I've been wracking my brain for days trying to think of something to do for the holiday. I'm not that romantic of a person and the idea of showering Dakota with candy and flowers is ridiculous and one of the more hilarious mental images I've had recently. I don't even know what I'd really call him to get a sentiment pre-added card. I still have it stuck in my head that boy-friend sounds too stupid and too gay. But I guess I am gay, I'm sleeping with another man. Technicalities I guess. I like Dakota's view on it, I'm just being myself and I don't need to label it. Why does it have to be as complicated as assigning rules and actions, can't it just be simple that this is the person I love? Happy Valentine's Day to my favorite thing ever and you're mine and it's the best.

Chewing on a pinstriped straw I watch the stage. There's a rock show happening around me and this is where my mind is. Dakota is filling in for some friend of his; the small venue is packed with people dancing to the music and screaming the chorus, and I'm in gushy land.

A female voice slides over my shoulder. "Another Dr.

Pepper?" the waitress asks, reaching over me to grab my empty glass. The skin of her arm is chalk-white and criss-crossed with a tattoo of climbing ivy.

"Sure, why not." I shrug and pull out my wallet as she slides the glass onto her cork-covered tray.

"Your date never show up?" she asks as I hand her a numbered bill. When she motions to the empty seat across from me I chuckle. "Don't worry, you'll have no problem finding a replacement." She reaches into the pocket of her apron and I can see the ivy twining around the front of her arm as well.

"Beautiful tattoo. Your favorite plant?" I ask.

"Ivy's a weed actually. It's for my sister," she smiles. Not that flirtatious smile, but a genuine one. "I had it done at Ink Heart's. I'll be right back with your drink." I watch her move through the crowd. She must sense my stare, because her hips sway hard.

The crowd screams as the song ends, and my attention pulls to the stage again. I watch the rest of the show, switching over to water. I'm still sitting there, studying my phone when Dakota slides into the chair across from me.

"Texting your hot girlfriend?" he teases.

Sliding my glass of water toward him I can't help but smile. He's panting but smiling through a sheen of sweat. His t-shirt is stuck to him like a second skin, hair plastered to his forehead. I can't help but see him like this, gulping down the water, and think he doesn't look sick. He looks just fine. Sweaty, but fine.

Somewhere in my brain I know it's a dangerous train of thought, but the tracks run straight to my heart. He can't be that sick if he's like this. One year was the average, but was there anything about him that was average? Maybe he had two, three, ten, infinite.

I drop my phone in my pocket and ask, "Plans later?"

"A shower. I'd ask you to join but," he trails off. There's a playful arch to his eyebrow but a woe in his expression. I reflect it, want and regret covered with a smile. We can't, not with Jase sharing our suite. Even with the truce.

I sigh. "He'd flip shit."

"I know. Anyway," he sighs and pushes the empty glass away. "Oscar is treating for dinner but I'd rather be with you."

"Don't want to introduce me to your friends?" I joke.

Dakota shrugs one shoulder. "Want to go? We can go."

"It's up to you."

With a roll of his eyes and a shake of his head he takes his phone out and taps at the screen. "You are way too amiable."

"If you'd rather..." I fiddle with my straw and try not to smile. "It's not the fourteenth yet but we could celebrate early."

His smile goes askew as he tilts his head. "For Valentine's Day?"

"Day of Love, Friendship, and Gang Massacres. Same day every year."

"You have something special planned?"

"Not really," I say, shaking my head and jumping off my chair. "I'm being spontaneous. Come on."

"Can I have a shower before the spontaneity?" he asks.

A large man in a Hulk t-shirt shows us to the lounge, pointing to a low red leather couch. The tattoo shop is brightly lit, rock music and humming needles floating from behind the tall counter space. It smells like incense and ink. Finger-combing his beard, the man points to a pile of portfolio books on the coffee table.

"Those are organized by price if you don't know what you want, and these are organized by style. Take a look and I'll go get the paperwork."

Dakota picks up the first book and starts thumbing through. "You seriously just decided this today?"

"Yep." I nod and pick up a book and hand it to him, taking the other out of his hands. "Here. I'm not that cheap."

We thumb through the portfolios for a few minutes before the bearded man comes back and offers us drinks as he sets two clipboards down. After he leaves again Dakota asks, "You're going to get one too?"

"Why not?" I shrug.

"What are you getting?" he asks, flipping through a page of bleeding roses.

I scan a page of intricate tribals before shaking my head. "No idea. Matching tramp stamps?"

Dakota laughs, his full-throated one when he's really happy. "No." After flipping through a few more pages he tosses the book back onto the table. "I don't know either. You pick one for me and I'll pick one for you."

"You'd give me something stupid like a sunflower on my back or something."

"No I wouldn't," he sighs.

I watch him for a moment, and clear my throat. "Being serious. You'd trust me to pick something permanent on your body?"

"I do. But if you're not I get it. You'll be stuck with it longer than I will."

"Don't talk like that," I glower at him. I wish he wouldn't mention it at times like this. Wish he never mentioned it, it is easier to pretend it doesn't exist then. Grabbing the pen off the clipboard I say, "Give me your left hand." Wordlessly he places his hand in mine and I turn it over so the inside of his wrist is exposed. "No peeking until it's done."

"Deal," he smiles and leans back on the couch, covering his eyes. Sliding the pen into position between my thumb and index finger, I pull back his white sleeve, my eyes wandering his forearm as it's exposed. Old scars criss-cross his skin, and my thumb runs over the newest scar on his wrist; the reminder of that night. Pressing the pen tip to his skin I carefully scrawl, leaving a line of blue across the inside of his wrist. Satisfied, I tug his sleeve down and cap the pen.

"Done?"

"No peeking."

Sitting up, he reaches for the pen and takes my right arm in his. "Alright, no peeking."

As hard as it is, I don't catch a glimpse while the tattooist works. I try to focus on the needles stabbing into my skin, imagining what it could look like, but I'm at a loss. Dakota's finished before me, and fidgets with his bandage while waiting for the artist to finish mine.

It's painful, and not done soon enough. Eventually the work is finished, my right wrist is bandaged, the bill is paid and we head back to our dorm. When we're in our room Dakota produces more gauze and tape.

Sitting on our bed with the supplies he points at his blood-stained bandage. "Have to change it, that means I get to see mine first right?"

"Tattoos were probably a bad idea for you and that whole slightly excessive bleeding problem," I frown.

"Worth it."

Folding one knee I sit beside him on the bed and take

the package of gauze. "Yours first." I open the gauze packets, then unwind the tape a bit before taking his wrist in my hands. I watch his expression carefully, hoping he isn't disappointed. Gingerly pushing his sleeve back, I hold my breath and peel off his blood-soaked bandage.

I see his eyes move across the design, reading my crisp handwriting that has become raised lettering. My thumb runs over his forearm, soothing his old scars. "You can't forget it. Every time you look at your wrists you'll see this, not these," I murmur and squeeze my grip.

He whispers the words, reading the tattoo out loud, "Remember I Love You." His two-toned eyes lift and meet mine, shining in the low lighting. "Look at yours." He pulls my right hand into his lap, fingers cold against my skin as he pulls off the bandage. I pull my hand back to examine my wrist and see a compass rose.

Dakota murmurs, "So you can always find your way."

"I found my way. You're my true north." Leaning in, I kiss him slowly, purposefully, the taste of his mouth easing the throbbing in my wrist.

* * *

Dakota is at his night class when I leave our room to shower, and I make a mistake. When I leave the bathroom freshly showered, I see our dorm room door didn't close. Jase is standing in the small hallway, his eyes glaring through the open door before lasering in on me.

"Ian," he breathes, rumbling my name like a waking dragon.

"What?" I ask, and glance at the door.

"You're fucking him, aren't you?" he seethes.

My mouth falls open. I'm not going to say no, but I'm

startled.

"You two shacking up all cozy in that bed?" He sneers. "You're sick. Just wait until I tell Shelly."

"What's she going to do?"

"They don't let opposite-sex couples live in dorms together, it's not fair to let you guys do it. Technically it's not even your room."

He looks so jubilant, it makes me want to hurt him.

"Is that going to make you feel better?" I growl. "You want me to pay a fine or something and you can gloat about it? Want me to move all my shit back into your room?"

He's taken aback by me, I can see it on his face. Pure surprise, again.

"You know, I spent last semester with you fucking girls in our room incessantly, and I never went complaining to Shelly about it. I'm away from you doing my own thing, why is it an issue? Because it's Jase now and your sensitivities are more important than mine?"

Striking like a cobra, his hands come out and punch my shoulders, causing me to fall back against the wall. "You're a sick fuck."

I hit his shoulders back, shoving him into his closed dorm door. "You're not going to push me around. Enough is enough, just leave me and Dakota alone."

Part of me wants this to escalate, I want him to throw a punch at my face so I can throw one back. He would get the best of me, but the temptation of releasing all my anger at him through my hands is thick.

The better part of me picks up my shower caddy and goes into Dakota's room, and slams the door shut.

Chapter Eighteen
March

It's a packed night for Cover-Ups, a thick crowd all around me as I stand at one of the tall tables near the stage. Dakota is front and center on stage, halfway through Incubus' song "Drive" when I feel a tap on my shoulder.

"Hey Ian. Mind if I join you?" Shelly yells.

I smile and point at the space next to me. She sets down her glass and gives me a return smile. I hope she doesn't attempt to carry on a conversation, it's way too loud.

She doesn't, until the song ends and there's a ripple of applause and hooting.

"He's good," Shelly states, as if she is surprised by this fact.

"You know he's a music major." I smile and roll my eyes.

"I know, I saw him at a concert on campus, but he wasn't playing a guitar then, he had a violin I think."

Dakota's voice cuts through my thoughts, drawing my eyes to him as he starts "Wish You Were Here". I shrug one shoulder. "He's freakishly talented at this stuff." I lift my glass and catch the straw with my lips, sucking down a gulp of water. It's so hot in the cramped room.

I shouldn't complain about the temperature in the room, Dakota's roasting under the lights. More so than usual, sweat dripping off his brow and down the sides of his face. It makes my stomach flutter with nerves as I wonder if he's okay. I pull out my phone and check the time. Usually they go on break by now.

Dakota's fingers trip, missing a beat. His voice is steady, detracting from his mistake, but my stomach heaves. The chord rhythm of the song is simple enough that I can play it. How can he mess up? His fingers trip again, and he's looking over at the other guitarist, holding some silent conversation as he continues belting out the verse.

Something's wrong. Dakota looks over the crowd, his eyes coming to rest on mine. There's panic in his gaze. I jump out of my skin.

Zach, the other guitarist, steps forward to the mic and picks up on the next line. I have to push through the crowd to get to the side of the stage. I hear Shelly behind me. The bouncer steps out in front of me when I get to the door that goes backstage, but he either recognizes me or sees my terrified expression and opens the door for me to slip through.

I see Dakota step out of view of the public, folding over himself as he staggers and drops his Ibanez.

"Kota!" I'm across the distance and catching him as he crumples. "What's wrong?"

"My head," he yelps as we sink to the floor. "It hurts."

As I look down at him, fear pushes bile up my throat. Blood is streaming out of his ear, around the angle of his jaw and down his neck. Holding him tighter, I pull the earpiece off his ear and let it fall to the floor.

"Ian, I'm gonna be sick," he moans.

"Shelly, call an ambulance," I bark at her, pulling Dakota

closer.

* * *

"The Tantar isn't working," I murmur to my phone. Around me the hospital room is dark, and Dakota is sound asleep in bed. I walk from the window to the bedside and back, giving my nervous energy an exit and checking for his breaths. Outside the window I see an amber glow from parking lot lights.

Troy sighs through the phone, a deep sigh. I imagine him closing his eyes and leaning back in his desk chair as he does it.

"What do I do?" I ask.

"Let me give you a number for him to call in the morning. It's a specialist at Duke University, it wouldn't hurt for Dakota to get worked up there."

"What will they do that you can't do at home?" I just want to throw Dakota in my Jeep and drive him straight to the Mayo clinic for Troy to fix him. There has to be some benefit to having a neuro-oncologist for a step-dad when your soulmate has brain cancer.

"I don't know for sure Ian, but they have the best brain clinic in the country. They can get him the most time."

My eyes sting at my stepfather's words. I haven't thought about it, I hate being reminded of it, and the last few hours have thrown it in my face. Time, time, time is numbered, short, running out. I need more of it. Suddenly dealing with the tumor isn't in the distant future, it's right now, and I'm not ready.

"I'll text you the number. It's after five in the morning, Ian, you need to get some sleep."

I swallow the boulder in my throat, letting it hit deep in

my stomach before I respond. "I'll try. Thanks Troy."

"Keep me posted, okay? Get some rest."

"I will," I promise, then say my goodbye and hang up.

Quietly as I can, I sit back down in the chair pulled up to the bedside. Despite the monitoring wires and intrusive IV, Dakota looks peaceful. Does he look sick? I hate to admit he does. But he doesn't look like he's dying. I know death's transportation, and it's what scares me the most.

* * *

The air outside is chilly, nibbling my cheeks and ears as I lug my giant rolling suitcase away from the dorms and down to the parking lot. Walking beside me, Dakota is clutching two coffees and is smiling into the cool wind. He bounced back from the Cover Ups incident with his usual chipper attitude, and it soothes my soul to see him 'normal' again.

We look completely normal, just two guys walking down to the parking lot. I've got my black Milford hoodie on with jeans, he's got a Carhartt zip jacket with jeans and his red Badgers baseball cap. With the oversized suitcase I look like any other student heading home for spring break. We're not normal though, we're trekking 800 miles to try and buy time because we're dying. At least it feels like I'm dying on the inside when I think about it, and I have no idea how I'm supposed to live without him. I won't, I'll die too figuratively. I can't lose him now.

"What's with that face?" Dakota asks, noticing my frown as he opens the back hatch door of my Jeep. "Thinking about this fourteen hour drive?"

"Trying to decide if we make a run for it straight through," I lie and smile to cover my thoughts. Hefting the black suitcase, I throw it in the Jeep's trunk space.

"Ready?"

"Let's go," Dakota smiles and hands me a coffee cup.

As I walk around the Jeep to the driver's side, I exhale in a hissing curse. Keyed into the driver's door of my Cherokee is the word 'FAG'.

"What's wrong?" Dakota asks as he comes around to my side. "Oh. Jase?"

"I don't know who else."

"Well," he says cheerily. "I know how to fix this right quick."

My eyebrows pinch together as I watch him take his keys off his belt loop. He kneels next to the SUV, and non-chalantly carves an 'S' into my door panel. "There, much better."

I laugh and shake my head. "Much more accurate."

"Much." He nods matter-of-factly and moves back to the passenger side.

I get behind the wheel and he slides into the passenger seat, and we're off and running for South Carolina. We get through town and onto the interstate when one of the stupidest questions rolls off my tongue, "Are you nervous?"

"About getting poked, prodded, and scanned again? A bit with the poking part," Dakota mumbles, his nimble fingers fiddling with the lid on his paper cup. "I don't want to know that the tumor's growing."

"Maybe they can do surgery," I say.

Dakota sighs, his breath growling through his mouth in frustration. "I don't want another surgery."

I momentarily forgot they already cracked his skull open once before. "I'm sure it sucked but it was worth it, wasn't it?"

"I still don't want another surgery," he says surely.

I blink. My foot creeps off the gas pedal a bit, my face

scrunching in disbelief. "If they can do surgery, you won't do it? What the hell?" How can he say that?

"It's not worth it."

"Not worth it?" I gape. "What's with this negativity bullshit? Dakota, you need to be positive, if they can do surgery-"

Dakota's moody eyes glare into the side of my face. "Ian, I'm sick and it's going to kill me whether or not they cut my head open and carve into my brain. I'm going to die and I don't want to live miserably up to that point."

"More time with me is living miserably," I ask flatly. In the back of my mind I know I'm being a selfish dick, but my emotions are getting out of control.

"What kind of time is it?" Dakota asks, his voice rising. "Six months just like this? Or a year of you staring at me while I lay around in some hospice place unable to talk, all I do is stare at the ceiling drooling while I shit myself or something. Ian, I want quality not quantity." He sighs deeply, expelling a tightness in his chest and shoulders. "I want to spend the rest of my life with you, but I want to participate in it and don't want to suffer. Is that really such a horrible thought?"

I bite my lower lip, letting his words hang in the air. God he's right, and it is his choice not mine, but I hate the options he has to pick from. I hate this whole situation, and that it happened to him.

After a long minute I murmur, "I'm sorry."

"Don't say sorry for stupid shit." Dakota smiles, and reaches over to take my hand in his.

He's comforting me. We're driving halfway across the country on a matter of life and death and it's him having to comfort me. I feel like a worthless piece of shit, but I tangle my fingers in his and hold on tight.

* * *

It's been a long day, and my head is throbbing by the time I exit the hospital building and take a breath of fresh air. It's a hot, sunny, disgustingly beautiful day. Shuffling my feet, I move away from the building to a grey stone bench. It's inscripted with the name of someone I never knew, a memorial bench. Which is weird when you think about it, as a memorial to you here's a bunch of people's butts sitting on your memorial. I don't ever want a bench in my honor anywhere.

Sitting down on the bench, I pull out my phone and ignore the missed calls and text messages, and call my mother on speaker phone.

"Hi Honey," my mother answers. I can just tell by her voice she's nervous. "Did you get my email?"

"No, I haven't checked my email."

"I know you were planning on driving back to school for the rest of your spring break, but Troy and I got you a vacation rental for the rest of the week."

"Thanks, Mom," I mumble. I feel like a spoiled rich kid, and perhaps I am, but I am so grateful for the gesture. "It'd be nice not to have to turn and burn back 800 miles right away."

"That's what Troy and I thought. How's it going down there at Duke?"

"Well," I preface. "His tumor has grown back. They can't operate on it again, it's too snarled up in his brain. Um," I pause to swallow as my throat thickens. "They're putting him on a different drug, Atavast. He's getting his first infusion right now, they said he can continue with the infusions when we get back to school, the one hospital can do them."

"He's intent on finishing the semester, isn't he?"

"Yeah, he's stubborn." I smile slightly.

"There's not much left of the semester. And I'm insisting he comes to Minnesota, no arguments from him. I'll have Troy look into setting up those treatments locally." We hadn't really talked about it, about summer break. Of course I want to take him home with me, but bringing it up with my parents has been hard. What am I supposed to say? 'Hey Mom, can my friend come stay with us? He might die at our house, is that cool?'.

"Mom…" My throat is so tight the word squeezes out. I look up at the bright sky, willing my tears away but they just seem to come faster. "They don't know how long he has."

"It's hard to judge things like that sweetheart, especially with the brain." God damn it, her voice sounds so calm. I wish I could be as steady as her, I need to be, but I'm falling apart.

"I don't know what to do," I gasp.

My mother draws a long breath. "Ian, honey, the only thing you have to do is be there for him. I know how much you love him, and I know he loves you sweetheart. Try to finish out the semester, then you boys come home and we'll get through this, okay?"

"I'm supposed to go back to work this summer," I babble as sharp needles tap-dance behind my eyes. I can't think straight.

"Dakota is so much more important than a summer job or taking summer classes, and we realize that and we're blessed to be in a position to give you your time together without any other worries. I want you both here when school wraps up."

"Mom…" I squeak, tears overflowing as I fold over

at the waist, head between my knees. I feel relief at her words, but at the same time I'm falling through a bottomless pit of self-loathing. "This is so hard, and it's not even happening to me. I'm so weak."

"Ian, you are not weak. You have strength, and you will use it. I love you so much and wish I could be there to tell you that in person. Showing the emotion you're feeling isn't weak, you're just being honest with yourself and honest with the world in expressing it."

I inhale hard, trying to rein my tears back.

"I want you to check your email and when Dakota's finished today you boys get there safe, okay? Spend some time together and call me if you need anything at all, alright?"

"Okay," my voice cracks as I agree. "I love you Mom."

"Love you too sweetheart, I'll talk to you soon."

Our conversation ends, and I end up bawling into my hands.

Chapter Nineteen
April

"April Fool's?" I ask, sitting down on the doctor's round stool and rolling it closer to Dakota's bed.

"I wish," Dakota grumbles, pulling down the collar of his gown to expose the bandage below his collarbone.

I stare at the bandage, knowing that beneath it the doctors had inserted a port under his skin to make his Atavast treatments a little easier. It sounds so alien and bizarre, putting a foreign device into his body like that and leaving it there.

"Worth it, they won't have to stab up your arms."

"They were so flawless before that," Dakota snorts and rolls his eyes. "This will be so sexy once it heals too."

"Your collarbone is quite sexy, but there are other parts of your body higher on my favorite list," I say and feel my stomach squirrel clapping its paws and fluttering its tail when he smiles back. I move in closer and take his hand in mine, squeezing hard. "It's worth it." It's so worth it, the treatments have made him better, livelier, his old rambunctious self, and this will make things easier to get those treatments into his body.

"It is," Dakota agrees, and our conversation falls quiet.

I'm staring at the pattern on his hospital gown, trying to decide what animal the blue shapes most resemble, and I hear a sniffle. My eyes follow his arm up to his eyes, which I'm surprised to see are gleaming. Since that first night when I got back to school I haven't seen him cry. He's been the rock and I've been the mess of loose bits ready to fall apart when it should be the other way around, but now he's breaking.

"Kota?" I murmur, running my hand along his arm. "Hey."

He covers his face with his other hand, and his shoulders tremble with a silent cry. I can't help it when I feel my own eyes start to sting, but I try to be strong. Standing up, I move my hand up to his shoulder. I don't know what to say, I can't tell him everything's okay or going to be okay because they're not.

"Kota? What's wrong?"

"I'm really going to die. This is going to kill me, and I don't want to die, Ian. I'm scared."

He's right, and there's nothing I can do to change it.

I gather his upper body in my arms, holding him tight to my chest. He fits so perfectly, being smaller built than me, and I can nuzzle his smooth hair as he sobs. Instantly I feel the dampness of his tears on my shirt, chilling my insides. I hope I feel strong and sure to him.

"Don't be scared, you're not alone. I'm right here, I'm not going anywhere."

I wish there was more I had to offer. Something, anything to make it better, but all I have to give is that promise. We're in this together.

I try to hold back the sob building in my own throat, and I kiss his forehead. "Don't be scared. I'm going to be right here."

Chapter Twenty
May

"Hey, Ian!"

I stop walking down the paved path, and turn to see Shelly jogging at me. I turn my suitcase handle upright to let the boxy luggage sit on the ground.

"Are you moving out already?" She asks when she reaches me.

"I finished yesterday, and Dakota's in his last final right now, so I'm getting most of the stuff in the Jeep."

"Oh." She frowns, then hooks her thumbs in the straps of her backpack. "You guys leaving tonight then?"

"Yep."

"Geez, already. Well, give me a hug in case I don't see you before you leave." I give her a polite hug, and she sighs heavily. "I don't know why but this seems like a hard goodbye."

It should be a harder goodbye, I'll probably never see her again, but I don't say it out loud. "It's been an interesting year."

"Well I hope you have a good summer, and I'll see you on move-in day. I'll be counting on you to haul all my heavy stuff up from my car."

"You got it." I smile and grab the handle on my suitcase. "Bye Shelly, and thanks for everything."

"No problem," she says cheerily, and I start walking toward the parking lot.

It feels strange, walking across campus and knowing I'm never coming back. I had imagined graduating here, and leaving with a degree and ready to take on the next part of my life. Instead, I'm three years short of my degree, and I'm not ready for what life has planned for me next. I don't know what I'm going to do about school, and I don't really care, it's not my priority right now.

Turning my face to the sun, I look out and see Milford's trademark tower. I am going to miss it, but I can't come back.

It's late when I steer my Cherokee up the driveway to my house. The sun has dipped below the horizon line, but its fingers of light are still pushing away the dark.

"You ready for this?" I ask. "Mainly Mia smothering you with affection."

Dakota smiles then rolls his peppermint candy around his mouth. "Everybody loves me."

"Everybody does love you." I pick up his hand I had been holding and firmly kiss his knuckles. "Just remember that I'm your favorite."

"Always," he laughs and shakes our hands.

I park in the driveway and quickly grab our bags, then lead the way into the house. It's as I expected, a lot of fuss over both of us which ends up with Dakota seated at the kitchen island for snacks and me hauling our luggage upstairs.

Entering my room, it feels like a decade has passed since I was here. I'm flooded with sharp memories of Dakota; soft kisses and touches, sharp kisses and touches. Finding him missing, erased out of my life. That one bites particularly hard at my heart, and not because it happened but because it's going to happen again. He's going to leave me, not on his terms, but fate is going to erase him from my life.

Inhaling deeply to force back the sting in my eyes, I wrangle back my emotions and heft the suitcases up on the spare bed. I don't need to think about it now.

I leave my room and trot down the staircase, and see Mia sitting next to Dakota, and my mom serving up some kind of leftovers that smells like her veggie pasta. This, this is what I need to think about now.

* * *

I am mildly surprised when someone rings the doorbell at two in the afternoon, but I'm shocked to open the door and see Dakota's brother Pen standing there, dressed in black, holding the leash of a black german shepherd.

"Uh, hey," I bumble. I hear footsteps behind me, and the shepherd's tail starts to wag at mach twelve speed.

"Pen! Shadow!" Dakota cries out, falling to his knees at the door so the dog can lick his face. "How?"

His younger brother is smiling now. "My friend Alicia works at the humane society, and I asked her to keep an eye out for black german shepherds. He came in two days ago."

"Pen, this is awesome."

"Told ya I'd find a way to pay you back for giving me your truck," Pen says.

Dakota rolls his eyes at that, his hands scruffling his

dog's neck. "You don't have to pay me back for the truck."

"Well still," Pen says with a roll of his eyes.

"Thank you, Pen," Dakota stands up and hugs his taller brother.

I lean down and offer my hand for the dog to sniff. I'm surprised when he licks my hand then sidles into me, leaning against my leg as he looks up at me with his oversized ears. He's a beautiful dog. Thinner than the last time I'd seen him, and his coat not as glossy, but still beautiful.

My mom appears beside me out of nowhere. "You must be Pen."

"Mrs. St.Clair," he nods.

"Please call me Faith," my mom insists. She leans down to stroke Shadow's fur and tell the dog what a good boy he is.

"Wait," Dakota says. "How do you two know each other?"

Pen smiles a little and shrugs. "I called to see if it was okay to bring Shadow. Otherwise I would have kept him myself, he's such a cool dog."

"Both of you," my mother chastises. "Don't leave him standing there, come in Pen. Are you hungry? I have sandwich fixings."

"Oh, I don't need to intrude," Pen waves his hand. "I'm going to be in trouble when I get home anyway, I skipped school to come out here."

"Well I'm not letting you leave on an empty stomach," my mom says firmly and marches to the kitchen.

My mind is rolling, making a list of things we need to get from PetSmart, when it screeches to a stop. Pen… this is one of the last times he'll see his brother. It could be the very last even. God, I hate how my brain keeps reminding me of these things instead of just letting me enjoy the moment.

"Hey Pen, come upstairs with me a minute," Dakota says and beckons his younger brother to follow him. Without any urging, Shadow follows at his hip, and the brothers go upstairs to our room.

I sit down at the kitchen island and pick up the container of sliced cheese.

"What a sweet boy," my mom hums.

"Dakota loves that dog. His dad sold him on Craigslist while we were at school."

"That's so sad. Save some cheese for other people."

"I had like one slice."

"And there's two more in your hand."

I roll my eyes and take a bite out of both slices.

It's only a moment later when we hear raised voices coming from upstairs. When my mother frowns I feel the need to explain what I am pretty certain is happening.

"I think Dakota is giving him his inheritance."

"Inheritance?" my mom questions.

"Dakota's been working these side gigs while he's been at school to save up money for Pen's college. He has almost thirty grand saved up."

"Oh my."

"Dakota's pissed he didn't make more. Pen wants to be a doctor so thirty grand is a drop in the bucket, but I keep telling him he's an amazing brother for doing it."

"Hmm." My mom hums and snags a piece of cheese. "Would you be an amazing brother and wait until your sister gets home before you guys go shopping? That dog is going to need a bed, food and water bowls, you're going to need to get tags, dog food."

I swallow my bite of cheese. "Thank you for being okay with the dog." I'm not going to ask what changed her mind from the 'no we don't need a dog' stance because I really don't care. My heart is too happy to have Shadow back.

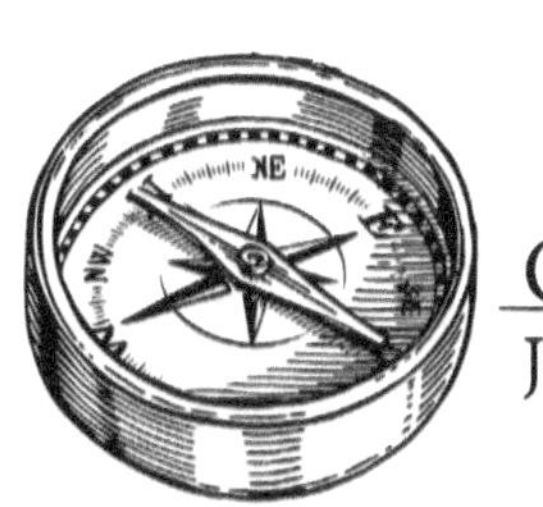

Chapter Twenty-One
June

It's kind of a nice change of pace when we get dressed up for a night out with my family. We have dinner at an upper crust restaurant, then head to the high school to see the art gallery for Mia's class. I'm surprised how nervous she acts throughout dinner and the drive.

"Ian?" she asks, tugging on my free arm as we walk toward the brick school building. "Promise you won't be mad."

"Mad?" I stop, and Dakota stops next to me. "Why would I be mad, Mia?"

"Because," she lets out in a woosh. "There might be pictures of you and I didn't ask you first. I'm sorry."

"As long as they're not naked pictures I'm not going to be mad, Mia," I laugh and fluff her ebony braids.

She doesn't look very assured, but keeps walking, leading the way inside.

Dakota tiptoes to whisper in my ear, "I hope there's naked pictures."

"Shut up you dork," I hiss back.

When we enter the gym-turned-gallery there is a woman speaking, who I assume is Mia's teacher. I half-listen as she talks about how the year-long assignment for the students was 'Change'. Glancing around the room I see a few paintings of the seasons, and I roll my eyes at the typicalness of them. Finally the woman stops talking and we can wander the gallery set up in the basketball gym. There are paintings, photos, and sketches of seasons, landscapes, animals and butterflies. There's a series of detailed pencil drawings of nickels, quarters, pennies, and dimes, which makes me laugh. There's always one smart ass in the class.

"Where's your stuff, Mia?" My mom asks.

"Over there in the corner." She points to the back of the gallery, where the teacher and a small crowd of people are standing.

"Well let's go see," my mom urges.

Mia shuffles as she leads us over, and I'm surprised when the first thing I see is, in fact, a large photograph of me. It's from the summer, and out of focus is Ben leaning over the engine compartment of my Cherokee. In focus is me, watching him, looking utterly lost. I know I'm lost because I have no idea what he is looking at, but it looks deeper than that, like a complete utter loss at where I am in my life.

The next photo is of me laying down, head hanging off the end of my bed looking contemplative. She had to have taken it from outside my room, I don't remember her taking it, and it makes me feel uncomfortable. My eyes move onto the next photo, one of Dakota smiling wide wearing a black beanie hat and a flannel shirt. It's from when he first came to Minnesota. The photo is in black and white, except for his two-toned eyes.

Moving over another photo and another, I see candid bits and pieces of my relationship with Dakota coming together in a visual story. As the story unfolds I'm surprised

I see the change in me, my smiles becoming sincere, the light in my eyes brighter. There's one she obviously snuck into my room for, as Dakota and I are curled up in bed spooning, my face buried into his shaggy hair. and I can feel my cheeks burning with embarrassment at such a private moment being stolen.

The last photo stops my heart, and I forget about the intrusive photo. It's Dakota from the back, holding his hands up over his shoulder in the shape of a heart, framing the setting summer sun. At first I want to say it's cheesy with the heart and all, but it hits me the depth behind it - a depth that no one else standing here with me, staring at the same photo, could possibly see.

Someone tugs on my arm, and I look down and see Mia's eyes wide and fearful. "Is he mad?" she whispers.

I look over at Dakota, but he's not standing next to me like he was a moment ago. He's walking away, and fast.

"No, Mia," I lie and take off after him.

I catch up to him in the men's restroom, but before I can say anything he's throwing up in the sink. Red covers the white porcelain, splashes onto his hand, his dress shirt.

"Kota," I gasp.

"Atavast," he garbles around a mouthful of blood. He coughs and spits, more red. "Side effect of the Atavast."

"This hasn't happened before." I run my fingers through my hair, and they tremble.

Silence stretches between us, Dakota bent over the sink and spitting red. The image of that setting sun is burned into my mind's eye, and my voice is choked as I ask, "It's not working anymore, is it?"

He doesn't look at me, and the overwhelming desperation I feel comes out in anger. I swing at the paper towel dispenser next to him, my fist denting the metal box. "God damn it."

Dakota ignores my tantrum, calmly turning on the

water, washing the evidence down the drain. He cups his hands to sip and spit, rinsing it from his mouth. Perfectly cool, he finally straightens his shirt and checks his reflection in the mirror. Looking through the mirror he meets my gaze, and I wish Mia had a picture of this. We're both dressed up, he's the one with blood on his shirt but I'm the one that looks ready to break.

"Come on, let's go," he says softly.

I want to object, but what alternative option do we really have? Where can we go? What can we do? Nowhere and nothing. We can't escape the building. There's nothing left if the Atavast is quitting on him.

Dakota slips his hand in mine, squeezing tight and pressing our tattoos together. "Come on, don't ruin your sister's night."

He leads the way out of the bathroom and back to the gallery, where more people than before are milling about. Some are casting us sideways looks, and I'm not sure if they recognize us from Mia's photos or they're staring because we're holding hands. I decide I don't care either way.

"Hey," Mia says with a tremble in her voice when we rejoin my family. I smile to ease her worry.

"Did you two hear? Mia won first place!" Mom blurts in excitement. "Her entry is going to a regional competition."

"Congratulations, Mia," I smile wider.

"You deserve it," Dakota adds.

"Thank you," she whispers, relief flooding her features. I flinch when she gives Dakota a spontaneous hug, worried she'll hurt him. "But I'm sorry, I should have said something to both of you. I didn't even realize I was using the pictures until I was looking through them on winter break. I'd been taking all sorts of pictures of everything since summer and I had no idea what to put together for this whole 'change' thing and it just jumped out at me. The biggest change around me was Ian."

Looking past her, at her photographs being gawked over, it does seem painfully obvious. I'm the visual definition of change, and Dakota's my catalyst. Squeezing Dakota's hand a little tighter, I look down at the floor.

Chapter Twenty-Two
July

July 1st

It's early morning, before it gets too warm, when Dakota and I head to the garage. I need to change the oil on my Jeep and Dakota insists I learn to be a man and do it myself. The comment makes me blush in embarrassment. My twin brother is a mechanic-in-training for piss' sakes and I can't even change the oil in my own vehicle.

"What's Ben going to do without me paying him sixty bucks to do this?" I ask, taking two creepers off the wall and placing them on the floor. I hold back the urge to help Dakota, and just watch him like a hawk as he sinks down to the floor and rolls onto his back. Shadow bellies down next to him, my second set of eyes.

"He was over charging you," Dakota snorts and scoots himself under the Jeep with slow, calculated movements.

I lay down on the second creeper and follow him under the vehicle. It just looks like a mess of metal and rubber snakes knotted together.

"Did you grab that oil pan over by the door?" Dakota asks.

"Nope." I scoot back out and grab the metal drain pan. I'm kneeling to the ground when Dakota makes this horrible noise, as if his breath was pulled out of his choked throat. "Dakota? Dakota!" I bark. Shadow jumps to his feet, whimpering loudly. When Dakota doesn't respond I grab his leg and pull hm out from under the Jeep.

His arms are pulled tight to his chest, his eyes staring straight ahead but unfocused, his entire body trembling. Seizure. I immediately roll him onto his side like I'd learned.

"Kota," I whisper, my word drowned out by his guttural moaning. All I can do is rest my hand on his abdomen, feeling the quiver in his muscles, and wait for it to pass. It makes my heart hurt; there's nothing I can do but watch him suffer. Just like the beginning of school, I wonder if this is now the end.

* * *

It's late, and the house is quiet when I leave my room. I don't hear television, music, or voices. Padding down the stairs, I eventually find myself at the doorway to Troy's study. My step-dad is sitting at his desk, staring at his computer screen, and he's exactly who I need to see.

"Hey Troy?" I ask, my voice rough.

He startles, but turns and smiles gently when he meets my eyes.

"Can I come in for a minute?"

"Sure Ian," he takes off his readers and motions to the other chair. I cross the room and collapse into it. "How's

Dakota?"

"He's sleeping. I wish he would have gone to the hospital."

"Well, that was his choice, and Ian, they're not going to tell him anything new at this point. You can't blame him."

"I don't. I'm just struggling with everything happening so fast. And it's not fair. And I'm not blaming you, Troy, but how do I, with a neuro-oncologist stepdad, end up with someone with a brain tumor, and not get a happy ending out of it?"

"Because life isn't fair, and sometimes it's ironic, and sometimes it's simply cruel."

July 2nd

I shovel dinner into my mouth without tasting it, and excuse myself from the table. My parents and Mia don't say anything, so I head upstairs to my room. The door is open, letting the sound of silverware kissing ceramic plates echo up the stairs and into my room. Shadow looks up from his spot at the foot of the bed, slowly wagging his bushy black tail.

"Hey buddy," I whisper, giving his head a quick scruffle. My eyes run over the lump in my bed that I know is Dakota, still sleeping off his seizure from yesterday. Seeing how much it took out of him worries me deep down, but I ignore it. I can't face it.

Stripping out of my shirt and jeans, I pull back the covers to reveal Dakota curled up into a ball and fast asleep. Careful not to wake him, I ungracefully slide into bed and wince when my probably cold skin touches his warmth. He doesn't wake, and I exhale in a long sigh and curl around him, making him my little spoon.

I lay there for a long time, committing the sensation to memory, forcefully burning it into my brain for all eternity. The awkward angle of my arm under the pillow, the weight of Dakota's head on the pillow and pinning my arm down. The minty smell of his hair tickling my nose. The softness of his shoulder when I crane my neck to kiss it, the feel of his waist when I lock my arm around it. I don't want to miss this.

But I am. It doesn't seem possible this body in my arms, so warm and real, is failing. This soul in my arms is going to disappear and I'll never find it again in my lifetime. Any second he could leave, and I can't go with him.

July 3rd

I'm sitting in the sunroom with Mia when Dakota appears in his pajamas despite it being four in the afternoon. He leans on the doorframe, looking utterly exhausted. Not exhausted, I have to remind myself, sick. His skin is an ashy grey that matches my black plaid flannel pants he's wearing. The dark rings circling his eyes are complimentary.

"What are you guys doing?" he whispers.

"I was making Ian be a captive audience," Mia smiles and strums her guitar. "Did I wake you up?"

"No. I was trying to read," he says, his voice rough as his hand comes up to rub his eyes. "Everything's blurry."

I open my mouth to ask a hundred questions, body tensing to jump off the couch, but Dakota beats me to the action. He pads across the tile floor and sits down next to me. Automatically my arm slides around his waist and he nuzzles into my shoulder.

"Keep playing Mia, I want to hear," Dakota whispers.

Mia forces a smile, her voice trembling a second before strengthening. "Alright." As her fingers pull the strings of her pink Epiphone, I tug the throw blanket off the back of the couch, tucking it around Dakota.

"What do you want to hear?" Mia asks.

"TSwift. Old Taylor Swift. Curly-haired Taylor Swift."

Mia strums for a few moments before finding her place. *"The way you move is like a full on rainstorm."*

4th of July

I'm not in the mood for celebrating, so when my family heads out to the lake with the boat I climb into bed with my sleepy soulmate. I lose track of the time, I might have even fallen asleep, and when I open my eyes my room is dark. Looking out the window I see dusky twilight and black shadows of trees.

"Miss fireworks?" Dakota murmurs.

"No," I answer honestly.

"You should have gone with them," he says, fingers rubbing at his eyes. His voice is rough from sleep.

"Rather stay here with you," I argue, pulling on his hip to roll him onto his side to face me.

"You're going to miss out on the fireworks. That's the best part."

"You're better."

It's quiet, Dakota studying my face with a faint smile on his lips. My fingertips are teasing under his shirt, absorbing the heat of his skin,

"Can we go watch fireworks?" Dakota asks.

"We're not going to catch everyone, they're in the middle of the lake by now."

"Just us."

I think it over for a minute. He seems in good spirits but I still don't want to drag him all over creation. "It's not the best of seats, but we could go down to the dock."

"'Kay."

Dakota climbs over me and moves to the dresser. He strips out of his white t-shirt and digs through the drawers to find one of mine. I can't help but notice how gaunt he looks. He's always been thin and trim, but his skin is tight over hollows and bone instead of muscle now. There's a sharpness to the geometry of his body, harsh lines replacing the strong angles of before.

He pulls one of my old lacrosse t-shirts on, then grabs his jeans off the other bed. I roll out of bed and take his hand, knotting our fingers together then leading the way out of my room and down to the garage.

"Thirsty? I ask, but he shakes his head.

I tap the garage door open then lead him over to the green side-by-side utility vehicle. I have to admit the night is beautiful when I back us out of the garage and into the quickly falling night. Dakota scoots in close to me as I cut across the backyard and find the trail that goes into our woods. It's just a minute drive to the lake, to my family's private dock.

I put the side-by-side in park and cut the engine. Pointing across the lake, into the darkness, I say, "That's where they're setting off the fireworks, so not too bad of a seat here."

Dakota slides away from me and swings his legs out of

the vehicle. "Let's go sit on the dock."

It's a short walk to the dock but my hand finds his again and holds tight. One, I like having the connection to him, and Two, I know his eyesight isn't that great and the last thing I need is him tripping and falling into the lake and giving me a heart attack.

I let him lead the way to the end of the dock, where we sit and take off our shoes and socks to dip our feet in the cool water. We sit in companionable silence, like two little kids holding hands and kicking our feet in the water. I can hear echoes from across the lake of laughter and small explosions from store-bought noisemakers.

So quietly, as if it was meant just for me, Dakota starts singing at a slow whisper. *"'Cause baby, you're a firework. Come on, show 'em what you're worth."* His voice and pace make the song hauntingly beautiful as he continues for a few more lines before burrowing into my side.

"I don't feel good," Dakota murmurs.

"Want to go back?"

"No, I want to see fireworks," he says stubbornly. "Just," he fusses for a second then finally lays back, his two-toned eyes now turned to the stars. "There."

I stretch back beside him, looking up at the sprinkled array of stars in the violet-black carpet of sky. It's beautiful, but I can't focus on it. I'm feeling the clamminess of Dakota's hand in mine, and listening carefully to his breaths.

A bright yellow light races up to the sky, then separates into a hundred dazzling streamers with a loud "POP". Another light races after it, then another, small comets exploding in color. They are breathtaking, so bright in the sky as they bloom above their mirrored reflection on the lake.

"They're fuzzy. I'm going to close my eyes, describe them to me," Dakota mumbles. I roll my head over to see his eyes closed, but his face relaxed.

Another loud pop cracks the air, and I look back to the sky. "This one's red. This one's perfectly cut in half, half white and half blue. This one's purple and green mixed together."

Dakota squeezes my hand, making me smile. "Another red one. This one's white but it's falling down on us like some giant chandelier. Trippy. Oh hey," I smile again as a piercing whistle fills the air. "The whistlers are my favorite."

There's a pop explosion, and the firework goes off with a shower of red and white lights.

"Which is your favorite?" I ask, watching the red and white embers fall back to the earth, winking out one by one. The sky goes momentarily dark. "Kota? Which one's your favorite?"

He doesn't answer, and when I look over at him he looks fast asleep. "Dakota?" I speak up, squeezing his hand.

A cold fist squeezes my heart, icy fingers digging into the tissue and piercing straight into my soul. "Dakota?" I flip onto my hands and knees, and I shake his shoulders. "Dakota! Wake up!" His head rolls from my violent shakes, his eyelids parting as another colored explosion lights the sky. No light reflects back in his eyes. "Kota, no, don't do this to me. Wake up. Wake up!"

* * *

There is no funeral, there is no grave. They took all the useful parts out of his body to save other people's lives, then shipped the rest off to the university to be cut up and examined. I know it was the right decision, it was his decision, but it doesn't sit right in my stomach when I think about it. I hate his body for failing him, I love it because it was his, and now it's completely gone. Just like him.

There's nowhere to put my grief except to hang it on my heart. I can't pour it out on other people at a funeral, or empty it out at a headstone, I have to carry it with me, feel it sticking to my bones, my heart. I'm scared it will reach my mind, touch all my precious memories and somehow take those from me too. All I have is memories and I'm so scared to lose them.

There's a knock on my bedroom door, but I don't answer. Someone coming to make me feel better, which is pointless on their part.

"Hey," a quiet voice follows the creak of my door. Mia tip-toes up to my bed, leaning over to see my face.

"What?" I croak, holding my pillow a little tighter. I hear Shadow whimper from the foot of the bed.

"Can I join you?" Mia whispers. I look up and finally meet her gaze, seeing loss in her deep brown eyes. She hurts too—nowhere near the pain I feel, but she feels something. She doesn't wait for me to answer either, she climbs into bed next to me, putting an arm around my waist and squeezing. "I miss him, Ian."

Her simple confession tears another shred of my heart, filling my eyes with fresh tears.

"Me too," I whisper.

Chapter Twenty-Three
August

I can't help but smile when I walk into Ink Heart's and see an overweight bearded gentleman wearing a Batman t-shirt. He gives me a polite smile, ignoring my wild hair and sloppy clothes. Why should he care if I look like shit and just drove seven hours to be there? I have cash in my wallet and purpose in my heart.

"What can I help you with?" the man asks, leaning his arms against the counter.

"I need a solid black band, right here." I tap on my right forearm, just below my elbow.

The artist's eyebrows lift in surprise. "Alright then, man knows what he wants. Let me grab your paperwork."

While I wait my eyes drift over to the upholstered couches in the front of the shop, remembering just half a year ago I'd sat there next to Dakota. We'd joked about sunflower tramp stamps and—

"Here you are."

I focus back on Batman, and take the paper and pen he's offering. Without reading it I sign the release, and he leads me back to the same room as before. My throat feels tight. I itch at the existing tattoo on the inside of my wrist.

"So a black band huh?" the artist asks conversationally.

I knew I'd end up having to explain myself, but my stomach still clenches at the idea. I have to keep it simple, otherwise I'll break down.

"I lost my best friend."

The man nods his head in understanding. I wonder if he really does understand.

"Show me how thick you want the band."

As thick as my layers of grief and as black as my heart.

Epilogue
One Year Later

Shadow goes crazy barking, and I look up from reading my book on the couch. My mom pads out of the kitchen and goes to peek out one of the front windows. I hear her exclaim under her breath, and I sit up a little.

"Mom?"

"Ian, come here."

I get off the couch and meet her at the front door. She opens the heavy wooden door, and looking through the storm door I see a beige Colorado sitting in our driveway, and a young man with a backpack coming up the walk.

"It's Pen," I say in disbelief. I saw him briefly after Dakota died, but it's been at least six months. I never thought I'd see Dakota's brother again, and it fills me with a strange mix of excitement and heartache.

My mom opens the storm door, greeting Pen with a smile and gentle hello.

"Hi, um," he says sheepishly, stepping into our house and shrugging his backpack off his shoulders and clutching it to his chest. "Hi Ian, Mrs. St. Clair."

"Faith. What a pleasant surprise," my mom grins.

"I don't want to intrude, I just had something to give Ian."

"Nonsense, come in." My mom herds him further into the house, into the kitchen where she sits us down and produces tall glasses of lemonade.

"Is your husband around?" Pen asks.

"No sweetheart, he's at work, but he'll be home around dinner time. You will stay for dinner, won't you?"

Pen squirms a bit uncomfortably. "I really just wanted to stop by and say thank you. I know it was you and your husband that sent me the education fund."

My eyebrows raise. I had no knowledge of this.

"Where did you decide to go then?" my mom asks.

"Minnesota State, I'm going for Pre-Med."

"Ian's working toward his psych degree at U of M," my mom adds. "I'm so glad to hear you're pursuing that Pen. I'm glad you took up my offer of stopping by, and I hope you'll make a habit of it if you'll be in the state."

Pen's blushing the slightest bit at my mom's overflowing kindness. I remember his brother having the same reaction.

"Thanks. Um," he shifts his eyes to me. "There was something else I came for. FedEx came about a month ago, and I was the one home to sign for him."

I tilt my head at his strange words. A moment later Pen pulls out of his backpack a plain matte black box, and sets it gently on the table before pushing it towards me. "He was dead to the rest of my family for years, so I didn't tell them I had him. I had the last month to say goodbye. I thought you should have a chance too."

Realization makes me shiver. Dakota's ashes. "They, they gave him back?" I stare at the black box for a long moment before I look up at Pen and smile the slightest bit.

"Dakota would have loved that, how they just FedExed him."

"He would have." Pen smiled.

I reach out and touch the box, feeling its smooth surface under my fingertips as I pull it closer.

"He told me he didn't want to 'sleep in the dirt', but he never said where he wanted to go instead." Pen says. "I thought about the tree thing, but if I did that at home my dad would probably cut it down. I thought about the swirly giant marble thing but then I imagined someone breaking into the house and taking him then he'd wind up at an antique store and some old lady would buy him and put him on a knick-knack shelf and then she'd die and her kids would throw him out then he'd be in the landfill sleeping in the dirt where he didn't want to be."

I smile sadly. "I remember."

* * *

I'm out of breath, for a few reasons. The hike up to this spot was intense and I'm out of shape, but the view is absolutely breathtaking. Dakota National Park spreads out in front of me in a stunning natural panorama. I unclip my backpack and set it down beside me, pulling out the black box that had journeyed with me to North Dakota.

I set it in my lap, staring at the deep black color as I catch my breath.

"If you were here right now you'd point out how creepy this is, me sitting on a mountain in the middle of North Dakota talking to a box of cremains," I laugh and wipe at a chilled tear escaping down my cheek. "But I guess this is finally it, I have to say goodbye. I had all the opportunity in the world to say it to your face, but I never did. I haven't said it in the year you've been gone either, but now you're making me. You're still making me do things I don't want to do, but I need to do," I chuckle and trace my finger along the edge of the lid.

"I miss you Kota, so much. I would give anything to have you here with me right now, but I know that's never going to happen. I just hope you can hear me say this, that I miss you and I'm so glad I met you and I wouldn't have changed one second with you. You changed me. I became the best version of myself because I met you. Even now you're making me a better person everyday."

I can't stop the tears flowing, my voice cracking as my fingers pry at the box.

"I had the time of my life, with you."

ABOUT THE AUTHOR

Stephanie Fox is an English Professor who loves animals, crafting, and spending time with her horse-crazy daughter. She has six cats and two dogs of her own, but she has also cared for a menagerie of other animals over the years. In her free time, she enjoys reading, writing, spending time outdoors, and attending horse shows with her daughter.